THE
JERUSALEM
PROTOCOL

Suzanne,

Enjoy!

Ps 122:6

David Orlo

DAVID ORLO

FLUENCY
TELLING STORIES THAT MATTER

Fluency Organization, Inc.
Design by Diane Kronmeyer and Lindsay Galvin.

ISBN 978-0-9908409-5-4

CAST OF CHARACTERS

From *The Cloud Strike Prophecy:*

Tyler Kensington – Former U.S. Marine pilot and part-time contract *Mossad* agent, private investigator

Regan Hart – Investment advisor, Global Wealth Advisors

Solomon "Solly" Rubin – *Mossad* agent and archeological tour guide in Israel

Dr. Hakeem Saad – Former Biological Weapons Director for Sadaam Hussein

Tony Parker – CIA Director

Arthur Flowers – President of the United States

Frank Taylor – White House Chief of Staff

New Characters:

Titus Flavius Josephus – Ancient Jewish historian, allied with Romans

Sophronius of Jerusalem – Patriarch of Jerusalem from 634 CE until 638 CE

Avi ben Tzion – Elderly Jewish man

Caliph Umar – Muslim Caliph, ordered construction of Dome of the Rock

Billy Frank Conroe – East Texas farmer
Ted Kensington – Tyler's father
Tony Myers – Airplane mechanic
Bakri Karimi – ISIS member embedded in the U.S.
Randall Pritchard – Sheriff of Smith County

Dr. Ibrahim Azzus – Leader, splinter Hamas group in Gaza and former assistant of Dr. Saad
Asher Hazzan – Director, Israeli *Mossad*
Natan Abrams – Israeli Prime Minister
Ziv Kessler – Civilian businessman, trusted advisor to Prime Minister Abrams
Chief Rabbi Yitzak Rabin – Chief Rabbi of Israel, High Priest
Abu Bakr al-Bagahdi, "The Fox" – ISIS leader
Captain Blair Blackburn – Cargo pilot
Colonel Ezra Hadad – *Mossad* Rescue Team commander

Dr. David Shvaz – Temple Institute Director, Jerusalem
Dr. Ariel Chavitz – Architect of the Third Temple
Dr. Akiva Hahn – Forensic archeologist
Dr. Uri Ravitz – Forensic archeologist
Sergeant Major Esther Meier – Jerusalem District Police commander
Walid Obeidat – Jordanian Ambassador to Israel
Leah Dayan – Ph.D. student of Akiva Hahn
Dr. Malak Cantor – Israeli astrophysicist
Gad Fielder – Assistant to Dr. Cantor

Captain Jim Powell – U.S. Army Chinook commander

Colonel Isaac Silverman – Israeli Defense Force Chinook liaison

King Mashallah – King of Jordan

King Nadeem – King of Saudi Arabia

Adeem el-Boutros – President of Egypt

Necmettin Bilal Gulbaran – President of Turkey

Khalifa bin Shakir al-Din – President, United Arab Emirates

Emir Omar Nurullah – Monarch of Qatar

Ali el-Gamal – CEO, *Al-Furqan* media

Ahmad Karim – ISIS videographer

Captain Abraham Kahn – IDF Bomb Disposal Unit expert

Fatih Nagi – Suicide bomber

Jalal Zaman – Suicide bomber

"As the navel is set in the centre of the human body,
so is the land of Israel the navel of the world...
situated in the centre of the world,
and Jerusalem in the centre of the land of Israel,
and the sanctuary in the centre of Jerusalem,
and the holy place in the centre of the sanctuary,
and the ark in the centre of the holy place,
and the foundation stone before the holy place,
because from it the world was founded."
Midrash Tanhuma, Kedoshim

PROLOGUE

SEPTEMBER 7, 70 CE
Mount of Olives, Jerusalem

Flavius Josephus wept as he stared across the Kidron Valley. He couldn't take his eyes off the massive fire racing through the Temple complex in his beloved Jerusalem. The smoke and ash blowing from the blazing inferno coated his face with soot. Tears plowed deep furrows down his cheeks as he heard the haunting cry of thousands of Jews being slaughtered by bloodthirsty Roman soldiers.

Watching the horrific scene from the safety of the Mount of Olives, he reflected on the events of the last three agonizing months of the Roman siege of Jerusalem that had culminated in this moment.

***

Born thirty-five years earlier as a Jew named Joseph ben Matityahu, Josephus had initially taken part in the longstanding Jewish rebellion against the Romans. However, for the past three years he'd become increasingly convinced that God was actually on the side of the Romans.

At the Battle of Jotapata the Romans captured him, and he had served as a slave until he demonstrated his allegiance and usefulness to General Titus, the son of Emperor Vespasian. Josephus was educated and fluent in Latin, Greek, Hebrew, and Aramaic. When Titus discovered this advantage, he granted Josephus his freedom and quickly assigned him the task of historian in order to record the Roman attack on Jerusalem. Titus also changed his name to Titus Flavius Josephus, assuming the family name.

Josephus' historical record would explain in detail how the Jewish Zealots under the leadership of John of Gischala had resented Roman authority in Jerusalem. They finally staged a coup and took control of the Roman-held Fortress Antonio and the Jewish Temple complex. Then they murdered the priests and stopped the daily sacrifice because they thought the High Priest and his underlings were too friendly with the Romans. The priests had only been trying to negotiate a truce, but John and his followers felt that the filthy Romans would only understand the tip of a sword.

In response General Titus surrounded Jerusalem, preventing food and supplies from entering and propelling its inhabitants into a devastating famine. A few Jewish deserters who supported neither the priests nor the Zealots eventually managed to slip out of the city under the cover of night to bear witness to the atrocities happening inside. They reported hellish conditions and famished mobs searching house-to-house for food. John and his thugs viciously robbed and murdered the wealthiest Jews remaining in the city, beating and torturing the residents after raiding their carefully hidden food stores.

Josephus recorded the Jews' evil behavior with these words: *"To narrate their atrocities in detail is impossible; but, to put it briefly, no other city every endured such miseries, nor since the world began has there been a generation more prolific in crime."*

The starving victims continued dying in staggering numbers, resorting to eating shoe leather and grass in desperate attempts to stay alive. Many witnesses told a grisly story about one of the Jews named Mary and her father Eleazar, a wealthy merchant from Bethezuba. A crazed mob demanded that Mary give them her newborn infant. They then roasted and ate her child.

Reports of such barbaric behavior enraged Titus, but he steadfastly rejected any personal responsibility since he had repeatedly offered peace in return for the Jews' surrender. In a final effort to negotiate a truce, Titus sent Josephus to the city walls to try and reason with the rebels. As Josephus paced outside the Eastern Gate of the Temple Mount, he shouted in Aramaic to the rebels keeping their posts overhead. He entreated them to surrender to the superior forces of the Romans and delivered Titus' assurance that any Jews who surrendered now would be treated well and their precious Temple protected.

But time was short, he warned.

Josephus considered himself a first-century Jeremiah, pleading with tears for his people to repent. God had used the Babylonians six hundred years earlier as His instrument to punish His rebellious people and destroy the First Temple that Solomon built. Much later, the exiled Jews had come back from Babylon and painstakingly rebuilt the Second Temple. Now the mighty Romans stood poised to impose His judgment again.

Realizing his fervent appeals were having no effect, Josephus made a bargain: *"I have a mother, a wife, and an ancient and illustrious house involved in these perils. And maybe you think it is on their account that my advice is offered. Slay them. Take my blood as the price of your own salvation! I too am prepared to die, if my death will lead to your learning wisdom."*

But the Zealots considered Josephus nothing but a traitor—a turncoat who had joined the enemies of God. After turning a deaf ear to his pleas, the Zealots on the wall started pummeling him with large stones. As Josephus ran to escape, one rock found its intended target and knocked him to the ground. Thinking they had killed him, their cheers rang out across the valley.

But Josephus had only been knocked unconscious and would recover after a group of courageous Roman soldiers dodged the continuous flurry of rocks and pulled him to safety inside Titus' headquarters. General Titus, further enraged at the audacity of the Zealots, subsequently dropped any notion of leniency.

That day the Romans vowed to begin ruthlessly

capturing and killing any Jews who escaped. They were tortured and crucified in a prominent venue just outside the city walls to intimidate any remaining Jews. As many as five hundred Jews a day were captured and crucified. Josephus would later record, *"So great was their number that space could not be found for the crosses, nor crosses for the bodies."*

The cruelty of the Romans had a chilling effect on some of the remaining Jews. Instead of surrendering to avoid the fate of their comrades, many declared that they preferred death to slavery and intended to fight with their last breath. On the other hand, thousands of frightened Jews started streaming like water through every opening in the city wall in hopes that the Romans could not capture all of them. Syrian troops, fighting alongside the Romans, caught several deserters who confessed they had sold all their possessions in return for gold coins, which they had then swallowed before making their escape. A rumor soon spread that all deserters were filled with gold. Many Jews who escaped the torture of crucifixion were captured by the Syrians and Arabs and sliced open in a mad search for golden loot. Josephus noted that in one night alone two thousand Jews were *"ripped up"* this way. He continued to witness this barbaric violence night after night—the hand of God falling hard upon His rebellious people.

Finally, Roman soldiers stormed the Fortress Antonio next to the Temple. For three bloody days and nights they attacked, only to be pushed back by the Zealots. When the Romans finally recaptured the Fortress, John and his

Zealots (now numbering two thousand) retreated to the Temple, blindly believing that God surely would not let His own house be destroyed.

It was now the beginning of the end.

With victory assured, Titus gathered a council of his leaders to discuss what should be done with the Temple. Some advised that it be destroyed because it was a safe house for the remnant of rebels. But Titus intended to preserve it as Rome's possession and convert the gold-adorned Temple to house the pantheon of Roman deities. The next day they would attack, Titus declared.

Early in the morning the overwhelming forces of the Romans attacked John and his fighters in the Temple. The Jews fought furiously, confident that God was on their side. After a three-hour battle, there were so many corpses that the Romans had to climb over piles of dead rebels to continue the onslaught.

In the heat of battle, a Roman soldier snatched a burning timber from a fire and threw it through the golden door on the north side of the chamber surrounding the inner sanctuary. Titus ordered the fire extinguished, but it was too late. The timbers and other combustible materials quickly burned out of control. God's holy Temple had erupted into flames.

***

This was the heart-wrenching scene Josephus was now witnessing ... the final moments of the Temple. He watched as some rebels desperately clung to the thick curtain hanging from the ceiling in front of the Holy of Holies, believing the Temple would prove to be as indestructible as God Himself. As fire engulfed the curtain, terrified screams rang out across the Kidron Valley. Josephus recorded, "You would indeed have thought that the Temple was boiling over from its base, being everywhere one mass of flame, yet the stream of blood was more copious than the flames."

Even as the Temple burned, a crazed false Jewish prophet convinced many to retreat into the inferno itself. Promising God would deliver them there, a crowd of six thousand civilians obediently climbed onto the porticos of the Temple complex. The fire soon spread, blocking any escape, and they were swallowed by the conflagration. All six thousand people perished. The battle was over.

All night the Romans chained and led their conquests away from Jerusalem, their prisoners staring in disbelief at the pile of ashes that had once been God's glorious Temple. The Romans captured over forty thousand Jews and sold them as slaves. Due to the excess of supply, the asking price would be almost nothing.

Josephus coughed from the thick smoke, his eyes burning. Wiping his hand across the tears streaming down his cheeks, he suddenly remembered that today was the Ninth Day of the Jewish month Av. To his astonishment, he realized that the destruction of this Second Temple was occurring in the same month and the very day that the

First Temple had been destroyed by the Babylonians.

As he stared at the soot and ashes falling all around him, he wondered aloud, "Will there ever be another Temple here in Jerusalem? Only God knows!"

Aelia Capitolina (formerly Jerusalem)
April, 637 CE

Six centuries after the birth of Christ, the Muslim Caliph named Umar entered the battle-scarred city that had been under constant attack by his Muslim hoards for years. *"So this is the Holy City everyone has been talking about?"* he mused. *"It's nothing but a broken down pile of rocks. But Insha-Allah, I will be the one to change that."*

His entourage of Muslim warriors cheered as he rode his white steed through the narrow streets of what remained of the Old City of Jerusalem. The Christian Byzantine leader named Sophronius had finally agreed to surrender the city – or what was left of it. His forces had been reduced to a few faithful officers and malnourished stragglers who had chosen not to flee, unlike most of their comrades.

Twenty-three years earlier, Persian Muslims had looted the city and destroyed the Church of the Holy Sepulcher. This classical Byzantine domed structure was built on the site that Helena, the mother of the Roman Emperor Constantine, designated when she visited Jerusalem in

327 CE. She'd had a dream the night before about the exact location where Christ had died and insisted the church be built there. Christian pilgrims had worshipped at the site ever since, believing it to be the true location of the crucifixion and resurrection. After destroying the church, the Persians massacred ninety thousand Christian inhabitants. Then their army began methodically killing the remnant of Byzantine warriors over time until only a few remained to defend the city.

Sophronius, called the Patriarch of Jerusalem, waited anxiously in the street and listened to the steady clop, clop of approaching horse hooves. As Caliph Umar rode up to within several feet of him, Sophronius knelt and offered up his sword in an act of unconditional surrender. Umar ignored the symbolic offer and commanded harshly, "Take me to the Jewish holy hill."

A translator communicated the request to Sophronius who asked, "Do you mean the site where the Jewish Temple once stood?"

"Of course, what else could I be talking about? Take me now!" Umar said.

Sophronius and his guards led the Muslim caliph through several winding streets until they arrived at a large, flat mount overlooking the Kidron Valley. After they climbed to the top, they saw where Byzantine monks had constructed a small chapel for private worship. The chapel now lay in ruins, and the rest of the site was a confusing maze of huge ancient stones tangled in green vines. Large trees grew in random patches of soil not covered by the massive blocks. Centuries of erosion and neglect had rendered the once beautiful Temple courtyards into a sad jungle of wild vegetation.

As Umar looked around, his eyes filled with the fire of religious zeal. "We must claim this mount for Allah and for his prophet, Mohammed. May his name be blessed!"

He turned to Sophronius and commanded, "Show me the exact place where the Jewish Temple stood."

Umar intended to build a shrine for Allah that mocked the domed design of the infidels' Church of the Holy Sepulcher. He would construct his dome four times larger to symbolize the superiority of Allah. "There is no God but Allah and Mohammed is his prophet," he exclaimed as he looked around the barren area, formulating his construction plans. "Islam is Allah's final and only true religion. I will build a great Muslim Shrine here. It shall stand forever so that another Jewish Temple will never take its place!"

Umar's soldiers shouted their approval of their ruthless leader's passionate speech. When the cheering died down, Sophronius explained to Umar that he was not sure of the exact location of the Jewish Temple. "It was destroyed hundreds of years ago by the Romans," he said. "I'm afraid the records have been lost."

"Who then can tell me exactly where the Temple stood?" Umar demanded impatiently, his eyes boring into his conquest.

Sophronius considered the question and replied, "There are only a handful of Jews left in the city, and some of them still speak of the Temple. Perhaps one of them will know."

"Bring the oldest and wisest one to me immediately. Be quick! We will not leave this place until I speak with him."

Sophronius' second-in-command returned an hour later with Avi ben Tzion. Avi was an old man stooped by age with startling white hair, a full beard, and curling sideburns dancing down toward his shoulders. He walked slowly with the aid of a staff. Generations of his family had protected the long-held secret of the precise location of the Jewish Temple. At the beginning of *Shabbat* each week, they would sneak into that area under the cover of darkness. Here they quoted the sacred words from the Torah, praying to the God of Israel just as generations of Jews before them had done. Long ago, Avi's great-grandfather had also been asked by the Byzantium leaders to point out the location of the Temple in order to build a church there. Wanting to protect the holy spot, he had instead directed them to an area far away from the actual location of the Temple.

Now it was Avi's turn. Sophronius' men brought Avi before Umar who demanded, "Old man, do you know the location where the Temple of the Jews stood?"

"I believe I do, sir."

"Show me."

Avi looked quickly to heaven for courage and then

led Umar and his soldiers to the ruins of the Byzantine chapel – a spot south of the sacred place where his family prayed each week. Avi assumed Umar and his forces hoped to desecrate the site with a Muslim shrine, so he silently vowed he would never reveal the actual location of the Holy Temple. He rapped his staff against a particular rock protruding from the rubble and confidently announced, "This. This is the spot."

"Are you sure?" Umar inquired.

"As sure as anyone can be, sir." Avi said this while directing his mind to asking God permission for his deception.

"That's all I need from you, old man. Tell me something. Will you convert to Islam and confess that Allah is the only God and that Mohammed is his prophet?"

Avi raised his head to gaze directly into Umar's cold eyes and said, "I cannot deny the God of Abraham, Isaac, and Jacob. He and he alone is the only true God."

"Kill the infidel!" Umar bellowed.

Before Avi could take another breath, Umar's bodyguard removed his curved, razor-sharp scimitar from its scabbard. The muscled soldier drew it back with both hands and smiled as he swung it toward the feeble neck of the old man. His sword had spilled plenty of infidel blood before. As Avi's head flew from his torso, pools of red soaked the ground. The blood spilled on the Temple Mount that day was not the first and it wouldn't be the last.

PART 1

1

PRESENT DAY

Israeli Prime Minister's Office, *Knesset* Building Jerusalem, Israel

Solly sat and stared at the priceless artwork adorning the outer walls of the Israeli Prime Minister's office. Solomon Rubin was his official name on a classified *Mossad* roster of the national intelligence agency of Israel. But everyone who knew him called him Solly.

He had never been invited to the Prime Minister's office before. He was a little nervous. Solly didn't own a suit and tie. In his cover role as an archeological tour guide, he preferred jeans, t-shirts, and hiking boots. For this occasion he had chosen his newest jeans, a clean dress shirt and had even shined his boots. He had washed his long grey hair, which he kept in a perfectly woven ponytail that hung down the middle of his back. His full white beard was clean and fluffed, and his deep, intelligent eyes stared out from skin that was tanned and lined from over thirty years under the desert sun. He had removed his black Stetson cowboy hat and was holding it in his lap when the door opened.

A young, well-dressed man stepped out and said in Hebrew, "Mr. Rubin, the Prime Minister will see you now." He held open the door and asked in English, "Would you care for coffee or water?"

Despite Solly's throat being dry with nerves, he muttered, "No thank you, mate." Even after being in Israel for thirty years, his native Australian accent was prominent.

The Prime Minister's office was large but not elaborately decorated. Solly saw Prime Minister Natan Abrams leaning over a map of the Middle East. His coat was off, his tie loosened, and his shirtsleeves rolled up to his elbows. He clamped a pipe between his teeth, but there was no smoke. He was a large man in his seventies who exuded strength and wisdom, yet his shaved head made him appear younger.

Solly instantly recognized the two men surrounding Abrams. A third man, obviously an Orthodox Jewish rabbi because of the way he was dressed, sat alone. Solly had never seen him before.

Solly's boss, Asher Hazzan, was the director of *Mossad* and he stood beside the Prime Minister gazing at the same map. Asher was a meticulous man whose suit and tie looked expensive. His Stefano Beyer shoes were shined to a high buff, and his slender frame and dark hair made him look more like a Hollywood actor than the chief of Israel's intelligence service. But his only consuming interest in life was the security of Israel. He had no wife, and it was even rumored he never dated. He was truly married to his job.

The second man by the Prime Minister was Ziv Kessler. He didn't have an official title but served as a key volunteer national security advisor. He wasn't paid by the government and didn't need any salary. He had made several fortunes building and selling software companies and was reported to be worth billions. Kessler was also the most knowledgeable man in Israel in regard to the Palestinian "problem."

A short, unattractive man, he wasn't one to stand out in a crowd, which gave him an advantage in business. But his extreme intelligence and encompassing grasp of world events in the Middle East were legendary.

As Solly stood at the door, Prime Minister Abrams glanced up and said, "Mr. Rubin, so glad you could join us."

Solly smiled. "It's hard to resist an invitation from the Prime Minister – especially when my boss is here."

"Solly, you know Ziv Kessler," Abrams said and the two men shook hands.

Then Abrams gestured toward the rabbi. "I don't know if you've ever met the Chief Rabbi of Israel, Rabbi Yitzak Rabin."

Rabbi Rabin was dressed in the traditional black suit and hat with a gray beard and uncut sideburns curling down beside his deeply furrowed face. He made no move to rise toward Solly but merely acknowledged his presence with a stiff nod. Solly didn't know whether to bow, shake his hand, or cover his head with his hat so he offered a simple, "My pleasure, sir."

Abrams continued, "That was quite an operation you launched in Georgia. If you hadn't stopped that attack at the Masters golf tournament at Augusta, we'd be living in a different world today."

Asher frowned. "But you really stuck your neck out there, Solly. You should have called for backup earlier. If you keep running around like an Australian cowboy, don't complain when your horse kicks you in the teeth."

Abrams threw back his head and laughed. "Give him some slack, Asher. I received a full briefing from the CIA, and believe me, Solly didn't have time to call in reinforcements. President Flowers was livid when he tore into me for allowing *Mossad* to run an independent operation on U.S. soil. He used language even I had never heard, demanding financial reparations for all the damage done and equipment destroyed."

"How did you cool him down?" Kessler asked Abrams.

"I knew he was bluffing. I just told him that it wouldn't help his approval rating if the U.S. public learned just how close they had come to another 9/11. And, I told him, if Parker had been in charge, they would have been a day late and a dollar short – and a few thousand leaders dead." Tony Parker was the CIA director, and Abrams preferred that Solly call the shots. "That shut him up pretty quickly,"

Abrams continued. "He finally agreed to take care of the cover-up and said to tell the agent involved 'thanks.'"

The Prime Minister looked Solly in the eye. "So, Solly, on behalf of the President of the United States, here's your one-word commendation – 'thanks.'"

"I didn't do it alone," Solly protested. "I had some pretty good helpers. As you know, Ty Kensington, the American I recruited as a part-time *Mossad* contractor, was the real hero. He crashed a perfectly good airplane to bring down the terrorist flying the crop duster filled with botulinum toxin. And don't forget my other American partner, Regan Hart. She was the first to suspect the true nature of the threat. That's women's intuition, I believe."

The Prime Minister said, "Well, we're grateful for both of them. We even pulled a few strings and helped establish Ms. Hart back in her investment business after her heroics."

"I'm glad to hear it," Solly said.

Abrams turned to the *Mossad* Director. "Asher, do we have any leads on the location of Dr. Hakeem Saad?"

Asher shook his head. "The CIA fumbled the ball, and he was able to escape from an ambulance before they could arrest him. We think we may have a lead on him, but it hasn't been confirmed. But wherever he is, he's angry. And you can bet that he is planning revenge against the U.S. and especially Solly."

The Prime Minister frowned. "Keep up the search for him," he ordered. "Solly, I didn't just bring you here to thank you. We need your help in a bigger operation. Ziv, why don't you explain it to Solly? He has top security clearance, so don't hold anything back."

"Solly, have you ever heard of the Jerusalem Protocol?" Kessler asked.

Solly smoothed his hand down his long beard and accessed his memory. "No, I can't say that I've ever heard that term before. What is it?"

Silence filled the room. That was a question none of the men wanted to answer. As on an invisible cue they all turned toward Rabbi Rabin who had yet to speak in the meeting. He stared at Solly with eyes full of fire and said in a low voice, "The Jerusalem Protocol is something that every faithful Jew prays for regularly. It will change our world."

2

Gaza City, Palestinian Territory

Dr. Hakeem Saad winced in agony as he walked across the small kitchen. A bullet fired by Solomon Rubin, a *Mossad* agent, had shattered his right kneecap. The Israeli agent had engaged Dr. Saad in a gun battle at a small airfield in rural Georgia during Dr. Saad's failed terrorist attack at Augusta National Golf Course. His hatred for this agent nicknamed "Solly" knew no limits. He would exact revenge or gladly die in the effort to destroy him and his illegal nation Israel.

Dr. Saad had been Sadaam Hussein's chief biological warfare developer at the pinnacle of Iraq's military power. After the fall of Hussein he had escaped to Yemen where he lived a peaceful life as a chemistry professor. His biological warfare skills were all but forgotten as he concentrated on his new career and his wife and two children. But his world had been rocked in flash the moment a U.S. drone-launched missile had stolen the lives of his wife and only son. He had sworn to *Allah* at that moment that he would extract revenge against the Great

Satan, the United States.

Dr. Saad had reconnected with some of the contacts of his past to formulate a plan. Al-Qaeda leaders approved and financed his aggressive strategy to strike America's elite leaders with a deadly attack that would rival 9/11. He had manufactured five hundred gallons of botulinum toxin, the deadliest poison known to man, and carefully loaded the liquid poison into the hopper of a hijacked crop duster that would fly over the Master's golf patrons and release a fine mist of the toxin. Everyone who ingested even a microscopic amount of the toxin would have died. But his sinister plan had failed.

Instead of being hailed a hero among Muslims around the world, Dr. Saad had found himself staring into the barrel of Solly's assault weapon. He had wished for death to enter Paradise as a *Mujahideen* martyr. But instead the Jewish pig had robbed him of glory by crippling him.

Before law enforcement personnel could arrest him, Dr. Saad had bluffed his way into an ambulance. On the way to the emergency room in Augusta, he had contacted his group of embedded *Al-Qaeda* operatives. They had hijacked the ambulance and killed the driver and the EMT before smuggling Dr. Saad away to safety.

Braced with heavy painkillers stolen from the ambulance, Dr. Saad had endured a tortuously long drive to Toronto, Canada. A nervous Muslim orthopedic surgeon, whose family in the West Bank had been threatened, had done his best to repair the damage from the gunshot wound.

The *Al-Qaeda* group in the U.S. had later identified Ty Kensington and Regan Hart as the other two infidels who had spoiled his evil plot. Even now they were tracking the whereabouts of those two. They knew Ty kept busy as a private investigator between the occasional contract jobs with *Mossad*, while Regan worked for an Atlanta investment firm, Global Wealth Advisors. Dr. Saad relished how Solly and his friends would all soon be begging for mercy from their captors.

Dr. Saad didn't believe in luck, but praise be to *Allah*, the bullet had gone cleanly through his kneecap without damaging any of the tendons. He would limp for the rest of his life, but at least he could still walk. The true damage from that incident was tied to the fact that his failure had angered *Al Qaeda's* top leaders in Yemen.

Several million American dollars from their Holy Land Fund, along with the required religious *zakat* offerings from Muslims worldwide, had been funneled into Dr. Saad's attack. The Holy Land Fund was disguised as a charitable relief organization in Texas until the discovery that it was actually supporting terrorism. The *zakat* is the alms offering that every religious Muslim is required to give to ease worldwide suffering. In their faith it is second only to prayer in importance. But investigative reporting has tied some of the *zakat* to supporting terrorism. *Al Qaeda* didn't tolerate failure, they didn't like wasting money, and they didn't believe in second chances.

Although he was now considered persona non grata in most Middle-Eastern nations, he had recently found acceptance in a former splinter group of *Hamas* led for eight years by Dr. Ibrahim Azzus, one of Dr. Saad's former assistants under Hussein who lived in Gaza City. Ibrahim's terrorist group was now one of several new ISIS groups in Gaza. After living under the radar in Canada for a few months until the manhunt for him had settled down, Dr. Saad had flown under heavy disguise to Cairo, Egypt. From there Ibrahim's men had smuggled him into Gaza through a tunnel. The Muslim Brotherhood, the parent organization of *Hamas*, had dug this tunnel under Israel's nose in order to further their destructive causes.

Ibrahim had eventually grown tired of the Brotherhood's repeated failures to wipe the hated Jews from Palestine. Firing rockets into the desert was no more effective than throwing pebbles at a barking dog to keep him quiet. But ISIS seemed to be an organization that was finally going somewhere.

Ibrahim and Dr. Saad had first met Abu Bakr al-Bagahdi when al-Bagahdi was a quiet student in Iraq and Dr. Saad was a guest lecturer. That quiet college student was now better known by his nickname "The Fox." Al-Bagahdi had joined *Al Qaeda* in Iraq and had launched missions against the crusading American forces before being captured and detained at Camp Bucca in 2004. When he was released years later he had begun to plan how to inflict the greatest damage upon the infidels who had invaded his homeland.

By 2014 "The Fox" had formed ISIS (Islamic State of Iraq and Syria) and declared a new worldwide Islamic caliphate. Ibrahim had been immediately interested in importing ISIS to Gaza and, with al-Bagahdi's approval, started forming a strong network of former *Hamas* fighters into a deadlier ISIS force. When Ibrahim's old boss, Dr. Saad, had contacted him for help, he knew of his failed plan in America. But he welcomed him into his burgeoning ISIS group because he knew Dr. Saad was a brilliant scientist. His skill set could still be utilized to kill infidels.

Ibrahim had been preaching the merciless doctrine of ISIS for the past few weeks when Dr. Saad arrived in Gaza. Ibrahim quickly recruited him under his command. Even though Dr. Saad pledged his allegiance to ISIS he thought to himself, *"Forget America and Israel. All I'm interested in is planning my personal revenge against Solomon Rubin, Ty Kensington, and Regan Hart."* Plotting how they would suffer consumed his thoughts.

Two days later he was thrilled when he received an intelligence update that the two Americans were now staying somewhere in the eastern part of the state of Texas. He convinced Ibrahim to activate four embedded ISIS fighters in the U.S. to eliminate the Americans as the first set of targets in a wider plot to destroy infidels. *"After the Americans are gone, I will turn my attention to the pleasure of killing this Solly."* Dr. Saad thought. *"He will suffer an especially slow and agonizing death for what he and his comrades have done to me and my family."*

3

5,500 feet Above Ground Level (AGL) above East Texas

The single engine of the Beechcraft V-35 Bonanza began to sputter and shake violently.

At the controls, Ty Kensington grimaced and his stomach muscles clenched in a knot. *"Oh no!"* he thought. *"This can't be happening!"*

"What's wrong?" Regan Hart shouted into her voice-activated headset.

"Don't worry," Ty said with more confidence than he felt. "The engine's running a little rough. I just need to adjust the mixture."

Ty twisted the red knob protruding from the firewall, hoping to find the right fuel-to-air combination to smooth out the engine. But the sputtering only intensified. The four-seat aircraft began to shudder.

Regan grabbed onto her armrest, bracing herself. "Tyyyy..." she began.

He tried increasing the throttle and there was no change. The manifold pressure gauge indicated that the engine was losing power—and fast.

"Tell me you know what you're doing!" Regan shouted into her headset. "Why did I *ever* get in another airplane with you?"

Ty was too busy trying to fly the airplane to answer. His airspeed was dropping and he had to lower the nose to keep from stalling. He tried switching magnetos, but the engine continued to cough and wheeze. By now his altitude was less than two thousand feet and his U. S. Marine pilot training automatically kicked in. It was time to look for a place to put the airplane down.

"Regan, don't freak out…"

"Don't freak out?" she interrupted. "Excuse me, but that's generally what people do when they think they're going to die in the next five seconds and…"

He cut her off. "We're going to make an emergency landing. Help me find a field or a road where we can land."

Regan was breathing fast and digging her nails into the faux leather of the armrest. "What's wrong with the perfectly good airport we left a few minutes ago?"

"Can't make it back," Ty said tersely. "You can complain or you can help me look for a place to land."

Regan began frantically scanning the ground below. She saw a few narrow, twisting roads and acres of thick trees everywhere.

"There!" she shouted and pointed her finger. "To the right. There's a field."

Without looking, he instantly banked the Bonanza to the right and spotted the short field near a stand of trees.

"Good eyes. I think we can make that."

Ty quickly keyed the microphone button on the yoke and said, "Tyler Pounds, Bonanza six four seven four Whiskey is making an emergency landing about thirty miles southwest of the airport." He didn't wait for a reply.

With a final cough the engine stopped and the propeller was wind milling, producing additional drag. Since the engine was producing no thrust, the Bonanza was now a heavy glider. He kept his airspeed pinned on eighty knots and lined up with the field. As he dropped to five hundred feet, he lowed his flaps. The field was approaching quickly. And so were the trees.

"We're too low!" Regan screamed.

"Trust me."

"You expect me to trust you?" Regan's voice dripped with sarcasm. "Do you remember what happened the last time we flew together?"

"You picked a lousy time to bring up old memories. Now tighten your shoulder harness and hold on. This could be rough."

Ty pulled back slightly on the yoke to raise the nose of his airplane-slash-glider. As he cleared the tall pine trees, he pulled the gear knob down. With no engine noise the whine of the electrically activated landing gear lowering was almost deafening.

The field ahead had been plowed, so he realized the landing would be soft. Ty just had to keep the airplane steering straight or it would easily flip over. He still had a few scars from when he flipped a crippled King Air months before.

As the airplane glided toward the field he gently raised the nose to reduce the airspeed. The airplane gear made contact with the bumpy ground and produced a loud bang. Ty fought the rudder pedals to keep it tracking straight. Luckily the field was running slightly uphill, causing the airplane to decelerate quickly. After only about twenty seconds of bouncing through dirt, the airplane came to an abrupt stop. There was only silence.

Ty breathed a sigh of relief. But he knew that as hard as that dead stick landing had been, he faced a tougher task of dealing with his passenger's wrath. After all, it had been his idea to take her up in his dad's plane for an afternoon ride in the clouds before their first official date.

They had recently driven in from Atlanta to Tyler, Texas, in order for Ty to introduce Regan to his parents. Since their first meeting under unusual circumstances, they had spent a lot of time together. But Regan refused to call their outings a date – she wanted to meet his parents before she agreed to date him. Before taking her home, Ty had wanted to surprise her by giving her an aerial view of East Texas. He had driven to Tyler Pounds Field. The mechanics at Johnson Aviation knew him well, so they gave him a key to his dad's aging Bonanza. After untying the ropes from the underside of the plane, they had taxied out for what was to be an enjoyable flight.

Eight months earlier Ty had been forced to crash-land a damaged Beechcraft King Air. Regan and their friend Solly had been passengers when Ty had caused an intentional midair collision to bring down a terrorist with a crop duster full of poisonous gas. The three of them had walked away with only minor injuries.

Since that fiasco Ty had worked hard to convince Regan that it was perfectly safe to fly with him again. And now, he was two for two—two takeoffs, two crash landings. Not a great average for a former Marine pilot.

Ty stole a sideways glance at Regan, expecting an outburst of anger. But to his surprise he saw a smile curving at the corners of her lips before she threw her head back laughing. Ty loved seeing her blue eyes full of mirth. Her long blonde hair was wild and tangled around her headset, but Ty thought she had never looked more beautiful. He was tempted to lean over and kiss her, but his training kicked in. His first job was getting out of the disabled aircraft.

"Open the door. Let's get out of here!" he ordered.

Regan unbuckled her seat belt and opened the single door on the passenger side and slid out onto the wing. She still hadn't stopped laughing.

After Ty extracted his lanky frame from the cockpit he said, "What's so funny?" But he soon dissolved into her contagious laughter as well.

"I'm just thinking it's no wonder you're still single. Do all of your dates end this way? Don't you believe in airports?"

"Airports are so dull. Nothing but a long, smooth runway. Isn't this more interesting?" Ty wasn't sure how Regan would answer that.

4

If Ty had been a praying man, he would have thanked the Man upstairs for the safe landing, but he left all the praying to Regan. As they stared behind the grounded airplane, they could see two parallel ruts in the dirt where the landing gear had gouged the dirt.

Ty walked around the Bonanza and said, "Everything looks intact. My dad is going to be very glad I didn't ruin his precious airplane."

"Yeah, congratulations, Mr. Lindberg. Your flying skills are legendary. But how are we going to get out of here?"

They both looked up in time to see a dilapidated pick up truck bouncing across the field toward them.

"Our limo approacheth, fair maiden."

"That could be some angry hillbilly with a shotgun. Didn't you ever see the movie *Deliverance*?"

"That was East Georgia," Ty corrected. "This is East Texas. We don't have hillbillies here. We have our share of rednecks, but most of them are just good ol' boys."

Ty watched the pickup truck as it shuddered to a stop. It appeared to be a Ford built sometime in the early 1960s. A blue cloud of dirty smoke belched from the exhaust pipe. The paint had faded to a dull shade that made it impossible to guess the original color. Freckles of unpainted Bondo decorated the badly dented fenders. A large bumper sticker adorning the front bumper read, "They can take my gun when they pry it from my cold, dead fingers."

As he carefully approached the vehicle, all of Ty's carefully honed skills as a private investigator kicked into high gear. Despite what he had assured Regan, he also knew these woods were filled with some pretty crazy people who still thought the South would rise again.

The driver's door creaked open and a man exited. It was hard to guess his age, but he looked somewhere far north of sixty. He was wearing faded overalls over an old plaid shirt. The pants of the overalls were stuffed into old work boots that were scuffed and untied. A sweat-stained green cap with a faded John Deere logo sat perched on a shock of white hair. The man's bottom lip protruded in an unnatural way.

As he walked toward Ty, the man turned to spit. Ty realized he had stuffed a wad of chewing tobacco in his mouth. The man wiped some drool with the back of his hand and said with a thick country accent, "Whut in the hay are you doin' landin' yor airplane in mah field?"

Ty held up both hands in a friendly gesture. "Sir," he said, "my engine stopped, and this was the only place to land." He reluctantly held out his hand and said, "My name is Ty Kensington and this is my friend Regan."

The man looked at Ty's hand for a second as if considering whether to shake it or not. Then he shot out his hand and said with a friendly grin, "My name's Billy Frank Conroe." When he smiled, Ty noticed that half of his teeth were missing, and the ones remaining were tobacco stained.

Ty shook the man's hand, which was as calloused as an old stump. "Pleased to meet you, Billy," Ty said. Regan smiled and waved.

As he pumped Ty's hand, the man explained, "Call me Billy Frank. My momma's name is Billie, and my daddy's name was Frank, so they call me Billy Frank," he said with a laugh that turned into a hacking cough.

He tipped his cap at Regan and said, "Ma'am."

Regan was glad that Billy Frank didn't offer her his hand – the same one that had wiped his mouth. She thought, *"If you looked up the word 'redneck' in the dictionary, you'd find a picture of this guy."* She swallowed a gurgle of inappropriate laughter that bubbled up into her throat. Regan was the queen of inappropriate laughter, and she didn't want to hurt this stranger's feelings.

She bit her lip and said, "I'm pleased to meet you, Billy Frank."

"Can I give you folks a lift?" he asked, looking over his shoulder to his old Ford.

Ty pulled out his iPhone. "Let me call my dad and let him know that we made an emergency landing. What's the name of this farm? Where are we in relation to Tyler?"

"Well, let's see. Tyler's about thirty miles north of here," Billy Frank said. "I don't really have a name for my farm. I got about twenty acres and raise a few hogs and some goats. I grow some corn in this field ... when I ain't got no airplane sittin' in it!"

Billy Frank started laughing again, culminating into a hacking cough so fierce he had to lean over and put his hands on his knees to catch his breath.

When he regained his breath, he stood up and said, "You two should just be thankful that you made it. They ain't too many bare fields around here – mostly pine trees. But like my old pappy used to say, 'Even a spotted pig looks black at night.' Yessir, I'd say you two's luckier than a rat in a cheese factory."

Ty and Regan glanced at each other with looks that needed no explanation. Was this guy for real? Billy Frank was just smiling, staring at them with eyes that suggested that the lights were on, but nobody was at home.

Ty pulled out his phone and called his father. After a few rings he said, "Hey Dad, it's Ty. Now don't worry, but I had to make an emergency landing in your Bonanza."

Regan couldn't hear the other side of the conversation, but she could tell from Ty's expression that his dad wasn't happy. Ty was cringing beneath the verbal tirade his dad was delivering.

"No, Dad, there's really *no* damage! The engine started losing power, and I put it down in a field a few miles south of Tyler." A few more minutes passed as Ty nodded silently and just listened.

"Well, we've met the man who owns the farm – and at least I didn't buy it by the way, right?"

Ted Kensington was in no mood for humor.

Ty continued, "Well, anyway, he offered to take us back into town. Where would you like to meet?"

After another minute of confirming their plans, Ty ended the call. "Billy Frank," he said, "my dad will send a mechanic out tomorrow to check on the plane. He said you can drop us off at Wal-Mart south of Tyler. Do you know how to get there?"

Billy Frank flashed a snaggletooth grin again and said, "Shoot, does a hog know how to find a mud hole? I used to take the missus, God rest her soul, to the Wal-Marx every Saturday."

Ty and Regan exchanged another glance, silently warning the other not to so much as crack a smile. Billy Frank never skipped a beat.

"The cancer took her two years ago. I shore miss her. Our trips to the Wal-Marx was like our weekly date. But you should see how some of the people dress there – like they got no class at all!"

Ty nodded in agreement and pointed to the truck. "Let's go then."

5

Billy Frank opened the door of his pickup, quickly brushing off the dirt and debris from the passenger side onto the floorboard. Regan slid into the middle of the worn bench seat and noticed that the windshield was cracked in several places. Empty Skoal tins littered the dashboard. The ceiling liner sagged toward her hair, and she wondered what kind of creatures might be living in there. She shuddered involuntarily and slid down further into the seat to get away from the flapping cloth.

Billy Frank hopped in next, and Regan instinctively scooted as close to Ty as possible. The engine came to life with a roar followed by a grinding noise as Billy Frank fought the gear handle on the steering column to find first gear. He laughed and said, "My pappy always said, 'If you can't find it, grind it!'"

"There it is!" he shouted and they were off.

They lurched forward and Regan noticed that the truck smelled strongly of gasoline. She felt every jolt and suspected that the shocks were non-existent.

"I can take this for a few miles," she told herself, already missing her C-class Mercedes.

They drove past a sad looking singlewide mobile home featuring a crooked deer stand in the backyard. Behind it a half-empty pond simmered down the hill.

Billy Frank followed Regan's eyes to the mobile home. "That's where I live, little lady. It's seems awful empty now with the missus gone. I only got fifteen more payments and it'll be all mine!"

As they drove past the mobile home and arrived at the front gate of the property, Ty was surprised to see Billy Frank use a remote control to open it. He also noticed two small video cameras mounted on metal poles next to the gate.

Billy Frank was one of those individuals who felt it was his responsibility to fill every moment of silence with his insight or opinion. He kept up a running commentary. Regan and Ty were too shell-shocked to interject.

"Yep, times are tough. But as my pappy used to say, 'About the time you get out on a limb, somebody'll pull the rug out from under you.'"

Ty and Regan started to laugh politely at his joke, but Billy Frank was serious.

"We been havin' an awful drought this summer," he continued. "It's so dry that the catfish have been knockin' at my back door askin' for a drink of water!"

Ty and Regan couldn't help but laugh at that one. This guy was really funny without even trying to be.

Billy Frank took their laughter as encouragement to keep going. "The only place I been hotter 'n here is

Vietnam – that there's a whole other country. I spent me a long time there with my best buds. We done a lot of killin', yessir. Not proud of it, but it was them or us."

"I was U.S. Marine," Ty said. "What branch did you serve in?"

"I was in the U. S. Army. One of 'em what was called Special Forces, but we weren't no more special than the other grunts there. They made us wear these green berets. I still got mine. I was always right smart at shootin', so they made me a sniper."

Ty wondered for the first time if there was more to this guy they first suspected.

Billy Frank changed the subject. "The Wal-Marx is just around this curve. I been meanin' to ask you. Are you two hitched?"

Regan blurted out a laugh.

Ty shot her the stink eye. "We're just friends. This was actually supposed to be our first date tonight. And you've certainly made it memorable, Billy Frank."

Billy Frank smiled a toothless grin as he stared vacantly just above Regan's hairline.

"She's a purdy one, fersure. Don't say much. That's a good thing. Don't let her get away."

Regan smothered her laughter with the back of her palm. Ty said, "Oh, I won't. She *is* rather meek and quiet."

This earned him a sharp elbow in his ribs.

"Ooof... I mean, here we are," Ty said. "Thanks, for the ride. I'll be back out tomorrow with the mechanic."

"Nice meetin' you folks. You can just continue your first date right here I reckon."

As Regan exited the truck, she smiled and waved at Billy Frank. With a smile still pasted on her face she turned to Ty and said through gritted teeth, "You know darn well, Buster, this isn't our first date. I actually don't know if we'll *ever* have one." Then she twirled around and stomped across the parking lot toward the large Wal-Mart entrance.

6

"There's my dad," Ty said as he pointed toward a silver Jeep Cherokee pulling up to the curb at the entrance to Wal-Mart.

Without saying a word, Regan hopped in the front passenger seat and introduced herself. "Hi, Ted. I hope you remember how to fly, because your son doesn't have a clue. I'm Regan by the way."

"It's not my fault!" Ty whined as he climbed in the back seat. "Dad, meet Regan. Regan, this is my dad."

Regan shook Ted's hand cordially, flashing her best smile, although she couldn't care less at the moment about making an impression on Ty's dad. Her hair was a wild mess, she was exhausted, and she was starving.

"Pleased to meet you, Regan," Ted said warmly. "I've heard a lot about you."

"When was the last time you flew the Bonanza, Dad?" Ty asked, eager to talk about something else.

"I don't know, Son. It's been tied down on the ramp at Johnson Aviation for the last six months or so. Since they found that heart murmur, I haven't been flying."

"I suspect that it probably had water in the fuel," Ty

offered as explanation. "I tried everything I knew, but I wasn't able to generate enough power to climb. The good news is that your pride and joy is still in one piece. We just have to figure out a way to get it out of this Texas redneck's field."

"Only two options there," Ted replied, making his way out of the parking lot and down the highway. "We either take off the wings and haul it out of there on a flatbed, or you fly it out."

"Me?" "Him?" Ty and Regan said simultaneously.

"I don't think I want to get back behind the controls of that old dog," Ty said. "No offense. How much would it cost to put it on a truck and transport it back to the airport?"

"You don't want to know, Ty," Ted said, making a right turn into the driveway at his home where Ty's mom was waiting on them with dinner.

"Well, Regan makes an obscene amount of money at her investment firm." Ty leaned forward on the leather console between Ted and Regan. "What do you say about financing our little rescue project? Everybody is trying to save the whales and save the planet. Don't you want to help save an airplane?"

"Forget it, Buster," Regan retorted. Ted laughed under his breath as the trio climbed out of the car. "You put it there, so you've got to get it out. You're zero for two with me when you're the pilot. There won't be a third time. I'm booking the next flight on Delta back to Atlanta."

"I can't say I blame you, Regan," Ty's dad said, holding open the front door to their home for their guest. "Why don't you at least join us for dinner?" She was starting to like Ted already.

"Come on, Regan," Ty pleaded. "I was just kidding. At least stay for a few more days and get to know my parents. Then we can drive back in my truck."

"No more small airplanes?" Regan inquired.

"Nope. We'll leave the flying to the pilots who fly the heavy steel."

7

Billy Frank Conroe was waiting at his gate for Ty and a mechanic from Johnson Aviation the next day. Ty had known Tony Myers since he had first learned to fly at age sixteen. Tony was one of several airframe and power plant mechanics who kept the private and commercial aircraft at Tyler Pounds Field in flying condition. Prior to moving to Tyler, Tony had worked for years in the flight maintenance department for American Airlines at DFW. He was rumored to have changed an engine on a Boeing 777 in less than two hours – a record that still stood. Since retiring from American, Tony had accepted a work-as-needed schedule at Johnson Aviation.

Billy Frank opened the gate and waved them forward to follow him. He climbed into his old pickup and after much grinding, found first gear and took off, leaving Ty and Tony choking on the pungent blue smoke.

Ty asked, "Tony, do you know anything about this guy?"

"Nope," Tony replied holding a rag over his nose and mouth. "But these woods are full of interesting people."

"What do you mean by interesting?" Ty asked.

"Well, let's just say that some of the family trees out here don't have many branches."

They both started laughing while still coughing from the smoke.

They followed Billy Frank to the back pasture until the airplane came into view.

"There's 6467 Whiskey," Ty said, reading the tail number off his plane. "I don't think she sustained any damage from the landing, but I'll let you be the judge."

Tony stared at the tall stand of trees at each end of the field, mentally planning an exit strategy. "You did a heck of a job getting her down safely," he told Ty. "Let's remove the engine cowl and see what the problem is."

Billy Frank met them at the airplane and launched a huge explosion of chewing tobacco juice into the dirt. He wiped his chin with his right hand and held it out to Ty. "Good to see you again, feller. Did you and Missy have a good date at the Wal-marx?"

Ty reluctantly shook his hand and said, "Not really, Billy Frank. We didn't have much time to enjoy it before my dad picked us up."

Ty quickly wiped his hand on his jeans and introduced Tony.

"Billy Frank, this is Tony Myers. He's an airplane mechanic."

Billy Frank walked over and held out his hand, but Tony just nodded, as he was already busy removing the screws securing the engine cowling.

"Hey, I can give you a hand if ya need it," Billy Frank offered to Tony. "I kin repair any kind of engine and have 'em running smooth in no time."

Tony thought about Billy Frank's truck. "Thanks Billy, but the law requires you to have a special license to work on airplanes."

"Call me Billy Frank. My momma's name is Billie, and my daddy's name was Frank. They call me Billy Frank so they could tell us all apart."

After lifting the engine cowling, Tony reached in and untwisted the safety wire that secured the bolt connecting the fuel line to the fuel pump. Then he repeated the action from where the line entered the engine compartment. Next he removed the short reinforced rubber hose and carried it back to his toolbox. As Billy Frank looked on, Tony took out a large empty glass jar and lowered one end of the fuel line into the jar. He put the upper end of the line into his mouth and gently blew until the fuel left in the line filled most of the jar.

Billy Frank, now peering over Tony's shoulder, whispered, "Make sure you don't suck on that tube. One time I was siphoning gas out of my truck for my lawn mower and I got a mouthful of gas. I was gaggin' like a cat swallerin' a hairball."

Instead of responding to Billy Frank, Tony held up the glass and watched as the liquid separated into two layers. "Just as I expected," he concluded. "Your fuel was contaminated with water. Water is heavier than aviation fuel, and this lower layer is all water."

"How did water get in the gas tank?" Ty asked.

"Well, there's usually some condensation that occurs in fuel tanks, especially when an airplane hasn't flown in a long time. Also, since this plane is tied down outside, if the seal around the fuel caps isn't tight, rainwater can seep in. You did sump the fuel tanks during your pre-flight, didn't you?"

"Sure I did. But I guess I didn't drain enough to remove all the water. What a dumb mistake. Can you fix it?"

"No problem," Tony said. "I'll just open the sump drains under the wings until there's no more water, and you'll be good to go. Are you sure you can fly this plane out of here?"

"I don't know. What do you think?"

Tony scratched his chin. "Well, if we can lighten up the airplane, I think you have enough room to take off, but I wouldn't try it myself. That one tall pine tree at the end of the field might make it impossible."

8

Ty turned and looked at the pine tree in question. He thought for a minute and asked, "Hey, Billy Frank, have you got a chainsaw?"

"Heck, does a cat have climbin' gear? I got me a big 'un."

"Would you be willing to cut down that pine tree?"

Billy Frank saw flashing dollar signs. "Well, my old pappy planted that tree and it's pretty special. But I guess I could cut it down ... if the price is right."

"How much is it gonna cost me?" Ty inquired.

"I think that there's a five hunnert dollar tree, best I kin figure."

"I'll pay you fifty."

"Done!" Billy Frank said as he quickly headed back to his truck, cackling at the easiest fifty dollars he ever earned.

"Okay, Tony, what else can we do to improve my chances of getting out of here?" Ty asked.

"I can remove the other seats and pull a couple of the avionic sets out. Every pound we can remove means a better chance of getting out. Then we can pump all the fuel out except for what you need to get back to the airport. I figure you only need about fifteen gallons."

"Let's do it."

An hour later Tony had replaced the fuel line and used the sump drains under each wing to drain the excess fuel into jerry cans. He crawled into the small cockpit and began to remove the two back seats and the passenger seat.

The sound of a chainsaw shattered the morning calm as Billy Frank battled with the single pine tree at the end of field. Soon the sound died and Billy Frank yelled, "Timber!" The pine crashed to the ground. Billy Frank cupped his hands around his mouth and yelled, "Any more fifty dollar trees you want cut down?"

Ty whispered to Tony, "If an idiot yells all alone in the forest, does anybody hear him?" Then he turned to and yelled to Billy Frank, "You're good, Billy Frank. That's the only one we need cut."

As Ty carried the airplane seats toward Tony's truck, he began to wonder if this was a good idea. He had flown F-15s for the Marines during the First Gulf War, so he was used to flying aircraft with power to spare. He remembered the pilots' adage: "There are old pilots and bold pilots. But there are no old bold pilots."

He thought, *Regan was right. I haven't had much luck lately in my flying career. At least she isn't here to witness this potential fiasco.*

He looked up just then to see his dad's Jeep Cherokee bouncing across the pasture toward him. Regan was sitting in the passenger seat chatting away with Ted, all smiles.

Tony walked over to Ty carrying the Garmin GPS and

the two Nav/Com radios. "I figure you can find your way back to the airport without the GPS. And you've still got a transponder and a handheld radio to call the tower. This is as light as she's gonna get."

Ted parked and walked up to the two men. "So you're going to try to fly her out?"

Regan was still in the car with the passenger mirror folded down, checking her makeup.

"Well, what do you think, Dad? Is this a dumb idea?"

Ted climbed up on the wing and crawled into the cockpit. He took a quick look around and said, "Let's don't leave anything to chance. Get the owner's manual out and calculate the takeoff distance. The wind is coming from that end of the field where it's pretty clear of trees."

Ty said, "Yeah. It cost me fifty dollars to have Billy Frank cut down his precious pine tree."

Ted looked at the man making their way toward them. "So that's the Billy Frank you and Regan have been talking about." He turned to the mechanic and said, "Tony, good job removing some of the weight. How much fuel is remaining?"

"About fifteen gallons, so that's ninety pounds."

Ted pulled the well-used owner's manual from the seat pocket in the back of the pilot's seat. He opened it and ran his finger down a chart. "According to this you need about twelve hundred feet to take off at this weight. But that's from a paved runway. I figure you need a third more distance on this dirt surface. That's sixteen hundred feet. It would be better if this plowed dirt could be graded flat."

Billy Frank had rejoined them and said, "I got me a flat blade that goes on the back of my John Deere. One or two times up this here field and it will be as flat as a pancake. I can do that for just a couple hunnert dollars."

"How about another fifty?" Ty said.

"Done!" Billy Frank got in his truck and drove off, crowing about the easiest hundred dollars he had ever made.

Billy Frank's truck may have been falling apart, but his John Deere tractor was almost new. He came roaring up, and within twenty minutes he had flattened the dirt in the middle of the field until it looked more like a dirt road than a plowed field.

Tony climbed down from the wing and said, "Let's walk off the field and we'll know for sure whether you have enough room or not."

Ty walked off distances on the golf course all the time, so he knew his stride was about three feet. He would need to make sure he had about five hundred thirty paces.

Ty started jogging toward the end of the field. When he got to the fence, he turned around and started walking and counting.

Regan had joined the men by now and asked sarcastically, "Ted, do you think he needs someone to help him count that high?"

Everyone laughed.

"Regan," Ted said, "you sure are refreshing. I like the fact that you give him a hard time. He needs someone to keep his massive ego in check."

After a few minutes, Ty came jogging back and said, "I think I can do it. I stopped counting at five hundred and thirty paces, and there was still some room left."

"Are you sure you want to try it, Ty?" Regan asked, genuine concern now in her voice. "It doesn't look like that much room to me."

"No problem," Ty said with more confidence than he felt.

"You're good to go," Tony said. "The fuel hose is replaced. Be sure to prime the engine a few pumps before you try to start it."

Billy Frank added, "I never been in one of them little flyin' machines. We flew in the big 'uns to Vietnam. Any chance you can let me ride with ya? I bet I kin fly one of these things. It looks pretty easy to me."

"I'd love to sometime, Billy Frank. But there's only one seat now. Sorry, buddy." Ty rolled his eyes as he climbed into the pilot's seat and buckled his seat belt.

9

Ty grabbed the pilot checklist and carefully followed every item. After pushing in the primer handle four times, he switched on the fuel pump and magnetos and yelled, "Clear prop!"

The engine turned over for about ten seconds before it roared to life. He made sure all the engine gauges were in the green and advanced the throttle. When he had enough momentum, Ty punched the left rudder pedal with his foot and the Bonanza began to turn left. He carefully taxied toward the end of the field bouncing over the dirt surface. *"Whew, this field is still pretty rough. If I hit a hole on the takeoff roll, I could snap the gear and this baby might flip over,"* Ty thought. He also noticed that he was beginning to sweat even though the morning air was still cool.

When he reached the end of the field, he punched the right rudder and the nose of the airplane swung around to the right until it was pointing into the wind.

He followed the run-up checklist and then reduced the power. By now he was having second thoughts. He wondered if praying would help.

Regan was a strong believer, but Ty had not yet decided

whether this whole God-thing was real or not. He had been raised in the church, but he rarely paid attention and his stint in the Marines had caused whatever faith he'd had to that point to fail. He wondered is this was a good time to start praying again.

"This isn't the time to think about God," the pilot in him reminded Ty. He had to get his dad's airplane out of this field. To accomplish a short-field takeoff he lowered the flaps 15 percent. He pressed his feet onto the top halves of the rudder pedals to apply the brakes. Then he smoothly advanced the throttle until the engine thundered. The airplane was shaking, straining forward. Ty released the brakes, and the airplane began to roll forward slowly. Too slowly. The old Bonanza eventually began to pick up speed, but he doubted he could achieve enough airspeed to lift off. He glued his eyes on the other end of the field, calculating in his mind at which point he could still abort the takeoff without crashing through the fence.

Bouncing along, he quickly glanced down at the airspeed indicator, willing the needle to reach the green arc that indicated an airspeed of seventy knots, the minimum speed for the airplane to fly.

"Come on. Come on. Oh, no," he thought as the fence rushed toward him.

He still didn't have enough speed to lift off. And now it was too late to stop. He was in deep trouble.

Regan and Ted watched with growing horror as the single-engine airplane roared down the field, the nose veering from side to side.

"He's not going to make it!" Ted yelled to Tony.

Regan's eyes filled with tears as she thought about Ty crashing through the fence. She closed her eyes, but tears squeezed through her eyelids and rolled down her cheeks. She prayed aloud with a confident voice, *"Please, Father! Help him. Help him!"*

Inside the cockpit Ty saw with alarm that the airspeed indicator was still lingering just below flying speed. He was beyond terrified. "Ty, you idiot! This was a stupid idea!" he yelled.

As he shouted those words, he yanked back on the yoke. To his surprise the Bonanza lifted off the ground just a few feet before reaching the fence. He quickly flipped the gear handle to raise the gear and cleared the fence with only a few feet to spare. As the gear tucked into the fuselage, the plane began to climb slowly. He retracted the flaps, and the vertical airspeed indicator showed him climbing at fifty feet a minute, then one hundred, then five hundred feet a minute. Suddenly the lightweight Bonanza was climbing into the blue sky like a homesick angel.

"Yes!" Ty whooped. When he reached one thousand feet he circled back around the field and waggled his wings at the four people standing in the field. He could see them jumping up and down for joy as Billy Frank tossed his green cap into the air.

Ty turned northwest toward Tyler Pounds Field and a real, paved runway.

On the ground, Ted put his arm around Regan and pointed to the sky. "Way to go, Son! He made it!"

Regan sniffed from crying and couldn't contain her smile. She whispered, "Thank you. Thank you. Thank you, God!"

Billy Frank picked up his hat, dusted it off on his knee and said, "Shoot. I thought he was a goner fersure. Now, whose gonna pay for my tree and my airport construction project?"

10

Gaza City, Gaza Strip

Dr. Hakeem Saad looked at the number of the incoming call on his cell phone. He recognized it as one of the ISIS members known as Bakri Karimi who was embedded in the United States.

Dr. Saad pushed a button on the phone and immediately said in Arabic, "Do you have encryption software on your phone?"

"Yes, it is working now," Bakri replied.

"What do you have to report?"

"We have located the man and the woman you are after."

Dr. Saad smiled for the first time in many days. "Excellent. Where are they?"

"They are visiting the man's parents in a city in the eastern part of Texas. What do you want us to do?"

"I want them killed and then beheaded. You will not receive your reward until I see pictures of their heads."

Bakri thought for a moment. "That will be difficult to do without getting caught. They are in a city with many people, and the local law enforcement resources are excellent. My team can't risk detection because we have other orders for a much larger operation. We are only doing this because you offered to pay. Perhaps we could simply kidnap them?"

Dr. Saad gripped the phone tighter until his knuckles were white. He replied, "You idiot! Kidnapping would raise an alarm and activate a massive manhunt. No, killing them is the best solution. I will only pay for their deaths."

Bakri sighed. "Perhaps we could follow them for a few days and see if they go to some isolated area where we can do the job. But we can't do anything where there are crowds and risk being caught."

"Do it anyway you want," Dr. Saad snarled. "Just send me the pictures of their heads when the job is over."

Bakri had spent time in England as a student, so his English was excellent. He had been thrilled to be accepted as a recruit for ISIS and had risen quickly through the ranks. Bakri had already taken his place in a death squad that had beheaded twenty-four Christians while someone filmed the atrocity. He repeatedly watched the glorious video of this act for Allah's sake.

Four weeks earlier he and his squad of ISIS fighters had flown out of Brussels, Belgium, into Cancun International Airport. Their phony passports got them into the city where they were provided a nondescript four-wheel drive SUV with stolen Texas license plates. It had been a simple matter to drive to the Texas border and slip across the border off-road. They had settled in a motel in East Texas for a few days while they waited for instructions. Their main target was in Dallas, but Bakri and his team were not due there for a few days and he was glad to have a chance to spill his first American blood in a more remote area.

Two nights earlier one of his team members had slipped a magnetic GPS unit under the back bumper of the American's truck that was parked at his parents' home. Bakri would look for the right time and a remote place where he could execute both of the Americans. He had visited a local Army Navy Surplus store and was surprised by the excellent choice available in swords. He had picked one that would do the job to his satisfaction and was looking forward to using it. He would have one of his men video it for the glory of ISIS.

11

The next night Ty and Regan reluctantly accepted Billy Frank's invitation to come out and share some barbequed ribs at his mobile home. They tried to decline, but he insisted. Because he had been such a help to them, they finally agreed, although Regan assured Ty that there was no way she was eating dinner at Billy Frank's. She would eat afterwards and just drink iced tea there.

Ty and Regan piled into Ty's pickup and made their way out to the country.

"Oh my gosh. I don't have my hand sanitizer," Regan said as she plowed through her purse.

"Call 911," Ty suggested sarcastically.

"Very funny," Regan said. She never went anywhere without hand sanitizer, and she wasn't entirely sure she could survive the evening without it.

As they drove up to the gate it opened automatically this time, and they drove down the dirt road to Billy Frank's mobile home. Billy Frank came out, wiped his hands on his overalls, and announced, "I guarantee that you ain't never had no ribs as good as I ken cook 'em. They so good, it'll make you slap yer grandma."

Ty had failed to notice on the drive out that a black SUV had been trailing him. Bakri was driving and had three heavily armed ISIS operatives with him.

As he drove past the gate to Billy Frank's farm, Bakri said, "I think we're in luck. I haven't seen another house close by. And it will be dark soon. We can slip in, do the job and be gone before anyone knows we're here."

12

Two hours later Ty sighed with contentment, patting his bulging stomach. "Billy Frank, you weren't wrong. Those were delicious ribs. How did you learn to cook like that?"

The three of them were sitting in lawn chairs behind the mobile home listening to the crickets and the sound of insects committing kamikaze in Billy Frank's two bug zappers. Even Regan had eventually broken down and had a few ribs. To her surprise, she actually enjoyed them!

"Well, there's two secrets to great ribs. One, you gotta make sure the meat's tender. Two, you gotta have the right sauce – I make it myself. And three, you gotta have the right heatage on the grill."

"That makes three secrets, Billy Frank," Regan said with a smile. "Are you going to tell us how to cook them?"

"Nope. Then it wouldn't be no secret no more! My sauce has got more secret ingredients than that General Sanders KFC! It's so secret that I forget it sometimes. But I got it right tonight!"

"You sure did!" Regan agreed, looking at her Apple watch. "It's getting late. Let us help you carry the dishes into the kitchen."

As she stood up, she was startled by a high-pitched beep coming from inside the trailer. "What's that noise?"

Billy Frank jumped up and said, "That's the motion sensor I have on my gate. I also got me a couple of motion activated game cameras set up. I mostly just like to look at deer these days instead of killin' 'em. Come on in and let's see what we got on the video!" Ty recognized this was quintessential redneck after dinner entertainment.

All three crowded around a monitor set up on the tiny kitchen table in Billy Frank's mobile home. What they saw on the display caused them to gasp simultaneously.

On the grainy video they could clearly see four armed men climbing over the gate and walking toward the trailer. They were dressed in black, their faces covered with black ski masks.

Billy Frank's voice suddenly turned authoritative, although he retained his East Texas twang. "They have night-vision goggles. And those look a lot like M92 pistols they're carrying."

It was as if Billy Frank morphed from redneck to weapons expert in a second.

"How do you know about those guns?" Ty asked incredulously.

"I know more about weapons than most people know about the back of their hand," Billy Frank responded, heading to a nearby closet. "Those are nasty semi-automatic pistols made at the Zastava factory in Serbia.

They carry a thirty-round mag and are the weapons of choice for terrorists. What are them guys doing here?"

Ty stood frozen in place.

"Billy Frank," he began, "we had a recent run-in with some really bad guys, and I wouldn't be surprised if they are after us. I'm sorry to bring you into this."

Ty whipped out his cell phone and began to punch in numbers. "I'm calling 911 for help. What's the location of this farm?"

"Just tell 'em it's the Conroe Farm eight miles east of Noonday."

Billy Frank was now holding a long rifle with a scope while he scampered back to his tiny bedroom. He shouted, "But there ain't no way 911 is gonna help you tonight. They's no way any cops gonna show up here within thirty minutes. And these fellers look serious about doing some damage real quick like."

Billy Frank ran back into the kitchen with a fist full of ammunition. "Don't worry none. I got a plan for those fellers."

"What's that?" Regan asked, pointing to the gun and nervously looking around the mobile home for an escape.

"This here is the M24. The best sniper weapon system the Army ever issued. Actually it's the modified version called the M24A2. Instead of a single-shot bolt action, it accepts this five-round magazine." He grabbed a flat, green magazine and slapped it in a slot on the underside of the rifle. "It's modified for a silencer, too, but I don't have time to put that thing on. It's gonna get noisy."

Ty was kicking himself for not bringing a firearm. "Don't be crazy, Billy Frank. There's four of them and only one of you."

"Yep, too bad for them," Billy Frank growled. "Now, here's the plan. I got me some spotlights mounted in the top of the pine trees around the trailer. I'm going to slip out the back door and move to the side yard. When I whistle, you hit that switch there by the stove. The light will temporarily blind them on account of them night-vision goggles they got on. When you hit the switch, drop to the floor and cover your heads. And stay down!"

Before Ty or Regan could argue, Billy Frank had slipped out the back door of the trailer.

13

Bakri whispered instructions in his com microphone. "Stay quiet. Spread out and stay low. We're almost within range. I heard voices. Don't shoot until I give the word, but then rush the trailer and empty your magazines. We don't know how many people are in there. We've got to get in and out quickly. But leave me time to decapitate the man and woman and get a picture. Radio silence from this point on."

Bakri switched off his com. Through his goggles he could see the silhouette of a couple of people inside the trailer. Only a few more steps and he would be in range.

Suddenly he heard a soft whistle. A moment later high-powered floodlights bathed the area around him.

Billy Frank had his rifle raised. He was confident because he visited a shooting range often and knew he could still easily hit a target three hundred yards away. The intruders were less than fifty yards from the end of his nose.

He sighted on the first target and gently squeezed the trigger. Before his target fell he was already aiming at his next bogie.

Even though the light temporarily blinded him, Bakri heard three shots less than a second apart. "Blam, blam,

blam!" He recognized an ambush and fell flat on his face as a fourth shot whizzed above the spot where he had been standing an instant before. He ripped off his night goggles and rolled quickly to his right as another shot whizzed past.

Billy Frank saw that his first three shots had found their target. Three of the attackers were lying motionless on the ground. But he didn't see the fourth man. He experienced that old rush of adrenaline that he hadn't felt since 'Nam.

He ejected his empty magazine, slammed a new one home, and peered through the scope. Nothing.

Bakri was breathing hard now. He knew he was in trouble. He was on the ground behind a small pine tree that afforded him a little cover. But he was still a sitting duck in the circle of the spotlights.

Staying low to the ground, he got up and ran to the next tree. As he ran, he sprayed bullets toward the lights in the top of the trees, shattering them. It was dark again. He heard two more shots thud into the tree he was hiding behind.

Inside the mobile home, Ty and Regan felt helpless. They had fallen to the floor and covered their heads when the shooting started, but they didn't know who was still alive. Just before the spotlights went out, they heard a burst of shots. Ty wanted to do something to protect Regan, but he was limited. The lights inside the mobile home made them an easy target, so he crept over to the wall and slowly reached up to the fuse box. He pulled the main breaker and plunged them both into darkness.

When Bakri saw the mobile home lights go out, he realized at least one person was still inside. From the shelter of the tree he slid to the side and began to fire into the trailer.

Regan screamed when the bullets began punching through the thin metal side. She futilely tried to dig a hole in the old shag carpet and bury her face. Pieces of metal and glass showered their bodies.

Ty was beside her in an instant, covering her with his body and doing anything he could to shelter her from the bullets and the flying debris. "Let's crawl into the bedroom," he whispered between gunfire bursts. "It seems to be farther from where the bullets are entering." Hanging onto each other, they crawled into the bedroom.

The stream of bullets started again, hammering the tiny trailer as powerful shots shredded the metal. Regan didn't really believe in luck. She believed in something much more powerful, so she began to pray. "Please, Heavenly Father, protect us. And please protect Billy Frank. We place ourselves in Your hands. Amen."

She thought she even heard Ty whisper, "Amen!" *"We must really be in trouble,"* she told herself.

Billy Frank had moved forward slowly when the attacker started peppering the trailer with bullets. He heard the shooter stop to reload once. He counted to four seconds before the next fusillade began. He didn't know if Ty and Regan were alive or dead. The shooting stopped once again. Billy Frank knew the attacker was reloading. He stepped out to search for the shooter, frantically looking left and right as he slowly counted the seconds.

"One, two, three."

Billy Frank caught a movement out of the corner of his eye and he sighted on it. It was the shooter. But instead of aiming at the mobile home, the shooter was aiming at him. Billy Frank squeezed the trigger.

14

Ty and Regan lay motionless, covering their heads and waiting for the next hurricane of bullets to pelt their hiding place. By now the sides of the trailer looked like Swiss cheese with dozens of bullet holes punctuating the walls. But then there was silence. Nothing. The silence stretched into several minutes before they dared to move.

Ty said in a half-whisper, "Billy Frank, are you there?"

No answer. That wasn't good. It could mean that one or more of the bad guys were out there waiting for them to stick their heads up.

After lying still for what seemed like an hour, but was actually only about five minutes, they began to hear a distant wail. It was the sound of sirens. They squeezed each other's hand as they realized that help was on the way.

"Don't move, Regan. If we hear the sirens, so do the bad guys. They may realize they are running out of time and storm the trailer. Let's just wait until we hear a friendly voice."

In about ten minutes they heard the emergency vehicles arrive and saw the reflection of the flashing lights on the law enforcement vehicles. Then they heard a voice over a loudspeaker. "Everyone come out with your hands held high. If you have any weapons, toss them out before you come out. I repeat. Come out with your hands up."

Ty and Regan stood up and walked slowly through what was left of Billy Frank's trailer. Their shoes crunched on the broken glass and metal littering the floor. They slowly opened the bullet-riddled front door and started down the steps. The headlights and searchlights of the police cars blinded them. The voice on the speaker commanded them, "Get on your knees with your hands behind your backs. Do it now!"

Ty and Regan complied.

As soon as they were down, two officers dashed around to their backs and shackled their hands with handcuffs. They roughly pulled them up to their feet and led them forward to the waiting police vehicles. Meanwhile, six additional vehicles arrived. It was a surreal scene with a myriad of flashing lights and the stench of cordite still lingering in the air.

As they were being escorted toward one of the cars, Ty and Regan couldn't miss seeing Billy Frank's body lying in a pool of blood. One of the officers was covering him with a plastic tarp, indicating there was no need for an ambulance.

As they approached the lead vehicle, Ty recognized the Smith County sheriff, Randall Pritchard.

Sheriff Pritchard said, "Aren't you Ty Kensington? Ted's boy?"

Ty said, "Yes sir. And am I ever glad to see you."

"Boys, get these cuffs off Ty. He's a Gulf War hero," Sheriff Pritchard ordered.

"She's with me," Ty told the sheriff, pointing his head toward Regan so the deputies would uncuff her, too.

"Son, can you tell me what in the name of Sam Hill happened here?" Sheriff Pritchard asked.

Ty shook his head as Regan rubbed her freed wrists. "It's going to take a long time to answer that question," Ty said. "I have been instructed to contact the CIA, the FBI, and the NSA in the case of any incident like this."

Sheriff Pritchard took off his cowboy hat and rubbed a hand through his thinning hair. "Shoot. Anytime you start calling in agencies that only use initials, I know I'm not going to bed anytime soon."

PART 2

15

Jerusalem, Israel

Two days later Solly was speaking to Ty over an encrypted satellite phone.

"I'm glad you and Regan are okay. Director Parker filled me in on the details of what happened the other night. This Conroe fellow must have been an expert marksman. All four ISIS soldiers were killed with headshots – which is fortunate because they were all wearing body armor. They were on Homeland Security's watch list. We're certain ISIS had something much bigger planned for them instead of just taking out you two. Sounds like our old friend Dr. Saad may have sent them. Your friend took out four potential terrorists on American soil."

Ty shook his head and smiled. "He told us that he was a sniper with the Green Berets in Vietnam, but we didn't take him that seriously. He ended up saving our lives."

Solly said, "He's a hero, but of course that incident has to stay off the record. Director Parker told me that the U.S. Army is going to posthumously award Billy Frank Conroe an Army Distinguished Service Cross. He's going to be buried with full military honors at Arlington National Cemetery."

"That's the least they can do," Ty agreed. "I checked with Sheriff Pritchard and he said Billy Frank has a nephew who can take over what's left of the farm."

"Good," Solly said before changing gears. "Ty, I've talked with my boss and he agrees that you two are going to continue to be a target until we can deal with Dr. Saad. I feel responsible for you being in danger. Apparently he has tracked you down in East Texas. Now we need to cover your tracks and get you some place safer."

"That sounds good. Regan and I don't want to go through another episode of dodging bullets. But where can we go?"

"You may not like my answer, but I think you need to be here with me."

"In Israel? Isn't that where attacks are happening almost every week?"

Solly laughed. "Would you believe there are actually ten times as many murders in Detroit each month than in all of Israel? The liberal American media likes to keep the conflict with the Palestinians on the front page."

"You're right about that!" Ty said. He always felt completely safe whenever he was in Israel. It was always comforting to see uniformed members of the highly trained guard, the Israeli Defense Force, so visible.

"Well, mate, I don't want to bash the U.S. government, but your borders aren't protected. Bad guys like those four ISIS blokes are slipping in from Mexico and Canada at an alarming rate. You know how vigilant we are about our borders here," Solly said.

Ty smiled and said, "Besides, I'd love to see you again. I've missed you, you old buzzard."

"Ha, this old buzzard can still give you a proper beating, you little pup."

Ty paused before he spoke next. "I'm all in, but I don't know about Regan. She would love to see you, but she's acting pretty distant right now. She said I attract danger like bees to a flower. She was even talking about returning to work next week."

"Why don't you try asking her and let me know what she says," Solly suggested. "Call me back as soon as you can because we need to get you two out of danger before something else happens."

16

East Texas

"Israel? Oh, I'd love to go!" Regan was beaming a smile Ty hadn't seen in days. "I've always wanted to visit there, and I'd like to see Solly again."

Ty was almost speechless. "I thought you said you were tired of me and wanted to get back to work."

"That was yesterday. I'm ready for a new adventure. And I can do my work from anywhere I have Internet access. I have only one requirement." She crossed her arms and frowned. "I will absolutely not go if you are flying the airplane!"

Ty held up his hands in surrender. "Don't worry. I won't be. I think Solly has a plan for getting us over there undetected." He glanced at his iPhone. "It's only 10:30 at night in Jerusalem so Solly will still be up."

He punched in the numbers and immediately heard the familiar Australian accent ask, "What did she say, mate?"

"She's all in. So what's the plan?"

Solly explained that flying on scheduled airlines

wouldn't be safe because Dr. Saad probably had other imbedded terrorists monitoring the passenger lists.

"I wouldn't be surprised if they attached a GPS tracker to your pickup," Solly continued. "That's probably how they knew you were in Texas. These guys are very good at hacking databases. We have evidence that their computer geeks have created a backdoor into many U.S. airlines. But we don't want them to know that we know this, of course."

Ty wasn't sure what transport options remained.

"As a part-time operative, you realize that we have a few of your fellow assets on the ground in the U.S. as well," Solly said. "I'll be in touch with a couple of them. Meanwhile, download an app called 'Confide' on your phone. It's a text app that uses military-grade end-to-end encryption and it is screenshot protected. The message disappears as soon as you read it. In about an hour I'll send you the details of smuggling you two into Israel."

"We're in your capable hands," Ty said as he disconnected and headed out to the garage to see if he could spot and remove any GPS tracker.

Two hours later, Ty's phone emitted a soft chime. He and Regan had both downloaded the Confide app on their phones. He saw a message from Solly and tapped it, revealing only a series of grey horizontal bars with no written message. But as he swiped his finger down the screen, each horizontal bar disappeared to reveal a line of an encrypted message:

Solly here. We have an extraction plan in place. Memorize these details because this message will disappear permanently after you read it. You are both booked in first class on Delta from Dallas to Atlanta. Departing at 8:40 tomorrow morning. But you aren't going to be on the flight. Two of our people who look enough like you will be on the flight with IDs that will easily pass TSA. Drive to the DFW airport and a Freedom Park valet employee will meet you at Terminal E. He'll take your keys before you enter the terminal. Proceed past the Delta ticket counter and go to door E116. It will say "Authorized Personnel Only." It has a keypad lock. The code is 874482. Once inside, a good friend of mine will give you further instructions.

After Ty and Regan read the message, he tapped "close" and the message disappeared from the screen.

"So if we aren't going to be on the plane to Atlanta, how are we going to get to Israel?" Regan asked.

"Don't worry, Regan. I'm sure Solly has a plan worked out."

"The last time you told me not to worry I ended up being used for target practice in a mobile home!" she retorted.

17

The next morning Ty drove them to the airport. The trip should have taken only a couple of hours, but an accident snarled the morning traffic in Dallas. They arrived at Terminal E parking and found the Freedom Park valet waiting for them.

As they walked slowly toward the terminal, Ty joked, "Well, we don't have to worry about missing our flight since we're not going to be on it." Regan laughed politely. The good thing about Ty was that he could entertain himself.

They found a door marked E116 and punched in the code from memory. There was a buzz and a loud click. Ty held the door for Regan to enter and he followed her. They passed through another door and walked into a room that appeared to be an employee lounge. To their surprise a crew of five FedEx cargo pilots were sitting around a table drinking coffee.

The oldest one stood up, walked over with his hand extended, and introduced himself. The rest of the crew kept talking to themselves.

"Good day, mate! I'm Captain Blair Blackburn. You

must be Solly's friends." He spoke with the same Australian accent Solly used. "Don't worry about introducing yourselves. Solly said it would be better if we kept our little ruse confidential. My flight crew has been briefed on a need-to-know basis. All they know is that you're a couple of friends of mine who are flying with us."

Regan said, "That sounds like our man of mystery all right. In fact, you sound a lot like him, too."

"Well, that's because we grew up together in Sydney. We've been mates since we were little lads in school. Through the years Solly has pulled me out of a few tough spots, so I owe him a favor or two. Getting you to Tel Aviv is a big payback to my friend."

"You aren't going to package us up and ship us are you?" Ty joked.

Captain Blackburn's eyes sparkled. "Well, we kidded about that being an option, but we decided you might be a tad uncomfortable. Instead, head into those two restrooms and you'll find company outfits that will fit you. Once you get dressed, come on back and we'll head out to our aircraft."

Ty and Regan came out of the restrooms wearing FedEx uniforms complete with caps and security IDs around their necks. They followed Captain Blackburn down some stairs and walked out onto a loading area where a cargo van was idling. The crew and the two stowaways boarded the van.

After a fifteen-minute ride to the other side of the

huge airport, they arrived at the cargo terminal. Eight large Boeing 777 200s were parked with their cargo doors open. Dozens of workmen dressed like Ty and Regan moved at a steady pace using forklifts to deliver dozens of metal containers through each plane's oversized doors. Workmen inside rolled the containers into place and tightened the straps to anchor the cargo so it wouldn't shift in flight.

As the van drove to the nearest jet, Regan commented, "Those don't look very comfortable to travel in."

"Beggars can't be choosers," Ty whispered under his breath.

Captain Blackburn explained, "We don't carry passengers, but we often ferry crew members to different locations. I think you'll be pleased with your accommodations up front."

The van stopped at the bottom of the airstairs that led to the cockpit. Ty and Regan pulled their caps low over their faces and hustled up the steps. Once inside they were surprised at the spacious cabin area directly behind the cockpit. There was only one row of six seats, but each seat was large enough to be in any airline's first class section. The seats were equipped to fully recline into flat beds. Behind the seats Regan saw a galley stocked with drinks and food.

As they checked out their travel space, Captain Blackburn nodded toward the galley. "I'm sorry," he said, "but you have to be your own flight attendant on this trip. There are plenty of choices there. I don't think you'll starve. There is also only one lavatory, but it is oversized and even has a shower if you feel the need to freshen up."

Regan was satisfied. "Well, Solly did it again. He sure knows how to travel in style." Turning to Captain Blackburn, she said, "This will be great. How long will the trip take?"

He glanced at his watch. "We are scheduled to push back in about an hour. Then we fly about fifty minutes to our hub in Memphis. We'll be on the ground there for another hour to refuel and reload. I'll get a new set of relief pilots and we'll be off. Once we're in the air from Memphis it will take us about thirteen hours to get to Tel Aviv – depending on the upper level winds. Solly said that it would be best if you guys stay on the plane until we get to Israel."

Ty walked up from the galley with a cool beer in his hand. He plopped down in the plush seat. "I think I can hang out with Ms. Hart here for the next eighteen hours. And Captain," he added, "I'm a licensed pilot, so if you need some rest, I'll be glad to take over"

Regan smirked and said sweetly, "There's only one thing he does better than flying airplanes—and that's crashing them! I wouldn't advise it."

Captain Blackburn nodded affirmatively. He didn't think Ty and Regan were a married couple, but they fought like brother and sister.

18

Ben Gurion Airport, Tel Aviv

The flight over the North Atlantic had been trouble-free. Captain Blackburn wasn't flying the first leg, so he sat with them and told stories about Solly's escapades as a teenager. Each seat was equipped with an iPad loaded with dozens of movies and a noise-cancelling headset. After Captain Blackburn took his shift in the pilot's seat, they settled in to watch movies, reclining their seats in case they fell asleep. The last few weeks had been full of adventures. They were coming down off an adrenalin high. Within minutes of hitting their pillows they were both sound asleep.

Regan awoke at the slight sound of a screech as Captain Blackburn expertly greased the jumbo jet onto the runway at Ben Gurion Airport in Tel Aviv. She was momentarily disoriented and couldn't remember exactly where she was. Just then a delicious smell tickled her nostrils.

Ty was standing in front of her with a tray of hot coffee and warm sweet rolls.

"I thought you were going to sleep forever."

"How long did I sleep? Did you get any rest?" Regan

stretched and yawned.

"I slept about four hours, but you were dead to the world for a full eight hours. I'll bet you're hungry by now."

"I am. But hold that thought. And hold that tray while I freshen up. Looks like you've already had a shower." Regan noticed he smelled good and wondered if he'd used aftershave.

Ty said, "I have cleaned up, and I left plenty of shampoo for you."

As Regan was refreshing her makeup, the first officer taxied the 777 to the cargo terminal across the airport from the passenger terminal.

Ty and Regan dug into their rolls. Captain Blackburn came back and asked, "How was the flight?"

Regan was chewing a big bite and couldn't manage a quick response.

"Excuse me," she said finally, swallowing a big gulp of coffee. "It was a great flight! No crying kids. No snooty flight attendants. This is the way to travel!"

"I'm glad you enjoyed it. We never have any complaints from our passengers or those in the cargo hold either!"

They heard a loud double knock from the exterior of the front exit door. Captain Blackburn disarmed the door, swung the handle down and pushed outward. The sun came streaming into the passenger area. Framed in the door was a familiar figure with a long, bushy beard and ever-present Stetson cowboy hat. He had a small suitcase in his hand.

"Solly!" Regan shouted as she jumped up and gave him a big hug. She thought again about how hugging Solly was like hugging a big, friendly bear.

Solly held her at arms length and smiled. "You're looking well, considering Ty tried to kill you on multiple occasions. Welcome to Israel, the land of miracles!"

Solly grabbed Ty's hand and pulled him in for a hug. "Welcome back, my friend. We have some good memories from your last visit."

"This was a pretty sneaky way to get us here," Ty said. "If those ISIS dudes tracked us here, then they have better tools than *Mossad*."

Solly's jovial manner turned serious in an instant. "No one is smarter than *Mossad*. ISIS is smart, but they'll never catch up to us before we wipe them out."

He tossed a small suitcase toward Ty and a smile returned to Solly's face. "Here are your new outfits. Sorry to say, you just lost your FedEx jobs. You're both going to be my assistant archeology guides, so you've got to look the part. Change in the lavatory and we'll be good to go."

As Regan removed the clothes from the suitcase and closed the restroom door, Solly turned to Captain Blackburn. Shaking his hand he said, "Thanks, mate, for helping me out again. Do you think anyone on your crew might talk about these two passengers?"

"Never happen, mate. These blokes are my handpicked pilots. This isn't the first time we've shuttled mysterious cargo."

Regan came out dressed in jeans, boots, a tan work vest, and a wide brimmed hat complete with oversized sunglasses.

"Your turn," she said to Ty in a singsong voice.

Ty changed and then Solly led them down the airstairs to a black Range Rover waiting on the tarmac. His driver zipped through a private airport perimeter manned by four heavily armored IDF forces.

Looking over the front leather seat at his guests, Solly got down to business. "Now that you guys are here, I need your help with an ultra-secret project that the Prime Minister has assigned me to cover. It's called the Jerusalem Protocol."

"I figured you must have had something up your sleeve, old man," Ty said. "No wonder you thought Israel would be the perfect hideout!"

"I'm in! What's the Jerusalem Protocol?" Regan asked.

"I don't even know too much about it yet myself. They mentioned it in a meeting the other day but kept all the details under wraps. We'll meet with Rabbi Yitzak Rabin late this afternoon. He's the Chief Rabbi in Israel, and he's supposed to start filling us in."

It took Solly and his guests a little less than an hour in light traffic to reach the King David Hotel in Jerusalem where they would be staying. Regan freshened up in her room while Ty unpacked his suitcase down the hall. Solly waited for them in the lobby, keeping a keen eye on his watch, as he did not want to be late for the temperamental rabbi.

19

Gaza City, Palestinian Territory

Dr. Saad was close to losing his temper as he listened to the voice on the other line of the phone. "You said you followed them to Dallas and that they were flying to Atlanta! How could you lose them?"

"We saw them enter the terminal," said an unnamed ISIS operative who worked under Ibrahim's command. "We hacked into the Delta system. It says that they passed security and boarded the flight. But our men waiting at the Atlanta airport never saw them get off the plane."

"Where is the American's truck?" Dr. Saad demanded.

"We think he must have discovered the tracker, so we had to follow him as best we could without it. We assume the truck is still sitting in the parking lot of the valet service that took delivery of it."

Dr. Saad was livid. "Tell your men to keep looking. I wanted to kill the Americans first and use them as bait to draw out the evil Jew who shot me. Now, thanks to your incompetence, I'll have to get our men in Jerusalem to start trying to locate the *Mossad* agent. I've got chemicals that will make that Solly tell us anything we want – even the location of his American friends. Then I will watch him die slowly and painfully."

"*Allah hu akbar*!" the man on the phone shouted.

Dr. Saad didn't respond. He hung up and paced around the small lab, wincing from the constant pain of his wounded knee. *"All these men Ibrahim gave me are stupid amateurs. I can see why he sent them. I bet they are poorly trained on purpose so that Americans will think that all ISIS fighters are that inept. I need someone with brains to help me get a man like Solly."*

He punched a number in his speed dial list. Ibrahim took the call but didn't speak. Instead Dr. Saad heard the encryption app being engaged. After a few seconds Ibrahim said curtly, "You know I don't like talking on the phone. I'd prefer we use couriers for our messages. What do you want this time?"

"I just need a name."

What name? I already gave you four operatives."

"That was a disaster and you know it," Dr. Saad said. "I need the toughest, best-trained, smartest ISIS fighter who is currently embedded in Israel."

After a few moments of silence Ibrahim replied, "I think I have just the right man for you. But you know I won't give you his name on the phone. I'll have a courier bring it to you. Now don't call me again."

As the call ended, Dr. Saad began to smile for the first time in a long time.

20

El-Wad Street, Muslim Quarter, Old Jerusalem

That afternoon Dr. Saad received instructions for a rendezvous in Jerusalem inside the Old City—the walled area within modern Jerusalem that is divided into four uneven quarters: Jewish, Muslim, Christian, and Armenian. Once more he found himself being smuggled over a border, this time in the back of an ambulance. He was now in Jerusalem sitting in a back room of a coffee house off the main street of the Arab souk, the famous market in the Old City area of Jerusalem. This Muslim quarter of the Old City was the largest and most crowded with people and shops. The narrow streets were always clogged with noisy vendors and shoppers.

Ibrahim had arranged for him to meet a new operative here, but so far he had been a no-show. Dr. Saad had already been waiting an hour and was getting ready to leave when a tall, young businessman came in and sat down beside him. He was dressed in an expensive suit with a silk tie and did not look like any ISIS operative he'd ever seen. This man looked more like he belonged in a fine jewelry store or behind the counter at a bank.

The handsome young man bowed and offered the typical Arabic greeting of peace. "As-salamu alaykum," he said. "You must be Dr. Saad. The name I most often use is Ali el-Gamal. Why don't you just call me Ali for now?"

Dr. Saad returned the greeting. "Wa'alaykumu salam," he said, but he frowned as he spoke. "I was looking for a tough fighter, and I get sent a male model?" he hissed over his coffee cup. "You look like one of those infidel Hollywood movie stars."

"The Americans have a saying, 'Looks can be deceiving,'" Ali purred like a cat. "Believe me, I am no stranger to violence and blood. What is it you need from me?"

"I need you to find an Israeli man and bring him to me. The filthy Israeli will lead me to two Americans who are going to pay for what they did to me."

Ali looked impatient. "Can you be a little more specific, old man?"

"I can do better than that," Dr. Saad said and opened his phone. He showed Ali a picture of Solly. "His name is Solomon Rubin. He is a *Mossad* agent whose cover is an archaeological tour guide. He's the reason I will always walk with a limp because last year he shot me in the American state of Georgia. And here are pictures of the two Americans. The man is Tyler Kensington. The girl is Regan Hart. We had the two Americans targeted to be killed in Texas, but they have escaped. I want all three of them dead."

Ali's eyes grew large. He looked at Dr. Saad with more

respect. "I know these names. We heard about a planned attack in Atlanta that could have brought the infidel Americans great suffering. That was *you*?"

Dr. Saad frowned and nodded, reliving his prior failure afresh. "It would have happened if not for this blasted *Mossad* agent and his two friends. Trust me, I plan to make all three of them regret interfering."

"This bearded one shouldn't be too hard to find," Ali said, pointing to the screen. "Text me the pictures. I have lots of trusted friends who live and work here in the souk. We'll be on the lookout for your Israeli Santa Claus and his two American elves."

21

Old Jerusalem, Jewish Quarter

Solly's driver dropped them off at the Old City, and they meandered through the narrow passages of the Jewish Quarter. Regan was fascinated by her first good look at Jerusalem. All the buildings were constructed from the same off-white sandstone. Solly led them up two sets of stone steps into a wide, open plaza. Regan stared as she looked at the ancient stone wall where dozens of Jews were praying. She had seen pictures of the Wailing Wall, but being there on site was an unexpectedly emotional experience where she strongly sensed God's presence.

"Why is it called the Wailing Wall?" she asked Solly.

He explained, "To the Jews it is called the Western Wall because it was part of the west wall that surrounded the area where the Jewish Temple was located. When our Israeli soldiers captured this area in 1967, they were so overcome with joy that many of them began crying and singing in Hebrew. It sounded to the Gentiles as if they were wailing, so the wall became known to the outside world as the 'Wailing' Wall."

Solly was never happier than when he was explaining history to an audience. As Ty and Regan listened, Ty noticed a fence that divided the area in front of the wall. The women crowded into a small area to the right. The larger area on the left was where the men were praying.

"Why do they keep the women and men separate?" he asked.

"This entire area is considered a Jewish synagogue. And in a synagogue men and women are separated," Solly explained.

"But why do the women only get a tiny area?" Regan wanted to know.

"I'll let you ask one of the Orthodox Jews that question. But don't expect to get an answer!" Solly chuckled.

They left the small plaza and walked a few steps up the narrow street to a door with a large sign over it. Standing outside the door waiting impatiently was a man dressed all in black. "Rabbi Rabin, it's good to see you again!" Solly said. He knew better than to offer to shake the Rabbi's hand. He'd learned his lesson the first time. "I'd like to introduce you to a couple of friends of mine. This is Ty and Regan."

Rabbi Rabin nodded his head in their general direction and said, "You're late. They're waiting for us inside. Let's enter."

The sign above the door was posted in English and Hebrew. It read "The Temple Institute." Solly read the Hebrew characters to them. "It's *Machon HaMikdash*. It translates literally into 'The Center for the Jewish Temple.'"

They walked down a short flight of stairs into an ordinary looking bookstore. Several tourists were busy buying books and looking at the pictures for sale.

"This way, please," Rabbi Rabin said, herding the trio to move along. He turned and walked through the main building past a large model of Herod's Temple that was inside a glass display case. Beyond this room was a small classroom where a guide for the Temple Institute was speaking in Hebrew to a tour group. They turned right and entered a small, empty movie theatre. At the front of the theatre they were met by a man who was dressed casually in slacks and a shirt but with a cloth *kippah* on the top of his head, the brimless hat worn by Jewish men who practice Judaism.

Rabbi Rabin wasted no words. "This is David Shvaz, the director of the Temple Institute. He is going to be your guide." Without saying goodbye, the rabbi walked out through the theatre door, closing it behind him. Solly guessed the rabbi had turned over the briefing to David instead of doing it himself.

David smiled a welcoming smile and held out his hand. "It's an honor to meet you, Solly. I've heard a lot about you." He shook hands politely with Ty and Regan. "We're glad to have guests here at the Temple Institute."

Solly looked around and said, "I've always wondered about this place. I've heard lots of rumors. And I don't know how much to believe."

"I was surprised to get a call from Prime Minister Abrams," David said. "He and Rabbi Rabin personally instructed me to brief you fully and show you some plans that only a few people in the world even know about."

Regan nearly shivered with excitement. She loved being among the first to know important information.

David held out a small remote the size of a key fob and punched a button. There was a beep and the entire movie screen moved up six feet off the floor. Behind the screen was a long hallway that sloped gently downward.

"Follow me," David said and headed down the secret passageway.

As they walked forward, the movie screen slid back into place behind them. Safety lights automatically illuminated each section of the passageway as they entered it.

After walking for what seemed to be about one hundred yards, the group arrived at a thick steel door with no evidence of a handle or means to open it. David looked into a retinal scanner beside the door and after two quick chirps, the thick door slipped open silently. On the other side an armed IDF guard waved them through. Solly, Ty, and Regan all stopped and stared around the brightly lit hall. It seemed to be larger than an aircraft hangar with a ceiling that soared at least twenty feet above the floor. Dozens of brightly lit workstations with state-of-the-art computers dotted the area. Each station was also equipped with several large flat HD screens. Building materials and wood crates of different sizes were stacked around the perimeter of the facility.

Solly took a deep breath. "I had heard that there was an underground warehouse near the Temple Mount, but I never really believed it."

David seemed delighted by his guests' reactions. "This is more than a warehouse, Solly. The Temple Institute technically owns it, but it is funded from a number of sources. The visitor's center where the public is allowed occupies less than 5 percent of the total square area of our operation center.

"So what is this, exactly?" Regan asked.

David beamed with pride as he stretched out his arms and said, "This is the nerve center for the plan to build the third Jewish Temple."

Solly, who had been stroking his beard and listening, stopped in mid-stroke.

"What did you say?" he asked, certain his hearing was failing him.

David continued, "Over the past twenty years, we have been focused down to the slightest detail on manufacturing all of the materials and implements needed for rebuilding and reinstituting ritual sacrifice in the Temple in Jerusalem."

Solly was really curious now. He asked, "Who knows about this? And why did the Prime Minister bring me in?"

"Only a handful of influential leaders in the government, *Mossad*, and in the religious community know. Prime Minister Abrams wants you to lead a team of archeologists onto the Temple Mount to determine the exact location of the Temple and the Holy of Holies."

"I don't need a team to determine that!" Solly assured David with a huff. "Everyone knows the Muslims' monstrosity called the Dome of the Rock is built right over the spot—"

David shook his head. "Well . . . not exactly."

"What do you mean?" Solly could not imagine another explanation. Ty and Regan were clueless and shrugged their shoulders at each other.

Without answering, David glanced at his watch and said, "We're out of time. I'll explain it in more depth tomorrow. You've had a long day. Get some rest and we'll get started with your full orientation tomorrow. Shalom!"

22

The Old City, Jerusalem

The next day Solly, Ty, and Regan walked through the Old City again, anxious to talk more with David at the Temple Institute. They weren't very enthusiastic about this grand scheme to build a Jewish Temple some day. Talking about it at the King David Hotel the night before, no one had thought the plan could possibly succeed. They imagined it would take years, possibly decades, to work through all the negotiations with Muslim countries and the red tape required for the Jews to pursue this idea. Even if they begin rebuilding the Temple under the nose of the Muslims, it would take decades for them to finish.

"It would start World War III," Ty had complained. Solly and Regan feared he was right.

Solly was Jewish, but he identified with a group of Messianic Jews who didn't see a need for a third Temple. Neither did Regan, who also considered herself a follower of Jesus. Christianity taught that Christ's final sacrifice on the cross had ended the need for animal sacrifice as an atonement for sin. Besides, as an animal lover, Regan was disgusted with the idea of sacrificing animals. Both Solly and Regan had talked to Ty about considering faith in Jesus at various times in their friendship, but he was far from convinced. And he was just stubborn enough to protest adopting their beliefs just to irritate them.

Despite their objections, they all agreed that undertaking an excavation of historical significance on the Temple Mount would be interesting work. So they were going to cooperate with David, albeit reluctantly. "And besides," Solly admitted, "it's hard to disobey an order from my Prime Minister!"

As they wove their way through the market, Regan said, "I haven't had a chance to shop yet. Is there anything interesting nearby?"

Solly smiled. "Are you kidding? The best shopping in the *world* is in Israel. And the best shopping in *Israel* is in the Muslim quarter of the *souk*. Come on, it's just around the corner."

Solly turned left and headed down a narrow lane. "Just remember, don't pay the asking price. You have to haggle with these guys. And watch your purse. There are professional pickpockets everywhere. What are you looking for specifically?"

"Oh, Solly, you know I only shop for two things. Anything and everything!"

Ty rolled his eyes. "You definitely have the shopping gene. I don't want to shop, but I'll tag along." He jogged a few steps to catch up with Solly and Regan. Then he started glancing around, imagining that every man in the narrow lane was a pickpocket.

Getting into the shopping zone, Regan felt relaxed for the first time since she'd landed in Jerusalem. The sights, sounds, and exotic aromas were unlike anywhere else on earth.

"Is it safe in here?" Regan asked, feeling almost claustrophobic among the vast array of draped scarves, purses, strands of garlic, jewelry, trays of nuts, fruit, and clothing packing both sides of the narrow walkway.

"As long as we stay together," Solly said, pushing a green scarf out of his face. "Besides, Ty and I are both packing if any trouble arises."

The shopkeepers were all shouting over each other to tempt the visitors to come into their stores. Regan ducked into a half dozen doorways and bought a few small trinkets.

She turned to Ty and said, "I'm looking for some olive wood boxes, have you seen any?" Ty looked around and wanted to say, "Just everywhere you look." But he only smiled pleasantly instead, knowing Regan didn't really want an answer anyway.

Regan was picking up retail momentum now. Ty was getting tired just trying to keep up with her and hold all her packages. He felt a little uncomfortable because it seemed that he and Solly were getting some strange looks from some of the shopkeepers. But he figured it was just because Solly looked so unusual with his puffy white beard and long braid dangling down his back. He was probably used to people staring at him.

A tourist couple stopped to ask Solly a question in the street just as Regan entered another shop stacked with Persian carpets. Ty followed and stopped at the door, trying to keep an eye on both Solly and Regan. Regan was talking with the shopkeeper about something in a special display case. Ty could usually hear her expertly haggling for a good price, but the noise in the street was drowning out her voice. When he stepped into the shop, he no longer saw her. Thinking she had probably slipped out to go to the next shop without his seeing her, he walked back outside.

Solly was now standing outside the door and asked Ty, "Have you seen Regan?"

23

The Muslim Quarter, Jerusalem

Ty shook his head. "I lost sight of her," he told Solly.

Neither man panicked. They were trained to stay calm during potential emergencies. They headed in different directions to search a dozen small stores close to where they last saw her.

"Regan!" Ty called.

"Ms. Hart, your tour group is about to leave," Solly said in a raised voice.

"Ms. Hart, can you hear me?"

Solly whipped out his phone and hit a speed dial number. He quickly explained the situation. Jerusalem District Police would soon surround that market looking for anyone matching Regan's description.

Ty and Solly returned to the store where they had last seen Regan. The surly storekeeper claimed that she had left the store without buying anything. He didn't see where she went. Solly didn't believe him.

Without a word Solly pulled the shade on the front door and turned the sign over to read "Closed." Above the loud objections of the storekeeper, Ty and Solly quickly shoved him back into the corner of his store. Ty grabbed his arms, but the man kept shouting that he knew nothing.

While Ty twisted the man's arms tighter, Solly reached behind his back and removed his .22 LRS from its holster. From another pocket he pulled out a silencer and screwed it onto the end of the barrel.

The storekeeper whimpered and tried to get away from Ty's grip. Solly placed the gun under the right eyeball of the quaking man. "I've killed before, and I'm ready to do it again if you don't tell us the truth," he said to the shopkeeper.

Finally, realizing that he was about to die, the man said, "My phone. Look on my phone."

With Ty still holding a firm grip on the squirming merchant, Solly searched the area around his cash drawer and pulled out a flip phone. "Here it is—now what?"

"If you promise not to hurt me, I will show you what you need to know," the man begged.

"If the information you give us will help us recover the girl, then you won't be harmed," Solly warned. "But if this is some trick, it will be your last mistake. These phones are used to detonate bombs, but you don't look like a suicide bomber to me. Just give him a good pat down, Ty."

After giving him a thorough search, Ty said, "No explosives. No weapons. He's clean."

"Not literally because this guy really needs a bath," Ty thought.

Solly gingerly put the phone into the man's hands while Ty kept a tight grip on his arms.

"Okay, slowly, what's on your phone that you want to show me?"

With trembling hands the merchant tried to open the phone, but it dropped to the ground on the hard tile.

"Sorry! Sorry!" the man shrieked.

Solly, keeping an eye on him, leaned over and picked up the phone.

This time the man held the phone carefully and touched an icon to bring up a picture. At first Solly didn't recognize the faces, and then to his utter shock he realized that he was looking at headshots of himself, Ty, and Regan with a cryptic message in Arabic underneath. The man explained what the message said. If anyone saw these three people, he was to call the number listed.

"When did you get this picture?" Solly demanded.

"Maybe two nights ago, I think."

"You better think. Tell us everything you remember," Ty said, giving one more squeeze on the man's arms.

"All I did was call the number when I saw you in the street outside my store. In about a minute a strange man I've never seen came in. He led the lady toward the back of the store and out through the back door."

"This shop has a back door?" Solly asked. "Show it to us right now!"

The storekeeper gladly led them behind a stack of colorful carpets. "It's not really a door. It's just a way to escape in case of an emergency."

Ty released the man's arms to let him move aside a cardboard panel, revealing a hole in the wall large enough for a man to crawl through.

Solly waved his gun toward the shopkeeper. "Ty, I'll keep my eye on this guy while you check out what's through the door."

Ty got down on his hands and knees and crawled through the opening. A terrible smell of rotting garbage assaulted his nostrils. He stood up and was looking down a narrow lane. Nobody was in sight.

He crawled back into the shop. "Looks like we're at a dead end. But we could trace that telephone number on the picture."

"Yeah, mate, I'd already thought about that. We can try, but I'm certain it's a throwaway phone. If we don't find her soon, I wouldn't be averse to calling the number just to threaten whoever answers. Meanwhile, we'll hold this scum until the Jerusalem District Police arrive. They have better methods to track his last call."

24

Regan was confused. She tried to wake up, but her eyelids refused to obey the repeated commands of her fuzzy brain to open. Icy tentacles of fear slowly wrapped around her mind. Along with the fear came the unwelcome pounding ache of the mother-of-all headaches.

Regan took a deep breath and shuddered as she tried to slowly exhale.

"Where am I? What's wrong with me?"

She could sense she was lying on her back on a thin mattress, but she didn't recognize the feel of the bed.

Her muddled mind wasn't interested in helping her think. Her thoughts struggled at the speed of thick molasses.

"Come on, Regan! Snap out of this! Think!"

But another part of her brain said, *"Are you talking to me? Sorry, we're closed today. Come back later."*

As Regan fought with all of her will to wake up, she had the sensation of being deep underwater where it was dark and cold. She kicked feverishly toward the surface where there might be air and light, but her legs became entwined in thick mental seaweed.

After what seemed an eternity of swimming, she suddenly broke through the surface of consciousness and slowly tried to open her eyes. Her heavy eyelids didn't respond at first, as if they had been sutured shut. But gradually, painfully, they peeled open. There was still only darkness—thick, oppressive, scary, darkness.

"Are my eyes really open, or is this just part of the nightmare?" she wondered.

Regan slowly raised her right hand in front of her face and waved. She felt slight air movement but couldn't make out even an outline of her hand.

Next she gently touched her eyelashes. Her eyes were open, but there was nothing for them to see except the terrifying darkness. So she closed them again and tried to think.

After several sluggish starts and stops, her brain decided to cooperate. As her jumbled thoughts lined up, she started to remember. In that instant her fright barometer shot up to terror-level and she started to scream. But her throat was so dry that only a pitiful choking sound came out. She quickly clapped her hands over her mouth to stifle the sound. If she were going to survive, she would need all her wits. She started to rewind her thoughts to replay the last things she recalled before waking up.

"I remember being with Ty and Solly in the souk in the Old City. The narrow streets were crowded and everyone was so loud! Storeowners were hawking their wares, especially to me because they guessed I was a rich American tourist. I had told Ty I wanted

shop 'til I dropped.' But I didn't literally want it to happen!"

Regan stifled a giggle that bubbled to her lips. She was the queen of inappropriate laughter at the most inappropriate times, but at least her sense of humor was returning.

"I've got to think! What happened?"

Regan started to remember more. She recalled that the last shop she entered was selling beautiful olive wood boxes. The tiny store had been stacked from floor to ceiling with carpets and carvings. The owner had been very friendly and must have sensed an easy sale. Another man had entered the store to browse. She'd glanced up to see Solly in the street and Ty posted just a few feet away in the doorway of the shop.

The excited owner had said that his best olive wood carvings were in the back corner of his store. He'd smiled at Regan, revealing a mouth full of broken teeth. In broken English he'd oozed, "I have something nicest just for you. I give you very best price. One of a kind. Very rare."

The shopkeeper had firmly grabbed Regan's elbow and escorted her around two racks of hanging carpets toward the back of the shop. Although it was only a few feet, she'd lost sight of Ty because of the thick carpets. As she'd knelt down to examine the large box, she'd felt a thick arm slip around her neck. Before she could scream, a rough hand had placed a strong-smelling cloth over her mouth and nose.

Regan had fought to get away, but the pungent odor in the cloth had made her light-headed. She'd felt a sharp prick in her neck. Then darkness.

Regan tried to remember more, but her brain was exhausted from the mental exercise. She tried to fight the drug-induced sleep, but she was soon drifting back into a land of terrible nightmares.

When she awoke again, she suffered the same dizzying disorientation. *"Where am I? Why can't I wake up?"* Then the reality of her situation landed on her like a huge boulder.

"Where are Ty and Solly? Have they been captured too?"

As she looked around, she noticed something different. A tiny sliver of light was peeking out from behind the one door in the room. It barely illuminated the few inches around the doorframe, but it was better than utter darkness.

As she crawled to the door, she realized that her street clothes had been removed and she was now wearing a plain gown of thick, rough material. Her head had been wrapped in a silk scarf. She had no shoes. As she got closer to the door, she saw a small plate with a piece of pita bread on it. There was also a wooden cup that contained what appeared to be water. She wasn't going to risk tasting it. Over in the corner she could see a plastic bucket. *"So that must be the en suite bath in his luxury hotel,"* she thought sarcastically.

She nibbled at the bread. It was moldy, but she knew she needed to keep up her strength. Regan stood to her feet, careful not to move too fast. Her head was still spinning from the drugs. She placed her ear to the thick door, trying to hear anything. But there was only silence. She banged on the door and shouted, "Hey! Is anybody out there? Can somebody help me?" There was no response.

Tears welled up in Regan's eyes. She let her body slide down the door until she was seated with her back to it. At least she could stay close to her tiny beam of light. She picked up another piece of pita bread and prayed, "Lord, I'm in trouble. I need your help and I need it soon, Father." Amen.

25

El-Wad Street, Muslim Quarter, the Old City

Dr. Saad was having Turkish coffee with Ali at the same private coffee shop where they had first met. As he sipped the thick sweet brew, he said, "I underestimated your abilities, my friend. Forgive me. I will not make that mistake twice."

Ali said, "It's all about technology. Everybody has a phone, and you can share a thousand copies of a picture in a few seconds. We got lucky to pick up your targets in only two days. Yet we were unable to capture the two men. They were armed and stayed exposed in a public area. But we have the girl."

"Can they trace the phone number you gave with the picture?" Dr. Saad inquired.

"Ha! We have hundreds of throwaway cell phones that we use once and then crush. There will be no way to trace that number to me or to you."

"So where is the girl now?"

"We have her secluded not far from here in a safe room we use for interrogations. We knew not to remove her from the Old City because the police set up barricades to examine everyone leaving the city that day.

"What is our plan to use her to draw the Israeli and the American to a place where we can kill them?" Dr. Saad was leading the conversation where he desperately wanted it to go.

Ali swirled the coffee in his cup thoughtfully. "You must remember something, Dr. Saad. You are respected because of your previous work for Sadaam Hussein and your recent attempt to terrorize Americans. But I don't work for you. I am only doing you a favor as a friend of a friend. I have a much bigger boss whose agenda I must follow."

"What are you talking about?"

"I'm sure you've heard of Abu Bakr al-Bagahdi."

"Of course. I know him from many years ago. He is the mastermind and the head of all of ISIS."

"He is the leader of the next global Caliphate!" Ali corrected. "And I have made him aware of this operation in Jerusalem. He thinks that we could use this American woman as a powerful propaganda tool against the infidels."

Dr. Saad didn't like this new direction of their conversation. He wanted Solly, Ty, and Regan to die. He didn't care about any propaganda agenda for ISIS.

Ali continued, "Al-Bagahdi saw the picture of the girl. He did some research and discovered that this Regan Hart is not married. He indicated a desire to take her as one of his wives. As the great leader of the Caliphate, you know he has the divine right to take up to six wives."

Dr. Saad feigned a cough, since he knew al-Bagahdi was rumored to have dozens of women he called wives.

Ali ignored the insinuation. "When he finishes with one wife, he puts her away. So he technically has only six wives at any one time. He believes if we can video him taking Regan Hart as his wife in Syria, it will demoralize the Americans. He'll then video her execution when he is through with her. This will prove that no one is safe from the powerful reach of ISIS."

Dr. Saad was seething, but he kept his outward composure calm. "But what about the other two? I wanted to use the girl as bait to draw them into our trap."

"That's your trap, not mine," Ali said as he stood up to leave, straightening his tie. "Good luck. We plan on removing the Hart girl from Jerusalem today. She will be disguised." Ali shared that she would be wearing the full *hijab*, including the *niqab* that would completely cover her face. "She will look like any Muslim woman on the street. She will be sedated enough to function but will not be able to talk or ask for help," he added.

"But this was not our plan," Dr. Saad objected, pushing back his chair. "I need this woman. How can I get in touch with you? Let's discuss an alternative plan."

"Our business is concluded," Ali said coolly. "If you try to sabotage our plans for this woman, you will be considered an enemy of ISIS. And, Dr. Saad, you don't want to become a name on an ISIS hit list. That's a label you won't live with for long."

Ali walked out of the coffee shop. But Dr. Saad wasn't ready to give up on his plans. His calculating brain was already working out a possible scenario to prevent Regan from being transported to Syria. He signaled his driver to return him to Gaza in the ambulance.

26

The Temple Institute, Jerusalem

Solly and Ty interviewed with the Jerusalem District Police before they left the market. The two men arrived at the Temple Institute later that day with heavy hearts because there was no trace of Regan. Unaware of what had happened to her, David was prepared to begin their training. Solly explained that it would have to be put on hold until they found out more information about their friend who had gone missing.

David said, "I am sorry about Ms. Hart. This operation is on a tight timetable. We don't have much time to spare. I can only give you a couple of days until we need to get serious about your role in this project."

"Thank you, sir. Shalom," Solly said. As they walked out of the Temple Institute, he confessed, "I feel awful about this. It was my idea to go into the *souk*."

Ty said, "Don't beat yourself up. You had no way of knowing they had distributed our pictures. Now I know why we were getting so many strange looks. It wasn't just your beard." Solly smiled weakly at Ty's attempt at humor.

"I can think of only one man who would be crazy enough to come against us on my home territory. It has got to be that deranged chemist, Dr. Saad. I've often regretted that day in Georgia that I didn't put the bullet between his eyes instead of through his knee."

"Well, we still have the phone number the shopkeeper gave us. Want to give it a try?"

Solly punched in the numbers and heard a pre-recorded message in Arabic.

"*The number you have dialed has been disconnected or is no longer...*" Solly disconnected the call before he heard the rest of the annoying message.

"Well, that's another dead end."

Ty said, "I think our best bet now is to search for Dr. Saad. If we can find him, we'll find Regan."

"Good idea, mate. The prey becomes the hunter. I like it. Where do we start?"

Ty laughed. "I'm pretty far down the food chain. But don't you work for a group that has a pretty good database on every bad guy on the planet?"

"I could answer that question, but then I'd have to kill you," Solly said. "Let me call my boss."

When Asher saw Solly's name appear on the screen, he was in a meeting with a dozen new *Mossad* agents. "Excuse me, folks. I've got to take this call."

All the young agents around the table nodded and continued talking.

"I need to take it *alone*!" Asher repeated. Within

seconds, the room was empty.

"What is it, Solly? I just dismissed a top-level meeting about monitoring Palestinian incursions into Israel."

Solly said, "Boss, I've never asked for too many favors, but I am asking for one now."

"No promises, Solly. What do you need?"

"As you, know I've asked Regan Hart and Ty Kensington to help me on the archeological mission on the Temple Mount."

Asher interrupted. "We owe them a great debt of gratitude for their previous work in Georgia, but as I said earlier there can never be any public recognition."

"No, no. A different favor. Regan apparently got kidnapped yesterday while shopping in the Muslim Quarter of the Old City. We're fairly sure that Dr. Hakeem Saad is behind it. He's probably using her as bait to get to Ty and me. We could sure use some Intel on his location and anything else related to this kidnapping."

Asher paused for a full ten seconds. "Solly, aren't you deeply involved in this Jerusalem Protocol plan?"

"Yes sir, I am."

"The Jerusalem Protocol has a much higher security level and priority than rescuing a damsel in distress from an old and bitter Iraqi chemist."

"I realize that, sir. But I don't believe we can proceed effectively with the Jerusalem Protocol until we have rescued Ms. Hart. She is an important part of the team."

"I see," Asher said. "Is she an archeologist, or a weapons

specialist, or a construction engineer whose expertise is needed for this project?"

"Well, not exactly, sir. But she is a brilliant tactician. She's part of a team that operates best when we have the symbiosis of our shared experiences."

"Solly, that sounds like psychobabble from that American, Oprah!" Asher chided. "But, because I have learned to trust your strange intuition, I will do everything I can to locate Dr. Saad and the third member of your symbiotic union. That's all."

He hung up.

Ty asked, "What did he say?"

Solly smiled, "He's going to try to locate Dr. Saad. If we find him, I think you're right—he can lead us to Regan."

27

After less than twenty-four hours in captivity, Regan was growing tired of her mindless routine. She would sleep for a couple of hours and wake up abruptly. Her captors had added a thin soup to the pita and water by the door. She ate gladly, although she figured the food must have small amounts of sedatives. When her lips became parched, she finally tried drinking the water. It was warm but seemed to be pure. She had even worked up enough courage to use the plastic bucket in the corner.

She continued to pound on the door, but there was no response.

Unaware of whether it was day or night, she tried to walk circles around the tiny room to build up her strength. She didn't know what would happen to her, but every scenario filled her with dread.

Finally, after what seemed liked days, but was actually hours, she heard some movement outside her room. Suddenly two women dressed in all black burst in. Regan screamed and dropped to her knees, blinded by the rush of light. They didn't speak a word but began removing her dirty cloth garments. Regan was too sluggish to fight. They brought fresh water and soap and gently bathed her sweaty body. Then they began to dress her, draping her in the same full black outfit they were wearing. They covered her head with a black hood that only had a slit for her eyes.

Regan tried to reason with these women. "Ladies, please. I am an American. I have been taken against my will. Will you please contact the American Embassy here and let them know that I need their help?"

The women ignored her pleas as they finished their task. Another man in a white medical jacket entered next. He raised Regan's black sleeve, roughly swabbed an area of her arm, and gave her an injection. At first Regan felt no effects. But within minutes her thoughts became blurred and she could barely stand. She tried to protest, but no words would form. The two women shouldered her limp body between them and led her out of the room.

28

Gaza City, Palestinian Territory

Regan woke up in a room full of fluorescent light. As she slowly turned her head, she saw windows around the tops of three of the walls. The first smell that filled her nose was the sterile scent of a medical clinic or hospital. Her hands were bound in front, and she was lying on an examination table. Now she had on a thin hospital gown and no shoes on her bare feet. Her head was covered in a silk scarf. The room was warm. She felt herself sweating from fear and the heat.

She had lost track of time and had no clue where she was or how many hours or days had passed. Her mind was still slightly muddled from the drugs, but she was beginning to think clearly. She heard no sounds, so she assumed she was alone. She slowly swung her legs around and slowly sat up on the edge of the table.

"Well, I see you're awake, Ms. Hart!" Regan recoiled in horror at the voice she immediately recognized as Dr. Saad's.

"This has got to be a terrible nightmare. I need to wake up right now! Wake up!"

Dr. Saad limped around the table until he was facing her. He looked as if he'd aged ten years since she'd last seen him. He was wearing a lab coat and holding a small revolver in his hand. "Don't try anything stupid. I need to keep you alive for a little longer, but I'm not beyond putting a bullet in your knee if you don't do as I say."

"Where am I?"

"Let's just say that you're no longer in Israel. You are now a guest of ISIS. I'm sure you've heard of us. If you are thinking about escaping, I have several trained fighters protecting our compound here. This is my personal lab where I use my training to make chemical and explosive weapons for our fighters."

"What do you want from me?" Regan spat.

"Oh, we're going to take very good care of you. Our esteemed ISIS leader has a special plan for his American guest. I'll let him break that news to you himself. I wouldn't want to spoil the surprise. Meanwhile, I need you here to lure Solly and your boyfriend into my little trap."

"He's not my boyfriend. And you can't make me betray my friends."

Dr. Saad smiled as he picked up a large syringe. "Have it your way. I've perfected my own recipe for a flawless psychotropic drug. With a small dosage of this, you will do or say anything you're told."

Regan felt nauseated at the thought of more drugs in her already weakened system. "Okay. What's the drug-free plan?"

"I thought you'd come around," Dr. Saad said, putting down the syringe. "I give you a throwaway cell phone. You call your boyfriend and beg the two of them to come and rescue you. Pretty simple, huh?"

"Don't expect those two to come walking straight into your ambush. They're smarter than that."

Dr. Saad's mouth curled with a wicked grin. "I wouldn't expect anything less from them, Ms. Hart."

29

Jewish Quarter, the Old City

Solly and Ty were at an outdoor café in the Jewish Quarter. Solly was reading an encrypted text on his Confide app. It was from Asher.

When the message disappeared, Solly turned to Ty and said, "Well, mate, that's the first bit of good news we've had in a bit. Asher has agents living as Palestinians in Gaza City. They've been keeping an eye on Dr. Saad as a person of interest. He has joined ISIS as a weapons maker. He's also recently made a couple of clandestine visits to the Muslim Quarter, but now he's back at his lab in Gaza City."

"Let's go pay him a friendly visit," Ty said.

"Not so fast. An Israeli or an American can't just go walking into the Gaza Strip. We'd be shot on sight. Even our IDF units in tanks meet heavy resistance whenever they're sent in to quell violence or to stop the rocket attacks. We need a plan. And besides, we can't be certain that's where Regan is."

Ty's cell phone rang. He didn't recognize the caller ID number, but he decided to answer it anyway.

"Hello."

"Ty? Ty? It's Regan!"

"Regan! Thank God you're alive!" Ty shouted. "Are you okay?"

"I'm okay. Dr. Saad gave me this untraceable phone to call you to come get me."

Ty put his hand over the phone and mouthed "Dr. Saad" to Solly.

"I'm at his lab in Gaza City. But listen, it's a trap..."

Suddenly Dr. Saad's voice came on the phone. "Both of you come alone and you won't be harmed. At least not at first. Bring anyone with you, and the girl dies."

The line went dead.

Ty's veins were raised on the skin of his reddened neck. He punched the small table hard with his fist. "If he harms a hair on her head, he's going to *pay* for it."

"Settle down," Solly said, not wanting to draw attention.

"He obviously wants to lure us into his trap to capture or kill us, Solly," Ty seethed.

"The preferred ISIS method of execution is something that they stage and video for shock value and recruitment," Solly explained. "They may be hoping to capture us rather than blow us away immediately."

"So what's your idea?" Ty asked.

"It's time to bring in the big guns."

"You mean the U.S. Marines?" Ty asked proudly.

"No, I mean the covert *Mossad* experts Asher already

has imbedded in Gaza. We have teams specially trained for these kinds of extractions. The quicker we move, the less time Dr. Saad will have to prepare his defenses. I'd say we go in tonight."

30

Gaza City, Palestinian Territory

Dr. Saad threw the cell phone against the wall and used his other hand to backhand Regan across her face.

"You pig!" he shouted. "I said no funny business."

Regan rubbed her cheek where she could already feel the swelling begin.

Dr. Saad was trembling with uncontrollable fury. "I know you and your friends think you can outsmart me, but you're dealing with a desperate man."

Regan knew it was true. *What did he have to live for? He truly was a mad scientist,* she thought.

"You have taken my family, my job, my leg," Dr. Saad raged. "And I have lived these past few months for just one thing. To see all three of you die!" He pointed the pistol at her with a trembling hand.

Regan was terrified and realized he might kill her right then and there.

"You think I joined ISIS because I believe in their twisted vision? No! ISIS works for my purposes. I have received orders to capture the other two and send the three of you to Syria. Hours from now you will be the newest bride of Al-Bagahdi, the ISIS leader."

Regan felt a wave of cold dread break over her.

Dr. Saad continued his maniacal narrative. "Oh, but he has 'married' dozens of women during his time. Once he gets tired of you, Ms. Hart, he will toss you away. You and your two friends will be Internet stars of your own videos where you'll be beheaded on camera!"

Dr. Saad's breathing slowed as he regained his composure in a Jekyll and Hyde transformation. "That, anyway, is the official plan from the ISIS leaders. But I have my own plan."

As Regan continued to rub her bruised face, she found herself nearly paralyzed with fear. She could only pray, *"God, we need You to intervene. This man is pure evil. Please help me, Lord!"*

Just as she closed her prayer, Dr. Saad walked toward her with the syringe in his hand.

31

Mossad Headquarters, Jerusalem

Solly and Ty stood with a dozen soldiers in a high-tech planning room. Another ten soldiers were seated at computer consoles around the perimeter of the room. Colonel Ezra Hadad was the commander of the rescue force. He was a tall man in his late forties with closely cropped gray hair. His face was tan with crinkles near his brown eyes. He looked like a man who had spent most of his life living and working outdoors.

When he spoke, the men came to attention. "Okay, men. Many of you know Agent Solomon. This is Ty, one of our contractors. He's an American and former U.S. Marine. They will be armed, but they are considered non-combatants in this mission. We will all be wearing Kevlar vests and communication helmets with night-vision optics. We'll also be carrying handguns. Along with your standard gear, you'll all be issued the newest generation oxygen system. It's small but powerful and bulletproof. The closed system converts your expelled carbon dioxide back into breathable oxygen. Remember, Dr. Saad's weapon of choice is poisonous gas."

He continued, "Our objective is to extract Regan Hart alive and to do so with no casualties on either side. As you are aware, we don't need tensions to escalate between Gaza and Israel at this time."

Pointing to one of the large flat screen monitors, Colonel Hadad noted the location of Dr. Saad's lab.

"We have a fixed-wing drone at ten thousand feet circling the area. The drone is equipped with powerful night optics including an infrared sensor. It has already revealed there are six persons currently inside the lab. We believe one of them is Ms. Hart and one is Dr. Saad. The other four are either lab assistants or ISIS guards. When we zoom around the building, we see nine additional heat signatures stationed at strategic points. These are most certainly heavily armed guards. Our plan is to take them out quietly and then allow Solly and Ty to approach Dr. Saad and negotiate for Ms. Hart's release."

"I thought you said you didn't want any casualties," Solly interjected.

"You're going to witness some of our newest high-tech toys tonight," the colonel answered. He explained that *Mossad* had developed small attack quadrocopter drones called Ravens. He turned and picked one up to from the floor to show them. The lightweight drone was painted black with a smooth surface to resist radar. The body of the Raven was no bigger than a laptop computer. It had four thin, black arms protruding from the body with black

Kevlar propellers at the tips. Ty and Solly were amazed.

"This may look like a toy," Colonel Hadad said. "But it's packed with the latest in microprocessors for communication and control. It is also designed to fly silently. A pilot in this room can control it remotely, or it can be set on autopilot to carry out a predetermined flight plan and mission. We'll have a dozen Ravens in the air around the lab just as we arrive. They are programmed tonight to deal with the guards while producing no causalities. Are there any other questions?"

Ty wondered how the colonel's "no casualties" order would work out. Instead he asked, "How are we going to get to the lab in the middle of Gaza City without arising suspicion?"

"The way most people get around in Gaza City. We're taking a city bus."

32

Ramallah Street, Gaza City

Ty had been on dirtier buses before, but he couldn't remember when. The old vehicle lurched and smoked, but he had to admit it was a good cover. It looked like any of the other Palestinian buses that Ty saw meandering through the city.

It was nearing midnight as they bounced down the highway, choking on dust. The rescue team had boarded the bus two hours ago in an underground garage in Jerusalem. Ty noticed that some of the soldiers seemed to be sleeping now, but he was too nervous to close his eyes. The ride was so bumpy that he didn't even think about rest. He was thinking about Regan. He wondered if she had been harmed. He thought about praying, but he really didn't want it to be a desperate foxhole prayer like the ones he'd heard others pray back in the Marines when they were in trouble. So he shook off the idea.

His fellow travelers were a strange-looking group. In order to pass inspection at a checkpoint twenty minutes earlier, they were wearing plain robes over their combat uniforms with the traditional Arab *keffiyeh* wrapped around their heads. They had stuffed their helmets and gear in bags at their feet. Seeing nothing amiss, the Palestinian policemen had waved them through the border without stopping.

Ty was shocked to see the stark difference between Israel and the Gaza Strip. Gaza City was a bombed-out mess, and the streets were littered with all kinds of trash.

Fortunately there was little pedestrian traffic at this hour. They had been given orders not to speak to anyone. Only the bus driver and a couple of the operatives spoke fluent Arabic.

The bus shuddered to a stop at a plaza not far from the known location of Dr. Saad's lab. The driver turned off the exterior and interior lights of the bus. Colonel Hadad whispered, "Robes off. Helmets on and connected."

The men, including Solly and Ty, complied with his order.

"Com check one. Com check one," Colonel Hadad spoke into his helmet mic.

Everyone raised their thumbs to indicate they were online.

The first phase of the mission was to neutralize the nine armed guards outside the building. As promised, the twelve Ravens were already in the air nearby, each one targeting a different guard. The Ravens had synchronized their weapons so that when the controller pushed the "fire" button, each target would be eliminated simultaneously.

"You indicated they were using non-lethal ammo, right?" Ty confirmed.

"That's right. The Ravens are equipped with lethal

ammo as well. But the non-lethal weapon is similar to a very strong electric Taser. The Ravens will approach undetected to within ten feet of each guard. They can't miss at that range. The electrical jolt isn't fatal, but the guards will be immobilized and unconscious for at least an hour."

Colonel Hadad lowered his night optical lens and motioned the group to follow him out of the bus into the city street.

Ty had used night vision goggles before when he served with the Marines, but these new goggles were extremely advanced without the blurry green images he remembered. He silently followed Solly who was trailing the group of soldiers. After turning two corners, they saw the lab. Nine prone bodies wearing traditional black ISIS uniforms were scattered around the building. Ty looked up in the sky to see if he could spot one of the Ravens, but if they were still there, he couldn't detect them.

The *Mossad* officers silently gathered at the back door of the lab. Colonel Hadad lit up a floor plan of the building on his small tablet. The larger fixed-wing drone interfaced with his tablet and confirmed infrared images of six people presently inside the building. Two images were in the front reception room, and four were in the larger lab at the back.

"We enter on the count of three." Colonel Hadad took a deep breath. "One ... two..."

The sound of broken glass and the thud of a metal object hitting the pavement interrupted his countdown.

"Grenade! Everyone down!"

33

Rather than a huge explosion, a loud hissing sound filled the air followed by a thick cloud spreading from the metal canister.

Dr. Saad had been watching the extraction team the entire time with his upgraded surveillance equipment he'd recently installed. He saw his nine guards mysteriously collapse and had been patiently waiting for the extraction team to get closer before he launched retrofitted smoke grenades. He had designed them to kill instead of merely distract the enemy. The thick smoke was a potent combination of a fast-acting phosphine and cyanide gas. It killed quickly, but after thirty minutes any remaining gas would dissipate into the air. He had no desire to kill everyone in the city, although he had the skill to do so.

Dr. Saad was wearing a sophisticated breathing mask and had also placed one over Regan's face, as she lay unconscious on a stretcher. At his signal the two ISIS guards in the reception area had tossed a second grenade at the extraction team, unaware that they were poisonous and not explosives.

Although Dr. Saad was happy to utilize one of his

lethal inventions, he was ultimately disappointed. He had really wanted to capture Solly and Ty alive so he could orchestrate a much slower, tortuous death for both of them. But they had foolishly chosen to attempt a rescue, so he had no other choice but to eliminate them immediately.

The thick cloud of gas now blocked his view on the security screens, but he was certain the two men who had tormented him were now dead by his hand.

Besides poisoning the Israelis and the Americans, the only collateral damage were the deaths of his two ISIS guards in the reception area who inhaled the gas and died. But that was of little concern to Dr. Saad. They would be honored as *Mujahideen* who died for the cause of Allah. *"Good luck with those seventy-two virgins,"* Dr. Saad thought sarcastically. He no longer believed the tenets of his faith since Allah had so clearly abandoned him in the past by robbing him of his family.

Always the meticulous planner, he had formulated an alternative plan to escape with the American woman. Now that his most vexing enemies were dead, he might still present her to Al-Bagahdi as a blonde bride. Dr. Saad pressed a button on a wall to open a hidden doorway into the building next door. His two remaining guards, also wearing breathing masks, picked up each end of Regan's stretcher. He motioned them through the door before he hit a switch by the doorframe. A series of small explosions ignited inside the lab, and soon it was fully engulfed in flames, destroying any evidence of Dr. Saad's work.

34

"Grenade! Everyone down!" Colonel Hadad shouted. Seeing that the grenade was actually emitting a cloud of gas, he yelled, "Hold your breath! Oxygen masks on now!"

The team complied, taking shallow breaths through their masks.

Just then they heard a loud explosion. In a few minutes they could feel the heat from the burning lab, so they stood up to investigate. "Everyone check in. Keep your masks on," Colonel Hadad ordered, confirming that none of his men had been lost. They moved away to a safe distance from the fire and removed their masks.

"Saad can't be in there anymore," Solly said to the colonel. "I believe he escaped and torched his lab to cover his tracks. How can we find him?"

Colonel Hadad pulled out his tablet again. "Our eye in the sky is still reading a huge heat signature from the fire in the lab. Let me take another look."

Colonel Hadad tapped more data on his screen and said, "Look, here. We have four heat signatures leaving the lab before the fire. It's as if they walked right through the wall. Our surveillance drone is still tracking them. They are already two blocks away from our position. They're moving quickly down *al-Mukhtar* Street toward a large parking garage."

"Once they get under the parking garage they will be hard to track," Solly said. "They likely have a vehicle there to make their getaway. Is there any way we can stop them before they escape?"

"We're not on exactly friendly terms with the Palestinian police," the colonel said.

"So it's not as if we can put out an APB on them," Ty offered. "How many Ravens do you have left on station?"

"We have three left in the area." He got on his encrypted cell and called the control center. "We're tracking four heat signatures on *al-Mukhtar* moving toward a parking garage. Position the three remaining Ravens over the target ASAP."

Colonel Hadad turned to Solly and Ty. "They will be there in less than a minute. It's your call, Solly. Lethal or non-lethal?"

Solly's face gave him all the answer the colonel needed.

"Light up the three men, but don't target the female," the colonel shouted into his cell.

35

Al-Mukhtar Street, Gaza City

Dr. Saad instructed his two ISIS fighters to remove their oxygen masks. They were safe now from the lingering effects of the gas. He kept the oxygen mask on Regan just to keep her breathing regular while under the effects of the sedation.

He could see the parking garage ahead. Once again he thought he had outsmarted the Israelis. He had made arrangements for a nondescript van with changeable license plates to be waiting for him in the garage.

Inside the van were fake Egyptian passports for himself and his three passengers. When they arrived at the border, Dr. Saad would administer another drug that would make Regan appear as if she were suffering the effects of muscular sclerosis and couldn't speak. When he arrived in Egypt, he would connect with old friends—members of the Muslim Brotherhood who now had connections with ISIS.

After hiding for a few weeks, he would carry his prize American bride to Syria in order to extend her suffering.

As they ran toward the garage, a new vision began formulating in his mind. Once in Syria his personal revenge would finally be satisfied, leaving him free to use his expertise to design coordinated multiple chemical attacks against the American infidels on their soil. He would make the 9/11 attack pale in comparison.

They were only about fifty feet from the parking garage. Dr. Saad never heard the silent approach of the three Ravens. For some reason his eyes were drawn to the clear night sky under a blanket of stars. There seemed to be a small portion of the sky where the stars were blurred out.

"Hmm. I wonder what that could be?"

It was his last thought. At that moment a nineteen-year-old Israeli soldier sitting at a computer terminal tapped an icon on his screen. One of the Ravens released a .40 caliber hollow point bullet from a range of twenty feet. It struck Dr. Saad in the middle of his forehead and left a huge exit wound in the back of his skull. He was dead before he hit the ground. Because of the synchronized software, two more identical bullets from the other Ravens took down the two ISIS fighters carrying Regan's stretcher. They fell where they stood. The Ravens remained on station to record that Regan was not injured when her stretcher tumbled to the street.

Six minutes later the Ravens recorded the Israeli extraction squad arriving at Regan's location. They picked her up and carried her back to the bus for the slow trip back to Jerusalem.

36

The Gaza-Jerusalem Highway

Once again, Regan woke up totally disoriented. She was lying on a stretcher. *"Am I dead? Where am I? What's that dusty smell?"* she wondered.

A strangely familiar voice said, "I think she's waking up. Here, let's give her a little water."

Regan felt the plastic lip of a bottle of water meeting her lips. She began to swallow. It was the best thing she had ever tasted. She drank deeper and began to choke.

"Take it easy now. That's plenty," the voice soothed.

Regan risked opening one eye and saw a friendly face with a huge white beard.

"Solly? Is that you?"

"It's me in the flesh," Solly said, winking at his friend. "And a rather pungent flesh, I might add. We've done a bit of sweating tonight."

Regan reached up and put her arms around Solly's neck. "Oh, it's so good to hear your voice. I thought I'd never see you again!"

Solly wiped away tears from his eyes. "You gave us

quite a scare, old girl. We thought we had lost you as well. I apologize for taking my eyes off you in the *souk*."

"No, no. It was my fault. I'm a big girl. I should be able to take care of myself."

"Nope, that's the man's job," Ty joked as he moved in beside Solly to talk to Regan. He explained how Dr. Saad had arranged her kidnapping and how Solly had coordinated with *Mossad* to get her out.

"We're on a bus now from Gaza back to Jerusalem," he told her as Solly made his way to the front of the bus again. "A doctor is waiting for us back at the hotel to check you over and make sure you're okay. We'll get you whatever you feel like eating, and you'll rest tonight in your own room in a nice, comfortable bed. How does that sound?"

Regan smiled weakly. She was emotionally and physically exhausted.

Ty wanted to tell her something else, but he couldn't find the words so he just looked at her for a minute.

"What is it?" Regan asked. "Do I have something on my face? Stop looking at me like that for heaven's sake." Ty took her spicy response as a good sign that she was going to be back to normal soon. He laughed and put his arm around her and pulled her close in a friendly hug. He waited another minute before speaking.

"Regan," he said softly so no one else could hear, "when you were gone, I thought I'd lost you forever. That's something I could not bear to think about. I'm so glad you are okay."

Regan was quiet for a long time. Just when Ty was regretting how vulnerable he'd been, he looked down and noticed Regan was sound asleep on his shoulder. He sighed, feeling very content and somewhat relieved that Regan hadn't heard him after all.

PART 3

37

The Temple Institute Visitors Center, Jerusalem

Regan awoke in the King David Hotel feeling refreshed after sleeping for ten hours straight. Ty and Solly urged her to stay behind and rest some more. But Regan stubbornly insisted she felt fine. Besides, she told them, the doctor had cleared her to do whatever she felt like doing.

"Like you've ever needed permission for that, " Ty joked.

"Ha ha, funny boy," she said smiling. "Let's get going."

After breakfast Solly, Regan, and Ty walked to the Visitors Center of the Temple Institute where Director David Shvaz was waiting for them.

"I hear you had quite the experience since the last time we saw each other. But I'm thrilled to see you have returned to us safely, Ms. Hart."

Regan beamed. "You're not as thrilled as I am!"

She held up her hand and pinched her forefinger and thumb in proximity. "I was *this* close to becoming the bride of Frankenstein!"

"You're getting married Ms. Hart?" David asked.

"Never mind. The wedding's off," Regan said, trembling at the thought.

"Hopefully that's all behind us now since that nasty fellow has been neutralized," Solly said.

"More like vaporized, I'd say," Ty said with a wry grin and fist bumped Solly.

Solly turned to David and said, "We're all yours now."

"Great, then follow me." David began making his way through the museum to what they had learned was secretly called the Temple Institute Annex. "You know the drill by now," he said as he passed by all the international tourists on the way to the theater. The Jewish guides who worked there gave the minimal information reserved for the public about the Temple Institute, but their guests had no idea that the museum was the actual nerve center for the future rebuilding the Temple.

When David led them into the theater, it was deserted once again. The screen opened at his command, and they walked down the sloping passageway to the underground center. Inside it was a beehive of activity as usual with dozens of engineers, scientists, and workmen grouped around several workstations. Several fully armed security agents in black uniforms kept a watchful eye for any unauthorized entry.

David led them over to a computer terminal with three large flat-screens filled with rotating 3-D architectural plans. A worker with a shock of wild white hair and wearing a white lab coat was sitting at the screens. He was bent over the keyboard furiously punching on the keys labeled in Hebrew. At the same time he was deftly manipulating a computer mouse to highlight different areas of the screens.

The group walked up to his workstation and stood for a few minutes, not wanting to interrupt someone so evidently lost in his work. After a full minute without even sensing their presence, David coughed to get his attention.

"Ahem, Dr. Chavitz, I'd like to introduce you..."

Dr. Chavitz kept typing.

"Dr. Ariel Chavitz is the brains behind the Jerusalem Protocol," David explained to his guests. He gently placed his hand on the man's shoulder and said in a low voice, "Dr. Chavitz? May I borrow your valuable attention for a few minutes?"

As if awakening from a dream, Dr. Chavitz stopped pecking away and swiveled around in his chair. He stared up at David as if looking at a stranger. Dr. Chavitz had a weathered and wrinkled face framed by big black eyeglasses with thick lenses that magnified his eyeballs. His age was a mystery. He could have been in his sixties or in his eighties, and his hair was a bird's nest that hadn't seen a comb since *Yom Kippur*. A multi-colored *kippah* perched precariously on one section of his head was anchored with several black bobby pins. But there was no mistaking the deep intelligence in his owl-like eyes. He blinked as recognition slowly registered in his gaze.

Sliding his glasses up his nose with one finger, he mumbled, "Certainly, Director. What can I do for you?"

"Dr. Chavitz, I want you to meet three new members of the Jerusalem Protocol team."

After he introduced them, Solly reached out a tanned hand and offered a hearty, "Nice to make your acquaintance, chap," although the handshake he received in return was more like a cold fish.

"Mmm hmm," Dr. Chavitz mumbled absentmindedly.

David cleared his throat again before saying, "I need you to bring my friends up to speed on the work you've been doing on the Jerusalem Protocol."

Dr. Chavitz scooted his glasses higher on his nose and asked matter-of-factly, "Do you have two months for me to give you the full story?"

"Please, just the short version this time," David said politely.

Dr. Chavitz seemed genuinely disappointed but took a deep breath and started speaking rapidly without making eye contact with the three guests. "Thirty years ago our Maker directed the rabbis who would later begin the Temple Institute to prepare to rebuild His Temple." He stopped suddenly. "Out of reverence most of us never mention the name of our Maker, but I assume you know about Whom I'm referring?"

All three nodded.

"You've read the Bible, I assume?"

Solly and Regan nodded vigorously. Ty shrugged his shoulders sheepishly.

"I see I've got to give *you* a little history lesson then, Mr. Kensington," Dr. Chavitz said, taking another deep breath and sighing as if he were in physical pain. "Without knowing the story of the Temple, you cannot know the story of the Jews. And you certainly cannot understand the significance of the Jerusalem Protocol.

"About three thousand years ago, our Maker instructed King David to build a Temple in Jerusalem. Before that time the sacrifices for sin had been offered in a temporary structure called the *mishkan*. You would say, 'tabernacle.' This portable tent was dismantled and rebuilt whenever Moses and the Hebrew people moved on their nomadic journey through the wilderness.

"David was a man of war with blood on his hands, so our Maker wouldn't allow him to build the Temple. His son Solomon was chosen to undertake that task. King David became the main fundraiser, giving much of his wealth to acquire a stockpile of gold, silver, stones, and wood for the construction. Money also poured in from the people because this was a time of great power and wealth.

He looked askew at Ty and asked, "Are you sure you don't know this story, Mr. Kensington?"

Ty raised his palms to plead guilty. "Sorry. I never paid attention in Sunday school."

Dr. Chavitz ruefully clicked his tongue and continued. "After King David died Solomon constructed the Temple and spared no expense. He located the stone quarry several kilometers away from the holy site so that it would not be tainted by the sounds of hammers hitting stone. He utilized slave labor and appointed over three thousand supervisors to carefully look over every detail. Still, even with this huge workforce, it took almost twenty years to finish. The Scriptures list the amount of gold and silver in Solomon's Temple as being worth 833 trillion shekels today."

"How much is that in good ol' U.S. dollars?" Ty asked.

Dr. Chavitz quickly performed the mental calculation. "About 216 trillion dollars, give or take a couple of million."

Ty let out a low whistle. "Wow, that was some building."

Dr. Chavitz talked to Ty as if dealing with a child. "Oh, no—not just a building, Mr. Kensington. It was the Temple!" His baritone voice reverberated in the open space. "Let's fast-forward. Solomon's Temple was in existence for around four hundred years. Then on the Eighth Day of Av in 586 BCE Nebuchadnezzar and the Babylonians overran Jerusalem and destroyed this beautiful Temple. They carried off the Temple treasures and some records claim they even removed the Ark of the Covenant."

"The ark? Like Noah's ark?" Ty asked.

Regan thought Ty must be really trying Dr. Chavitz' patience by now, but she realized something had changed in Dr. Chavitz' terse expression. He had a captive audience and was taking great pleasure in his pedantic explanation.

"The word ark or *tebah* in Hebrew simply means a box. Noah escaped the flood in a big floating box. Yes?"

Ty nodded.

"The Ark of the Covenant is also a box, but this one contains reminders of our Maker's covenant with His people. Personally, I believe it still exists somewhere. Many of my peers believe that Solomon's priests wisely hid the Ark before the Babylonians could get to it. At the proper time our Maker will return it to us."

"What was in it?" Ty asked.

"The Ark contained the two tablets of the Ten Commandments given to Moses, a bowl of manna, and Aaron's rod. The lid of the box was decorated with two golden cherubim facing each other with spread wings. The very *Shekinah* glory of our Maker dwelt in the presence of that Ark, Mr. Kensington."

Ty furrowed his brows and asked, "Manna? What's that?"

A tiny smile traced Dr. Chavitz's lips. "*Finally*, you're right."

"Huh?" Ty quizzed.

"When the Israelites were wandering in the wilderness, the Maker gave them bread-like flakes from heaven to feed them. When they first saw it, they didn't know what it was so they asked, '*Manhu?*' That's Hebrew for, 'What that?' So you see, you got it right."

Solly looked at Regan and passed his hand over the top of his hat as if to say, *"It's no use—it's over his head."*

Regan tried to steer the conversation back on track. "That had to be a terrible day for the Jewish people to see their Temple destroyed before their very eyes."

"To be sure, Ms. Hart," said Dr. Chavitz. "But in hindsight we see that our Maker used this godless ruler to get our ancestors' attention. They had turned away from the true Maker and were worshipping idols. The prophet Jeremiah warned the residents of Jerusalem that unless they repented they could lose the city and the Temple, but nobody had believed him. Some of the finest, brightest Israelites were deported to Babylon to serve in the court of Nebuchadnezzar. One of them was named Daniel. I'm sure you've heard of him."

Ty smiled and raised his index finger, "Daniel in the Lion's Den. I know that story!"

Dr. Chavitz smiled like a father watching a toddler learn to walk.

"So he *does* know a little of the Bible," David said to the group.

They all laughed, except Dr. Chavitz whose face had grown suddenly serious. His owl-like eyes stared ahead, now aglow with spiritual fervor. It seemed as if he had once again forgotten anyone else was there. After a few seconds of awkward silence, his mind returned to the present.

"Pardon me. But when I think of the magnitude of what we are about to do for the glory of our Maker, I can hardly take it in."

David stepped in. "It is a staggering thought, as he said. The story of the Temple is essential to understanding the historical significance of the Jerusalem Protocol."

"Where were we?" Dr. Chavitz asked. "Oh yes, now we are getting to the good part."

38

The Temple Institute Annex, Beneath Jerusalem

Dr. Chavitz trained his swivel chair directly on his young pupil and continued his orientation.

"After almost seven decades of exile, our Maker influenced the Persian king to allow our people to return here to Jerusalem. Their first job was to rebuild the city walls. After several years they laid the foundation for the Second Temple. It was a time of joy and weeping. The young men rejoiced, but not the oldest men who remembered Solomon's Temple as children. They wept for the lost glory of the former beautiful house of worship. Under the leadership of Ezra and Nehemiah, the people completed the Second Temple in just four years in 515 BCE. But it was a basic, unadorned building that some rabbis thought of as nothing but a shadow of Solomon's majestic work. Yet our Maker once again made His presence known among His people."

"Without an Ark?" Ty interjected.

"The Ark of the Covenant was never used in the Second Temple," said Dr. Chavitz. The priests placed a large seven-branch Menorah to stand in the Holy Place instead. A beautiful thick curtain separated the Holy Place from the Holy of Holies, called the *Kodesh Hakodeshim* in Hebrew. But the Holy of Holies was empty – except for the *Shekinah* glory of our Maker."

"Did anything ever happen inside that room?" Ty asked.

"Finally, a good question!" Regan said. "Congratulations, Ty."

"She's right," Dr. Chavitz agreed. "This is the most important part, so listen quickly."

The Jewish Temple, he explained, contained only two rooms separated by a thick curtain. The outer room was called the Most Holy Place where the priests burned incense and offered sacrifices. The inner room was the Holy of Holies. Only the High Priest was allowed to enter that room once a year on Yom Kippur. On *Yom Kippur*, the Day of Atonement, the High Priest would take the blood of a ram and enter the Holy of Holies to make atonement for the sins of the people. But during the Second Temple period the priesthood had become corrupt. Except for a brief season of independence after the Maccabean revolt, the Jews were always under the heels of the Persians, the Syrians, and later the Romans—none of whom cared anything for God.

"They were so careless that they often awarded the office of High Priest to the highest bidder," Dr. Chavitz explained. He went on to describe the deadly consequences that followed this unholy barter. If the High Priest entering the Holy of Holies wasn't spiritually pure and able to focus on the task, he would not survive the encounter with the *Shekinah* glory of God. "Moses himself, when asked to see God's face, had been told he would surely die," he said. "Even he could only be shown the afterglow of God's goodness. In fact, during the Second Temple period the priests tied a rope to the leg of the High Priest on *Yom Kippur.* That way, if he died in the presence of the Maker, they could retrieve the body."

"You're kidding!" Regan said. "I've never heard that before."

"It's true," Solly nodded affirmatively.

"We have complete records of the names of all the High Priests since the beginning of Solomon's Temple," Dr. Chavitz explained. "During the four hundred years of Solomon's Temple, there were only eighteen High Priests—an average term of over twenty years each. But during the four hundred years of the Second Temple, they had more than three hundred High Priests!"

"I don't get it," Regan said. "Why so many priests?"

Dr. Chavitz eyes twinkled, "You do the math. Either the High Priest got outbid each year, or they *died* in the Holy Presence of the Maker! There are many accounts of having to drag bodies from the Holy of Holies. You don't want to mess with our Maker!"

"Who would want that job?" Regan asked.

"Right you are, Ms. Hart," Dr. Chavitz answered.

"Toward the end of the Second Temple, some of the High Priests refused to enter the Holy of Holies even on *Yom Kippur*."

"What happened to that Second Temple?" Ty asked.

"The Romans eventually destroyed it in 70 CE," Dr. Chavitz said. "But before it was destroyed it received a major upgrade. In 63 BCE the Romans captured Jerusalem and the surrounding territory. About thirty years later a half-Jew named Herod was named as ruler of the area. He hadn't been born a Jew, so he had to impress the Jewish people in order for them to accept him as their king."

"Are you talking about Herod the Great?" Regan asked.

"Yes, and that's probably a title he gave himself!" Dr. Chavitz chuckled.

Dr. Chavitz explained that when Herod looked at the modest Temple in Jerusalem, he made plans to enlarge it in about 20 BCE to enhance his reputation and rival some of the temples he had seen in Rome. He expanded it and built beautiful courtyards around it.

"There wasn't much flat ground around the Temple because both the First and Second Temples were located on the pinnacle of Mt. Moriah," Dr. Chavitz noted.

Solly turned to Regan and said, "He's right. Not everyone makes the connection. The Temple was built on the same mountain where Abraham went to sacrifice his only son, Isaac."

"Better yet," David interjected, "Dr. Chavitz can show

you that the altars of both Temples were built on the exact spot where the Jews believed Abraham was prepared to sacrifice Isaac."

Ty held up his hand, "Wait. Do you mean to tell me that God had Abraham kill his son?"

Dr. Chavitz was not put off by the question, as he'd been asked a similar question many times in the past. "No. But Abraham was willing – that's the kind of man the Maker was looking for to build His nation. The Maker never truly intended for Isaac to die. It was a test. At the last moment an angel stopped Abraham, and he sacrificed a ram caught in a thicket instead of his son."

"What's that story got to do with this Herod guy?" Ty asked.

Dr. Chavitz was really getting into the story now. "Instead of a mountaintop, Herod needed a much larger, flattened area to enlarge the Temple. So his first architectural challenge was to turn the peak into a huge dirt platform to surround the Temple. This area is called the Temple Mount today.

"Herod hauled in millions of tons of dirt and rubble to form a platform the size of about twenty football fields or forty-six acres by your western measurements. That's the current size of the Temple Mount today."

Ty, Solly, and Regan nodded.

"He also needed to build a retaining wall around the platform to support all of the rock and soil he brought in, so he cut massive rectangular stones and put them on place to form a wall on all four sides. Considering the topography, it wasn't a perfect rectangular shape but more like a trapezoid ... wider at the northern end than at the south."

David said, "When you have ten thousand slaves to provide free labor, you can get a lot done. Parts of that retaining wall can still be seen surrounding the Temple Mount today."

"Yep. I showed them the Western Wall the other day," Solly explained. "Now that you know more about the Holy of Holies, you can appreciate that this Western Wall is the closest wall to the Holy of Holies. That's why our people pray there."

"Jewish scholars claim that Herod restored the Temple to the glory of Solomon's Temple," Dr. Chavitz noted. "This was the very Temple in place at the time of the Jewish rabbi, Jesus. He was angry over the corruption of the priests I spoke about. Perhaps you know the story of how he drove out the merchants and moneychangers?"

Solly thought it important to offer an explanation to Regan and Ty. "Some of us believe Jesus was more than a teacher. We believe He was the Messiah, but others like Dr. Chavitz disagree. We all get along for the sake of rebuilding Israel."

Without moving his body, Dr. Chavitz turned his head and peered over at Solly with unblinking round eyes. "So you're one of *those* Jews? There are a lot of you around these days." He shrugged. "You may be right. When the Messiah comes, the first question we're all going to ask Him is, 'Have you been here before?'"

Solly, David, and Dr. Chavitz shared a hearty laugh together. Regan and Ty exchanged blank looks. They didn't quite get Jewish humor.

After the laughter died, Regan asked, "So how long did it take for Herod to complete his facelift of the Temple? Does anyone know?"

Dr. Chavitz nodded. "We don't have to wonder because the Jewish historian, Flavius Josephus, left us detailed information about the project. Herod lived through the first twenty years of the renovation, but it continued long after he died. In fact, the work wasn't completed until 63 CE, just seven years before the Temple was destroyed. So the total project took about eighty years."

"There hasn't been a Jewish Temple in Jerusalem since 70 CE?"

Dr. Chavitz shook his head. "No, and remember there are no coincidences with our Maker. The Romans destroyed the Second Temple on the same day, of the same month that the Babylonians destroyed Solomon's Temple! You remember I told you it was the Eighth Day of Av. To this day the Jews around the world observe *Tisha B'Av* as a national day of mourning for the loss of both Jewish Temples. We fast and pray and read the mournful sections from the book of Lamentations. We declare our repentance for the sins of our ancestors in fervent hope that the Maker will allow us to build a third Temple to His glory."

Like many people outside of the Jewish faith, Regan had never realized the significance that a third Temple carried for the Jewish people. She was beginning to see the relevance surrounding thousands of years of history that Dr. Chavitz had compressed into the past few minutes. All of it seemed to be pointing to this very moment in the twenty-first century, and she would somehow be a part of it!

39

Temple Institute Annex, Beneath Jerusalem

Without warning, Dr. Chavitz swiveled his computer chair back toward his keyboard and array of flat screens. The history lesson was over. He had work to do.

"Sorry. I'm still a little confused," Ty said to Solly. "Why did the Muslims build their Golden Dome of the Rock where the Jewish Temple was? And doesn't that make it impossible for the Jews to rebuild the Temple there?"

David Shvaz led the group toward a nearby conference room. "That is the crucial question, isn't it? If you'll join me, I'll try to give you an answer while Dr. Chavitz completes some of his design work."

They entered a glassed room and sat at a large conference table made of polished wood. The group settled into three of the two dozen or so plush leather chairs around the table. David stood at the other end near a large screen. Solly noticed a long, horizontal slot parallel to the edge of the table in front of each seat. David picked up a tiny remote and touched it. Thin flat screen monitors silently arose out of the slots. A virtual attendant appeared on screen, asking if anyone would like water, tea, or coffee.

"I am rather dry after that long history lesson," Ty joked. "I'll have some bottled water."

Regan and David requested hot tea while Solly asked for coffee.

"My pleasure," spoke the woman.

David scrolled a wireless mouse on the table and an image of a bird appeared on the ultra HD 4K screens.

David began, "I'm an amateur birdwatcher. Thousands of species of birds migrate through Israel each season. There is a particular bird species known as blood parasites. They never build their own nests; they hide their eggs in the nests of other species. The cuckoo bird you see here has even evolved so that their eggs replicate the appearance of their preferred targets. If the host bird isn't mindful, the cuckoo hatchling will take over the nest for itself, pushing the other eggs out."

"Sorry, you've already lost me. What to birds have to do with the Dome of the Rock?" Ty asked.

David answered, "Muslims have a conquering mindset and a long history of claiming holy sites for themselves. It has been said that Islam spread at the tip of a sword. That's true. When Islam first developed in the Arabian Peninsula in the sixth century, Muslim warriors carried the message of the Prophet Mohammed. Their ultimatum was simple, 'Convert or die.' Some offered a third option called the *jizya*. Jews and Christians could pay a hefty annual tax to the Muslim rulers, thereby saving their lives. However, common people couldn't afford this exorbitant tax. Unable to fight against the Muslim armies, they could only watch as they conquered their cities and destroyed many of the local churches and synagogues. Instead of building their own mosques in their place, they claimed the most elegant churches and synagogues for themselves and converted them to mosques. As you see, they are much like the cuckoo."

Solly, Ty, and Regan were listening intently.

David scrolled again and displayed a picture of a huge mosque. "For instance, when they conquered what was then called Constantinople and is now Istanbul, they captured the beautiful Church of Holy Wisdom. The Muslims drove out the Christians, built minarets around it, and turned it into their main mosque. They didn't even change the name. It became the *Hagia Sophia* Mosque, which means 'Holy Wisdom Mosque.'"

The display changed again to show an aerial view of the Temple Mount dominated by a golden dome in the center and a black mosque on the left side of the screen.

"But the Muslims' biggest rip-off took place right here at the Temple Mount in Jerusalem when they conquered the city in 637 CE," David continued. "The Muslims claimed the entire Temple Mount as their own, knowing full well it was the most holy site for the Jewish religion because it had already served as the location of the two Temples. They built the Dome of the Rock anyway. Today Muslims consider it the third most holy site in Islam, behind the *Kaaba* in Mecca and Mohammed's tomb in Medina. They justify their claim to it by insisting that it was from this spot that Mohammed ascended into heaven to meet Allah."

Solly interjected, "But, according to the *Qur'an*, Mohammed never even visited Jerusalem, right?"

David smiled and nodded. "Right again, Solly. Mohammed was born in 571 CE and died at the age of sixty-two in 632 CE in the house of his latest wife, Aisha. By the way, she was eighteen at the time of his death, and he had married her ten years earlier. Mohammed is buried in Medina. When you study the *Qur'an*, there is no indication that Mohammed ever left the Arabian Peninsula."

"Why do the Muslims embrace the story of Mohammed being in Jerusalem?" Ty asked.

David put down his remote and said, "Let me give you a little background that few people know."

He went on to explain how the sacred scripture of Islam, the *Qur'an*, is considered the words of Allah given verbatim through the prophet Mohammed. The *Qur'an* never mentions Jerusalem. "But there are other writings that appeared after the death of Mohammed," said David. "These are called *hadith*, which is Arabic for 'reports'— verbal reports that circulated by word-of-mouth after the death of Mohammed. These reports were not collected and organized until the 8th and 9th centuries."

"I've heard of the *hadith*," said Solly. "I've even heard there are so many of these reports that they have really caused confusion in the Muslim faith."

"Indeed," David nodded. "There are about four thousand different *hadith*. Sunni and Shia Muslims are divided over which *hadith* are reliable. In a certain *hadith* called *Sahih al-Bukhari,* we find a story of a night journey of Mohammed to Jerusalem. In the story, Mohammed was asleep when the angel Gabriel woke him. After cleansing his heart, Gabriel placed him on a strange angelic beast called a *Buraq.* Some traditions say it was a giant horse with the head of an angel and the tail of a peacock. He then flew on this beast from Mecca to Jerusalem. This journey is called *al-Isra,* or 'night journey' in Arabic. Once in Jerusalem, the *hadith* reports that the horse-like creature placed his hoof on a rock marking the very spot where Abraham sacrificed Ishmael."

"Whoa! I thought we just talked about Abraham sacrificing Isaac. Who's Ishmael?" Ty asked.

"Ty," Solly scolded. "You really should read the Bible if for no other reason than you could carry on a conversation about religion. You do realize we're talking about the three foremost religions of the world—Christianity, Judaism, and Islam? David, do you mind if I fill in the gaps for this bloke?"

David seemed bemused and sipped his tea. "Go ahead."

Solly relished the opportunity to do some instructing of his own regarding Jewish history.

"All Jewish husbands love telling this story," Solly explained, talking as much with his hands as his voice.

"God had promised Abraham a son who would be the father of an entire nation. But as the years passed Abraham's wife, Sarah, hadn't conceived a child. She grew impatient and decided that God needed her help to make His promise happen. She told Abraham to go to bed with her young maid, Hagar, so perhaps she would conceive a son."

Solly's eyes darted to and fro. "Can't you hear Abraham saying, 'Yes dear'? Well, he went along with Plan B, of course. Hagar did become pregnant and gave birth to a son. They named this boy Ishmael, which means 'God listens' in Hebrew. It's somewhat of a joke because while God may have been listening, Sarah and Abraham definitely were not."

Regan smiled. Solly paused and stroked his long beard. "Meanwhile," he said, "when Ishmael was around thirteen years old, and Abraham was almost a hundred years old, ninety-year-old Sarah finally got pregnant. Can you imagine? She gave birth to a son and they named him Isaac. It means 'laughter' because she'd laughed at the notion when she'd overheard an angel promising Abraham a child."

"So what happened to this Ishmael?" Ty inquired.

Solly's eyes twinkled. "Sarah became jealous of Hagar, so she demanded that Abraham send away the boy and his mother. Abraham loved both of his boys, so he was reluctant to do it.

"But I bet he said 'Yes, dear' again," Regan threw in.

"I'm afraid so. He banished Hagar and Ishmael to the desert. After they went several days without finding water, Hagar cried out to God for help. 'God listened' and directed her to a well. Although he was not the son God promised to Abraham and Sarah, God told Hagar that Ishmael would also be the father of a great nation. Indeed, all Arab Muslims trace their heritage back to Abraham through Ishmael. That's the long answer to your question about why Muslims claim it was Ishmael who was the start of the show on Mt. Moriah."

"So when you think about it," Ty said, "this whole Arab-Israeli conflict is just one big family feud."

"That's one way to look at it," Solly said. "It's also important to remember not to settle for Plan B when God has a Plan A for us."

Regan looked at Ty and smiled. "Amen, Solly. And God has a Plan A for you, Buster. You'd better get in on it."

Solly turned to David apologetically. "I seem to have chased that *Buraq* out of the stall! Why don't you continue telling us about Mohammed's mythical journey to heaven?"

40

The Temple Institute Annex, Beneath Jerusalem

"Where was I?" David asked, setting down his teacup.

"Mohammed and his giant horse had just landed on the Temple Mount," Regan reminded him.

"Right. And, by the way, did you know that's why it's called the Dome of the Rock? The Muslims claim there is a rock called the Rock of Sacrifice under the dome with the actual hoof print of the *Buraq*."

"I have some Muslim friends at work. I've not heard that particular story about Mohammed's night journey," Regan admitted. "But didn't Mohammed also supposedly visit heaven? What's the story there?"

"It's actually quite interesting," David explained. "They say Mohammed ascended up through seven heavens to the presence of Allah. That's where we get the expression 'seventh heaven.' People think that's in the Bible, but it actually comes from this same *hadith*. When Mohammed reached the seventh heaven, Gabriel and the *Buraq* could go no further, but Mohammed continued into the presence of Allah.

"Allah commanded Mohammed to return and tell his followers that they must pray fifty times daily. Mohammed left Allah and was getting ready to take that message back to earth when he passed Moses. The story implies that Moses basically asked Mohammed, 'So what did the Boss tell you?' When Moses heard about the fifty daily prayers, he told Mohammed to go back and try to negotiate a smaller number. Fifty daily prayers would be too much of a burden on his followers.

"According to the *hadith*, Mohammed went back and forth between Moses and Allah until they settled on five daily prayers. And that's why Muslims pray five times a day. It's called *sadat*. That tradition comes from this *hadith*, not the *Qur'an*."

"So the Muslims built the Dome of the Rock to enshrine the place where they believe Mohammed ascended to heaven?" Regan asked.

"That's the official story," David said. "But the numbers don't add up."

"What numbers?" Ty asked.

David continued, "The *hadith* that tells the story was compiled by Imam *Muhammed al-Bukhari* who died in 870 CE...over two hundred years after Mohammed's death! But the Dome of the Rock was completed in 691 CE. This is at least a hundred years *before* the *hadith* story of Mohammed's ascension to heaven was even compiled. In other words, they had to come up with a story much later to explain why they chose that location for the Dome!"

"Then why was the Dome of the Rock really built?" Regan asked.

"Good question," Ty agreed.

"That's why I told you the story of the cuckoo," David began. "Muslims will completely deny this logic, but the Dome of the Rock was completed in 691 CE by Caliph *Adb al-Malik*. As was their custom, he simply wanted to stake claim to a Jewish holy site for the Muslim faith."

David habitually took another sip of his tea. "They reverse engineered the story to justify the location."

"But you just said the *Qur'an* doesn't mention Mohammed in Jerusalem. Doesn't that squelch the story?" Ty asked.

"Some Muslim scholars discount the inerrancy of the *hadith*, but none of them doubt the *Qur'an*," David said. "So in order to legitimize their actions they had to twist an interpretation of the *Qur'an* that identifies Jerusalem in the text."

"Wait, wait. Does the *Qur'an* say anything about the Dome of the Rock being in Jerusalem?" Ty asked.

"Absolutely nothing. But Muslims identify one verse in the *Qur'an* that they *claim* identifies Jerusalem." David scrolled his mouse, and the image on the screen changed to a digital version of the *Qur'an* in English.

"Before we read this, you must realize that the Muslims claim that the *Qur'an* can only be read and understood in Arabic. There are no acceptable translations in any other language." David scrolled down the text until his cursor stopped on a heading identified as *Surah 17*.

David nodded to Solly. "Solly, would you read *Surah 17.1*?"

Solly said, "Sure. *'Glory to (God) Who did take His Servant for a Journey by night from the Sacred Mosque to the Farthest Mosque whose precincts We did bless, in order that We might show him of Our Signs: For He is the One Who hears and sees all things.'*"

Ty kept expecting Solly to keep reading and eventually arrive at a statement about Jerusalem. "That's it?" Ty said. "I don't see Jerusalem anywhere in that verse."

"The plot thickens," Solly commented.

David then explained that the translation of the phrase 'Farthest Mosque' is *Al-Aqsa*. He scrolled his mouse again, and a picture of the Temple Mount appeared from the eastern perspective of the Mount of Olives.

"See that black mosque near the Dome of the Rock?" he asked. "Many people do not realize that the Dome of the Rock is not a mosque at all."

"It's not?" Regan asked.

"No. The Muslims named this black building next to it the *Al-Aqsa* Mosque. Why did they do that? To fit the story of Mohammed going to the 'farthest mosque' and to place Mohammed in Jerusalem. But again there is a problem with the math. *Al-Aqsa* Mosque wasn't built for almost one hundred years after Mohammed supposedly took his mysterious journey. So how could he have traveled to this 'farthest mosque' when it did not yet exist?"

There was silence around the table as this information sank in. Ty was the first to speak, connecting his thoughts aloud. "So if your theory is correct that the Muslims claimed this spot just because it was a Jewish holy site, and then later they made up a story to justify being here, then…?"

Solly interrupted. "Then the Muslims have no legitimate right to be on the Temple Mount. The Jews are free to rebuild the Temple wherever they wish."

David's face turned somber. "I'm afraid that's exactly right, Solly. And that's why you're going to help us launch the Jerusalem Protocol."

41

Western Wall Plaza, Jerusalem

Solly, David, Ty, and Regan left the Temple Institute and walked out in the bright sunlight kissing the Western Wall Plaza. Questions swirled in Solly's head. David's presentation had called into question everything he'd ever understood about the history of the Dome of the Rock and the Temple Mount. If David's cuckoo explanation was right, then the most likely theory was that Muslim warriors had purposefully built the Dome right over the Holy of Holies inside the Jewish Temple. But hadn't David hinted the other day that the original location of the Temple may have been somewhere else? What if someone centuries before had been mistaken— or even misled the Muslim conquerors regarding the location of the Jewish Temple? Even if the Muslims had no historic right to the Temple Mount area, they were not going anywhere soon. How could a rebuilt Jewish Temple and a Muslim holy site co-exist yards away from each other? He had no idea, but he was certain it would not be accomplished in his lifetime anyway.

As they looked around the wide expanse they saw hundreds of people milling about—tour groups with their leaders, Catholic nuns, and people of every ethnicity who had been drawn to this powerful and emotionally laden site. Closer to the Wall itself, hundreds more people prayed.

While they watched the parade of people come and go, David explained a little more background on the Wall. He pointed out that most Westerners think that the Western Wall is a recent attraction, but it has been important to Jews for several centuries.

"There are records about Jewish pilgrims coming here in the sixteenth century," he said. "As early as the 1800s, wealthy Jews in Europe offered enormous sums of money to purchase the right of access to the Wall. But the Muslims rejected all of these offers. Remember Jerusalem was under Jordanian control until 1967, so they made all the rules."

He went on to tell them about the rise of the Zionist movement in the early 1900s. The Wall evolved into a source of conflict between Jews and Muslims. Muslims began committing acts of violence against the Jewish pilgrims who attempted to pray at the Wall. In 1929 several hundred Jews gathered at the Wall to protest, but Muslim warriors massacred them. They killed one hundred thirty-three Jews and injured almost four hundred people. After the Israeli War of Independence in 1948, they won independence from Jordan, but it was a limited victory. Israel only gained control over the territory up to the outskirts of Jerusalem. That left Jordan with strategic control of the Temple Mount and Wall, and they promptly expelled any remaining Jews from the Old City, including the Jewish Quarter.

"For the next nineteen years the Muslims banned the Jews from praying at the Wall," David said.

"But then the unexpected happened," Solly said with pride. "Tell them about the Six Day War when Israel got it all back!" Solly had not yet arrived in Israel from Australia at the time of the war, but he knew its significance among his fellow Jews.

"Ah, yes. The Six Day War in 1967," David agreed. He went on to explain how Israel finally gained sole sovereignty of both the Wall and the Temple Mount for the first time since the days of the Maccabees in 160 BCE.

"I've been told that the open plaza we see here at the Western Wall today was completely buried under the filthy hovels and shops of the Moroccan Quarter," Solly added, nodding his head in shame.

According to David, the Israelis first relocated the residents living there into nicer housing in East Jerusalem. Then they brought in heavy equipment and bulldozed the area to create the plaza.

"If you look closely at the Wall, you can see a change of shade about eight feet up. That's how far under the dirt the Wall was buried!" David added.

As they looked across the way, Ty asked if they could

touch the Wall.

"Sure," David agreed. "Guys, we'll go to the left of the wooden barrier. Regan, you'll go to the right."

David pointed to the small, circular *kippah* on the peak of his head and said, "Ty, you'll need a *kippah* to cover your head. There's a container at the entrance where you can get one to use. Solly, your cowboy hat is fine."

As Regan walked away she said, "See you guys in a few minutes." She smiled at Ty and pointed her finger in his direction. "You can be sure I'm going to be praying for you, Big Boy."

Ty displayed a crooked grin and said, "Thanks, I'll take all the prayers I can get!"

As Regan approached the Wall, she saw thousands of pieces of crumpled paper shoved into every crevice between the stones. Each one contained a written prayer request. Women of every nationality crowded into the section to pray. Regan found herself shoulder to shoulder with dozens of Jewish women in black dresses with grey hair buns. She reached in her purse for a pen and something to write on. Finding an empty gum wrapper, Regan scrawled a prayer on it. She was still thinking about the words Ty had whispered to her when he'd thought she was asleep on the bus a few days ago. "God, please make a way..." she finished writing her prayer, folded it and slipped it into one of the cracks in the wall.

The men entered the ramp leading down to the Western Wall. Although he felt awkward, Ty obediently removed a small silk *kippah* from a container and placed it on the crown of his head. He said to Solly and David, "I know I'm asking a lot of dumb questions, but why do Jewish men cover their heads?"

David said, "The only dumb question is the one that you don't ask, so ask away." He touched the *kippah* on his head and said, "There's nothing in the Bible that tells us to cover our heads. But a famous rabbi started the custom in the Talmudic period. He claimed it was a way to remind ourselves that there is Someone above us who is watching over us. At that time only the rabbis covered their heads. Later, all Jewish men who observe the tenets of our faith started wearing head coverings." David also explained that secular or non-observant Jewish men don't wear the *kippah*.

"However, since this area is considered a synagogue, all men of any faith or no faith are asked to wear one," Solly explained.

As they approached the Wall, David pointed to the right and said, "That covered walkway that rises from the plaza is the only public entrance to the Temple Mount. Hopefully when we finish all the paperwork, you guys will be up there in a few days. If we receive final approval, you'll be a part of the first archeological team to work on the Temple Mount in over one hundred years."

Solly said, "The Temple Mount has been strictly off-limits for excavations since I've been in Israel. How are you going to swing getting us up there, much less digging?"

"Let's just say we have friends in high places, and friends

in even higher places. I'll explain later."

The three men now approached the face of the Wall. The Orthodox Jewish men in black suits and long beards bobbed up and down as they held small books in their hands. Others held their hands up on the stones trying to get as close to the Wall as possible. Small boys of all ages wore the same black outfits. Their hair was short on top, but their sideburns had been left untrimmed. Ty noticed the tentacles of long hair that spiraled down toward their shoulders as they swayed back and forth, deep in prayer.

As if reading his thoughts, Solly said quietly, "Part of the reason they sway is because the rhythmic movement helps keep them focused on their prayers and what they are reading. But a wise rabbi gave me the best reason I've ever heard. There's a verse in Psalm 35 where King David sings, 'All my limbs shall proclaim Your praises.' The rabbi called it 'full-body' praying.'"

"So what are they praying?" Ty asked.

David said, "They may be praying for the coming of the Messiah, or they may be reading prayers from the Bible. But you can be sure they're praying for something specific that involves what we're doing."

"What's that?" Ty asked.

David turned to the Wall, placed his hands on the stones rubbed smooth from millions of touches and said, "Every day, faithful Jews pray for the building of the Third Temple." He removed a small worn book from the back pocket of his pants. "Here, let me read it to you out of the

Jewish Prayer Book."

He thumbed through several pages, starting from the back of the Hebrew prayer book. "Here it is. Listen to this, *'Because of our sins we were exiled from our country and banished from our land. We cannot go up as pilgrims to worship Thee, to perform our duties in Thy chosen house, the great and Holy Temple which was called by Thy name, on account of the hand that was let loose on Thy sanctuary. May it be Thy will, Lord our God and God of our fathers, merciful King, in Thy abundant love again to* **have mercy on us and on Thy sanctuary; rebuild it speedily and magnify its glory.'"**

David closed the book, put his hands on his friends' shoulders and pulled them close. He whispered, "Gentlemen, we're going to be a part of the answer to prayers that are thousands of years old. And whenever we start rebuilding the Temple, you can bet we're going to do so speedily as the prayer says. My friends, that is the Jerusalem Protocol."

42

Office of the Prime Minister, Western Jerusalem

The next morning David met Solly, Ty, and Regan at the Israeli Prime Minister's office in Western Jerusalem. As they waited in the outer lobby, Regan smiled nervously. "I've never met a Prime Minister before. I hope I'm dressed properly," she said, smoothing her plain skirt.

"Don't worry, you look fine. I've met Prime Minister Abrams before, and he's a solid chap," Solly assured her.

"Frankly, there are many people in leadership who are uncomfortable with us including any non-Jewish people in this project," David said. "But Solly insisted that you are a team, and he carries a lot of weight with his boss in the *Mossad*. And his boss has the ear of the Prime Minister."

Solly nodded at his friends. "That's right. I need what each of these two unique people has to offer. Regan is a brilliant problem solver, and Ty isn't afraid of anything. I'm just an old tour guide who knows my way around any archaeological dig."

A door opened and a young man in a perfectly tailored dark suit welcomed them inside. "Prime Minister Abrams will see you now," he said and extended his hand toward the door. They walked into the Prime Minister's massive workspace.

Prime Minister Abrams had removed his suit coat. His red silk tie was loose around his neck. When he saw them, he walked around his desk and greeted them warmly. "Miss Hart, it is my honor to meet you finally!" He shook her hand firmly. "Your work in foiling the terrorist plot in Georgia was quite a feat. I don't think your President quite appreciates the magnitude of what you prevented."

Regan blurted out with nervous laughter, "It's a pleasure to meet you, sir. You look a *lot* taller in person than you do on television!" She mentally kicked herself for saying something so inane to the world leader.

"Why, thank you," Abrams said. He looked at Solly and quipped, "Indeed, one must be head and shoulders above some of the unshaven throngs with whom we share this land."

He turned to Ty and gripped his hand tightly. "Captain Kensington, it's an honor. I have read about your skills in the First Gulf War. But those missions were only a prelude to your flight last year in Georgia. It took a lot of guts to ram that crop duster."

Ty realized that the Prime Minister had done his homework. "I was pleased to serve my country, and I am honored to be a partner with *Mossad*. Like many Americans, I deeply believe in the preservation and continuation of the State of Israel."

Abrams seemed pleased. "Thank you, my boy. It's good to have someone like you on our side. We have many enemies who are intent on exterminating us."

He shook Solly's hand next. "I see you haven't found your razor since the last time we met," Abrams joked.

He greeted David Shvaz and welcomed them all to sit down, pointing to two couches facing each other with a low coffee table set with coffee and tea.

"I'm waiting on my main adviser to join us and give us a final briefing before we go any further. May I interest you in some coffee or tea?"

The group talked softly until they heard the door to the office open. Abrams stood up. "My friends, please allow me to introduce Ziv Kessler to you. He is my most trusted advisor. Solly, I believe you met the other day in my office."

Kessler shook hands with everyone, removed his coat, and draped it over an armchair behind the couches. He poured himself a cup of coffee and turned to the Prime Minister. "After studying the latest intelligence reports," Kessler said, "I'm convinced conditions are right to proceed with the Jerusalem Protocol. Dr. Shvaz, why don't you begin by filling in our friends about the true nature of the Temple Institute?"

Ty, Regan, and Solly looked surprised, since they thought they'd already discovered what was going on behind the scenes there.

David placed his coffee cup on the table and leaned forward with his elbows on his knees. He took a deep breath as if this was a briefing he had been waiting a long time to deliver. "Over the past few days you've learned only some of the details of the Temple Institute and the Jerusalem Protocol. Now it's time for you to know the whole story."

He paused and took a deep breath. "It's true that over the past three decades the Temple Institute has been committed to the rebuilding of the Jewish Temple. But no one outside of this room knows how close we are to executing it. As you know, our rabbis, engineers, and technicians have been working for over twenty years to create every single object and implement used in the Temple worship. Each one is based upon the exact specifications in Scripture and in other Jewish writings. Part of that effort is ostensibly for the sake of our massive tourism industry, which is why we have put some of the objects on display for the public to see. Millions of Christians visit Israel each year, and they are fascinated by the idea of a third Temple. But as you have seen, the purpose of the Temple Institute goes far beyond tourism."

He paused and looked at Kessler for approval. "With the generous donations of Jews around the world, we have successfully completed the entire process."

Solly raised his thick eyebrows and swallowed hard.

"Our final project was to recreate the robe of the High Priest," David continued, "complete with the precious jewels on the breastplate that comprise the *urim and thummin*."

Ty was poised to raise his hand and ask what those were, but he thought it would be better to listen first and ask questions later.

"We have reconstructed the enormous bronze altar, also called the brazen altar, where the animal sacrifices were burned inside an area known as the court of the priests. We have created the immense golden Menorah. It is made of pure gold, so it is worth millions of shekels. Our agricultural engineers in the Galilee have also genetically created a red heifer without a single white hair. In fact, they have a herd of them! The initial research and experiments were conducted by your own Texas A&M University. Our engineers took that data and built upon it to perfect it."

David turned to Ty, held up a palm, and said, "I know you're wondering what a red cow has to do with all this. According to Numbers 19 in the Old Testament, we need the ashes of a red heifer, or *para adumma* in Hebrew, for the ritual purification of the area that will be the Temple. The rabbis demand that there not be single white hair in order for the red heifer to qualify."

Regan smiled as she pictured a group of rabbis going over every square inch of a poor cow with a magnifying glass. She almost laughed but was able to control it.

David turned to look at the Prime Minister as if seeking approval to go on. The Prime Minister nodded imperceptibly and David continued. "Over the past two years we have also been training over one hundred *cohen*, or priests, on how to conduct the worship and sacrificial system based upon the Old Testament. But the most exciting news is that Dr. Chavitz has created 3-D architectural plans to rebuild the next Jewish Temple. He has also drawn the plans for the Hall of Hewn Stones, a wing beside the Temple. During the time of the Second Temple, the Sanhedrin met in this building that was attached to the northern section of the Temple. It was called that because it was constructed of carefully carved stones, and the buildings in the Temple were constructed of unhewn stones per the Maker's instructions.

"The new Hall of Hewn Stones will be the meeting place for the seventy-one members of the re-established Sanhedrin, the Jewish religious authority that originally operated in Israel in biblical times. Of course, Prime Minister Abrams will still exercise legal control over Israel alongside the *Knesset*, the legislative branch of the Israeli government. The Hall of Hewn Stones will have the outward appearance of the ancient chamber, but it will be equipped with the most modern high-tech communication devices."

David paused, reluctant to reveal the final part of the puzzle. Prime Minister Abrams sensed his hesitation and said, "I'll take it from here, Dr. Shvaz." Abrams turned to the guests seated on the couch facing him and said, "All of the building materials for the Temple structure are currently in storage a mere ten minutes from where we are."

"But the big question is still unanswered," countered Solly. "I know David told us that the Muslims have no legitimate claim to the Temple Mount. But how in blazes can you build the Temple when the Dome of the Rock is shining there in all its golden glory right on top of the Temple's original location?"

Kessler smiled at the Prime Minister and received a permissive nod in return. "Solly," Kessler began, "we have a strong hypothesis that the original location of the Temple was actually north of the Dome of the Rock. We need you to help lead a handpicked archaeological team to verify that hypothesis."

Solly was incredulous. He wasn't eager to put his team in danger. "I've never been up there, and the last archaeological team on the Temple Mount was in the 1840s. How are we going to be there without the Palestinians raining down holy terror on us?"

Kessler responded, "Most people around the world assume that the Palestinian Muslims control access to the Temple Mount. But that's not true."

Regan and Ty exchanged surprised looks.

Kessler continued, "When we captured Jerusalem from the Jordanians in 1967, we claimed possession of the Temple Mount as well. But since we were surrounded by millions of irate Muslim enemies, we allowed the Muslims to continue to use the Temple Mount. The Dome itself was covered in faded bronze until 1994 when King Haman of Jordan approached us for permission to cover it with gold plating to the tune of a cool eight million U.S. dollars at the time."

"Wow," said Ty, amazed at what he was hearing.

"That was nothing for a billionaire king, mind you," Kessler explained. "In exchange for permission to beautify the dome, we signed an Israeli-Jordan peace treaty that kept the Temple Mount under the military control of Israel but transferred the religious control back to the Jordanians."

"I'm beginning to see this take shape," Solly said. "Relations with Israel and Jordan used to be chilly, but today they are quite balmy. Haman's son, King Mashallah, has strengthened the ties between the two countries. I understand that we're even supplying millions of cubic meters of natural gas for Jordan from our Tamar gas field in the Mediterranean."

"That's correct," Kessler said. "King Mashallah is an extraordinary man and very much like his father. In 1997 a deranged Jordanian gunman opened fire on a group of Israeli junior high school children on a field trip to Peace Island—an area of the Jordan River near the border of our two countries. Seven schoolgirls were killed and six were injured. King Haman offered an official apology to Israel and the families. But then he actually sat *shiva*, the traditional Jewish mourning, with every family who had lost a daughter. That was never in the news, but it was a huge sign of the growing peace between the Jordanian king and Israel. His son, Mashallah, has continued in that same spirit."

Prime Minister Abrams added, "That's true. It's

a new day. King Mashallah and I have each other on speed dial. Jordan, Egypt, and Israel now share intelligence information about ISIS. King Mashallah has firmly rejected any hint of radical Islam in Jordan. He even recently shut down the offices of the Muslim Brotherhood in Jordan's five largest cities. I believe he is committed to helping broker peace between the Israelis and the Palestinians. And now we have received official permission from King Mashallah himself for a team of Israeli archeologists to access the Temple Mount. He had only two stipulations. First, the team may not enter or disturb the Dome of the Rock or the *El Aqsa* Mosque. If our hypothesis about the true Temple location is correct, that will be no problem. Second, there must be at least two members of the team to serve as observers who are neither Jewish nor Muslim."

He turned to Ty and Regan. "That's where the two of you come in. You qualify to be a part of the team. But Solly's right. There is some danger involved. The *Waqf*, the Muslim authority in charge of the *Al Aqsa* Mosque and the Temple Mount gatekeepers, are livid. We can expect some resistance. They have launched their objections to the Jordanian government in the capital city of Amman, but their protests are falling on deaf ears so far." A huge smile peeked through Solly's thick beard. He clapped his hands. "Okay folks, we're back in business! When do we start?"

Abrams stood up to signal the end of the meeting. "Is tomorrow too early?"

43

The Temple Mount, Jerusalem

Not long after the morning sun rose over the brow of the Mount of Olives, a team of sixteen people entered the covered wooden walkway up to the western entrance to the Temple Mount. To work alongside Solly, Ty, and Regan, Ziv Kessler had recruited two of Israel's top forensic archeologists.

Dr. Akiva Hahn was in his mid-thirties. He was six feet nine inches tall and as thin as a pencil. The young man had a quick smile and a quicker wit. He had received a Ph.D. in Forensic Sciences at Cranfield University in the U.K. and spoke with a refined English accent. After graduation he served in the Israeli Defense Force for eight years. After he left the IDF, he taught forensics at Hebrew University. Always full of energy, he hardly ever remained still. He hadn't slept much after receiving the news that he would be digging on the Temple Mount.

Uri Ravitz was in his early sixties and the physical opposite of his colleague. Barely five feet four inches tall, he was thick around the middle. What appeared to be fat was actually solid muscle. He had worked as a crime scene investigator for the New York City Police Department for over thirty years where he earned the nickname *Bulldog* both because of his shape and the tireless tenacity that he applied to every case. Once he got a case in his jaws, he never let go until it was solved. After retiring from the NYPD, he had immigrated to Israel three years ago. He was still taking Hebrew classes, as required for every Israeli immigrant, but he still preferred to speak English. His words came out in a torrent with a thick Brooklyn accent. Because of his background in forensics, and his NYPD pension, he worked as an unpaid consultant for *Mossad*.

The other ten members of the group were Israeli Police officers dressed in black uniforms and matching helmets connected with a personal intercom system. They wore Kevlar vests and were equipped with M-16 assault rifles and Jericho 941 handguns. Sergeant Major Esther Meier was the commander of the group. She was in her early thirties and had dark hair that she kept cut short. She appeared to be petite, but she too was packed with muscle. Esther had competed and won the Israman 226 Ironman competition three years straight. Contestants swam 3.8 kilometers followed by 180 kilometers biking up and down the mountainous region of Southern Israel. Then they finished with a grueling marathon run of 42.2 kilometers. Esther had won the respect of all her young male officers. In spite of her gender, they all called her "sir."

After the team climbed the walkway, they arrived at

the narrow entrance to the Temple Mount. This was the *Moghrabi* Gate, the only public entrance to the Temple Mount.

A dark-haired man with olive skin wearing an expensive suit met them at the entrance. He seemed to be overdressed for the occasion. His name was Walid Obeidat, the Jordanian Ambassador to Israel. Solly had met the Ambassador before, but he was surprised to see him on the Temple Mount.

"Mr. Ambassador, what a privilege to have you meet us," Solly said.

Walid shook Solly's hand. "It's good to see you again, Solly. I see you still haven't found your razor."

Solly emitted a hearty laugh. "Why does everyone greet me this way? So, Mr. Ambassador, may I ask you why you are here?"

Walid gestured toward the three Palestinian members of the *Waqt.* The three men looked at the team with utter contempt, their expressions appearing as if they had eaten something sour. "Something told me that these guys weren't going to allow you access, so I'm here with a signed document from His Highness himself. I've already spoken to them, so you won't have any trouble moving about the Temple Mount."

"Thank you, Mr. Ambassador," Solly said, gladly ignoring the three guards.

The group moved past them and through the entrance. The *Al Aqsa* Mosque was to their right, and the gleaming

Dome of the Rock was to their left. At this early hour the Temple Mount was deserted except for a few dozen Muslims saying their morning prayers in the mosque.

The group turned left and walked up several steps until they arrived at the ornate *Al-Kas* Ablution Fountain. This was a large circular fountain protected by a decorative metal fence. Twenty-four spigots protruded from the bottom of the fountain. Muslim men came to the fountain to perform *wudu* in preparation for their prayers. They would sit on the steps surrounding the fountain and remove their shoes. Then they would wash their hands, feet, mouth, arms, and legs as a purification ritual.

The team walked up several more steps until they stood in front of the Muslim shrine, the Dome of the Rock. Akiva turned to Solly and said, "This is really a dream come true for me. I've always wanted to be here."

Solly looked around at the sparse surroundings and said, "It's pretty underwhelming, huh?"

Akiva shook his head and replied, "No, it's exciting to think we're standing close to the location of the two Jewish Temples."

"I suppose you're right," Solly conceded. "Tell me something. What exactly is a forensic archaeologist anyway?"

Akiva looked pleased to have a chance to explain his lifelong passion. "I'll try not to give you the whole lecture," he said. "We use forensic methods to sample the soil and detect human and animal remains. For instance, forensic archaeologists were used in post-war Germany to determine the locations of the mass graves of the Jews."

"I see, but I can't believe that there are any bodies of people or animal carcasses buried here on the Temple Mount," Solly said, still confused as to why Uri and Akiva were assigned to the team.

"You're right—no animal remains are here. But I was part of a team that uncovered an ancient city dump just outside the walls of the city that contains thousands of animal bones. We believe it is where the priests buried the remains of the thousands of animals that were used for sacrifice. By analyzing nitrogen and carbon isotopes, we were able to compare the DNA of the bones to modern animals. From there, we could determine which bones belonged to sheep, rams, bulls, or other animals."

"But as you said, that was outside the walls of the Old City. Just what are you looking for here?"

"Blood," interjected Uri bluntly. "We're looking for blood. When we find the soil containing massive traces of animal blood, we know we're near the location of the bronze altar inside the court of the priests."

"I get it now," Regan said, joining their conversation. "Traces of blood ought to be in the soil from centuries of animal sacrifices that took place there."

"If we can believe Josephus, we're talking millions of animals, not thousands," Akiva explained.

Uri explained how in 2 Chronicles 7 in the Old Testament King Solomon sacrificed twenty-two thousand cattle and one hundred twenty thousand sheep and goats on a single day when he dedicated the Temple. "That had to create a river of blood near the place where the animals were sacrificed," he said.

Ty let out a low whistle. "That's a lot of beef and mutton! What did they do with those animals after they were sacrificed?"

"There was very little waste," Akiva said. "For example, the priests baked twelve loaves of bread each Sabbath from the grain offerings. They called it showbread and kept it on wooden racks in the Most Holy Place. In Leviticus God told Moses that Aaron and his sons were to eat the meat and the showbread after ceremonially offering it to God. This tradition of consuming the offerings continued through the Second Temple period. After presenting the animals and grain offerings to God, they roasted the slain animals over a fire. The priests and their families ate and distributed the extra meat and bread to feed the residents of Jerusalem."

Ty grinned. "That sounds like the Texas barbeque I grew up with."

"So, Akiva, what methods will you use to find the traces of animal blood?" Regan inquired, ignoring Ty's comment.

"Well, since Ty mentioned Texas, it's a little like drilling for oil. We will take core soil samples at several locations. We're looking for two levels of blood traces. The deeper level will be from the First Temple. Then there should be a thin layer of untainted soil. Then we ought to find another layer representing the Second Temple period."

"How deep will you have to drill?"

She could see Akiva making mental calculations. Finally he said, "We shouldn't have to drill more than four meters, or about twelve feet. Over the centuries civilizations built on top of one another, layering new buildings and streets on the ancient rubble of the old. But the level of the Temple Mount is closer to where it actually was in 70 CE when the Temple was destroyed. Obviously there has not been much construction here."

Solly put down his bags and said, "Well, let's start digging."

44

The Temple Mount, Jerusalem

Akiva led the team just east of the Dome of the Rock to a spot he calculated would have marked the approximate distance between where the animals were sacrificed and the Holy of Holies presumed to be underneath the Dome of the Rock's location. When he arrived at the spot, he stuck a small flag into the ground. He said, "Let's set up our drill here."

Four Israeli Police officers unstrapped their assault rifles and removed large backpacks. They began to unpack the contents of an American-made Shaw 25-millimeter portable drill. Akiva and Uri began assembling the four-foot sections of the aluminum tripod that would support the drill. Fully assembled, the top of the tripod was eight feet above the ground. Once it was in place, Akiva hung a Tanaka two-cycle gasoline powered drill engine to the peak of the tripod. The engine looked similar to a chain saw engine, but instead of a blade it had a single pipe protruding downward that was capable of spinning at a high rpm. There was a sturdy butterfly handle on each side of the engine.

One of the officers removed a large plastic water tank from his backpack. Akiva directed him to go to the *Al-Kas* fountain near the entrance and fill it with water to cool the drill bit as the friction created heat.

When the officer returned with the tank full of water, Uri attached a plastic hose from the tank into the top of the drill engine. He pushed down on a plunger on the top of the tank to pressurize it.

Akiva picked up a three-foot long hollow stainless steel tube and began to attach the diamond bit into the end. Once it was in place, he attached the other end of the core barrel to the bottom of the engine.

"That looks pretty short. How are you going to drill deeper?" Ty asked.

Akiva kept working as he explained. "Once the lead pipe has drilled down until the top end is near the surface, we'll stop the engine and disconnect it. Then we'll raise the engine on the tripod and attach another tube to the engine and to the lead barrel in the ground. We have enough additional core barrels to drill deeper than our goal of twelve feet."

Akiva took a small red plastic tank and used a funnel to carefully fill the engine's tank with a mixture of gasoline and oil.

"Anything we can do, mate?" Solly asked.

"Not really. This is a two-man operation. Uri and I will each take a handle and provide downward pressure." He twisted a couple of earplugs into his ears. Uri did the same.

Uri said, "This engine is pretty noisy, so you might want to stand back." He turned to Akiva and yelled, "Are we all set?"

"I think so." Akiva grabbed the pull cord to start the engine.

Before he could pull the handle, a staccato of gunfire erupted from somewhere in front of them. Akiva screamed as a bullet tore through his left shoulder. His body twisted and he fell to the ground motionless in a grotesque heap.

At the same instant one of the Israeli Police officers fell as a bullet tore through his unprotected throat. In seconds, bullets were flying everywhere.

Uri reacted with pure instinct. As he took cover, he whipped a Desert Eagle automatic pistol from a holster under his arm. He began firing the .44 Magnum bullets toward the sound of the shots until the eight bullets in his clip were depleted. Ducking behind one of the many large stones in the area, he jammed in another clip and looked for a target.

In the same instant, Esther and the Israeli Police squad jumped behind the cover of several nearby rocks. They started firing off a fusillade of rounds from their M16 assault rifles. Bullets from the assailants pinged all around them, and the air thickened with the smell of cordite. Rock chips exploded from the shots and covered everyone with white dust. Esther pulled out a small electronic remote and changed the frequency of her intercom to the police dispatch. "Mayday! Mayday! This is Sergeant Major Meier. Officer down. I repeat. Officer down. We are under attack on the Temple Mount. We are pinned down and need reinforcements."

Solly, Ty, and Regan had also sprung into action at the sound of the first shot. They hit the ground, bullets ricocheting off the rocks, and crawled to shelter.

Ty put his arm around Regan. "Are you okay?"

"I think so," Regan said breathlessly. "Where are these shots coming from?"

Solly had pulled out his pistol and was holding it up ready to fire, trying to gauge the location of the incoming fire. He lifted his head slowly, glanced, and ducked again. Bullets ripped into the rocks. "There's a concrete-reinforced guard shack near the entrance. It looks as if they're firing from there. From the sounds, I'd guess there are about three or four gunmen. We're pinned down for now."

Ty grimaced at the sound of bullets striking all around them. "And I'm unarmed again! I feel like the guy who brought a knife to a gunfight."

"What?" Regan asked.

"Never mind. Just keep your head down. And now would be a good time to do some of your best praying."

"Believe me, I've been doing that for the past two minutes."

"Me too," Solly chimed in. "You should try it sometime, Ty."

Solly glanced around the other side of the rock and saw

Akiva's body nearby in the dirt. "I think Akiva is still alive. I can't say the same for the officer."

Solly turned toward Esther and her squad and yelled, "I'm going to try to get Akiva to safety! Give me some cover fire."

Esther shouted, "Wilco! We have reinforcements on the way. If we can hold out for a few minutes, the cavalry will be here."

"Akiva is too big for you to carry alone, Solly," Ty said. "I'm going with you."

Solly handed his pistol to Regan. "I'm sure you remember how to use one of these. When we leave the safety of the cover, hold it up and empty the magazine toward the sound of the attackers. But don't put your pretty head up there."

Regan took the pistol and expertly snapped back the top slide to make sure a bullet was in the chamber. "Locked and loaded!"

Solly paused and shouted, "One, two, three!"

Regan ducked and held up the pistol. She started firing the automatic until the clip was empty. Esther's squad laid down a withering wave of bullets toward the guard shack. Rounds tore out huge chunks of concrete as they connected. The attackers ducked for cover. Solly and Ty ran to Akiva with their heads down. Ty quickly picked up Akiva's legs while Solly grabbed him under the shoulders.

"Let's go!" Ty shouted.

Within seconds, they were back behind the sheltering

rock with Regan. She quickly examined Akiva and said, "He's still breathing! Let's look at his wound."

Ty grabbed Akiva's shirt and ripped it apart. A large wound in his shoulder was leaking blood at an alarming rate.

"Sit him up and let's find the exit wound," Solly said.

They pulled Akiva to a sitting position, and Solly examined the larger wound on his back. "He's blessed. It was a through and through shot. There's no bullet. But he's losing a lot of blood. We need to apply pressure until help comes, whenever that may be."

45

The Temple Mount, Jerusalem

After what seemed to be an hour of exchanging fire, Esther heard the sound of sirens coming from the Western Wall Plaza below. She glanced at her watch and realized that they had been pinned down less than five minutes. Then she detected another sound that made her blood chill. Over the sirens she heard yelling that seemed to come from a thousand angry men. She had worked in Jerusalem long enough to recognize a Muslim mob starting a riot. She looked to the south and could see hundreds of men spilling out of the *El Aqsa* Mosque like ants on an anthill. They were running toward them, raising their fists in defiance and screaming with outrage. Esther realized in a panic that the mob was moving in a direction that would soon provide a human wall between the shooters and her squad.

Over the squad intercom she said, "Hold your fire. We can't fire into that unarmed mob." Soon the firing stopped as the mob stopped in the direct line of fire. They stood there, raising their fists and screaming their protests toward the intruders who had desecrated their holy site.

Esther heard a voice over a bullhorn yelling instructions in Arabic. She knew enough Arabic to recognize that the voice was ordering the mob to stand down. She glanced up to see an Israeli Police officer shouting instructions on the bullhorn as several dozen Israeli policemen in riot gear started streaming through the public Temple Mount entrance her team had entered earlier. They were carrying new Tabor assault rifles— pointed directly toward the mob.

The infuriated Muslims continued to yell in defiance as the Israeli policemen formed a line between Esther and the mob. There was a tense standoff as neither group dared budge. The officer with the bullhorn repeated, "Return to the Mosque immediately!" But the crowd ignored the order.

Solly ripped his shirttail and made bandages to press into Akiva's wounds and stop the flow of blood. But Akiva's tanned skin appeared pale, and his breathing was slow and ragged.

"If we don't get him medical attention soon, he could die!" Solly yelled, trying to be heard above the sound of the riot.

Regan looked over her shoulder toward the Mount of Olives. "Look!" she yelled. "It's a med-evac helicopter!"

Within seconds, a Bell 412 helicopter was hovering over the Temple Mount about thirty yards north of their position. Dust and dirt swirled as the helicopter pivoted above a section of level ground and settled down. The rotors continued to spin as two additional riot police members and an emergency medical tech jumped out, ducking their heads low. They unloaded a gurney and ran to Akiva. While the med tech inserted an IV, the policemen strapped Akiva to the gurney. It was too dangerous to attempt rescuing the downed police officer.

One of the officers yelled, "Follow us! You're getting a ride out of here, too!"

Solly, Ty, and Regan scrambled to their feet and ran. Once they were all aboard, the policemen slammed the door shut and made their way to join Esther and her squad while the med tech tended Akiva.

The Bell 412's twin turbo engines whined in protest of the heavy weight on board but then rose quickly. The pilot pivoted, went straight up, and then banked hard left. When he gained some altitude, he pointed the nose down and raced at a top speed of 150 knots toward Hadassah Medical Center on Mount Scopus. They were there in less than three minutes. Another medical crew was on the landing pad waiting to take Akiva into the emergency room.

Solly noticed with relief that Akiva's color and breathing were already improving from the replaced fluids. He said, "I think he's going to make it. Regan, our prayers are being answered!"

***

Back on the Temple Mount the standoff continued. The mob had grown as word spread about the protest.

They started chanting in Arabic, "God is great! We defend the holy place with our blood!"

The line of riot police had slowly backed away from the mob until they were directly in front of Esther and her remaining squad members. The shooting seemed to be over, so her squad left their hiding places behind the rocks. They kept their weapons ready.

Uri joined them with his pistol in hand. He couldn't stop thinking about his colleague and had watched helplessly as they loaded him onto the helicopter. *"Is he dead?"* Uri thought. *"If he is, someone is going to pay."*

Esther rushed over to the body of her fallen police officer. One look at this face indicated he was dead. But she knelt quickly anyway and placed her finger over his carotid artery. No pulse. He was gone.

In a combination of anger and sadness, she silently vowed that she would avenge the death of her teammate. She glanced up to see the Jordanian Ambassador marching into the area between the two groups followed by his contingent of six Jordanian security agents. Walid walked boldly over to the officer with the bullhorn and spoke to him privately.

The Israeli policeman handed the bullhorn to Walid and moved even farther away from the surging mob. Walid started yelling in Arabic over the bullhorn, but the chanting drowned out his voice. The mob was now at a fever pitch. Esther began to wonder if they were going to make it off the Temple Mount alive.

When Walid nodded at his security detail, they pointed their AK-47s to the sky and begin shooting rounds into the air. It only took a few seconds for the mob to become silent. Their shouts digressed to angry murmuring.

Walid paused for a moment and said into the bullhorn, "I have just spoken to His Highness, King Mashallah. He had personally assured the safety of the team working on the Temple Mount. He has been shamed by the behavior of those who attacked them. He commands you to leave the Temple Mount peacefully, or he will close the *Al-Aqsa* Mosque indefinitely! He has ordered my men to shoot anyone who doesn't comply. Now move!"

There was loud bitter complaining as some members of the mob discussed their options. Walid stared them down as the security agents leveled their weapons toward the mob. The protesters realized the security agents would have no qualms about mowing them down. Gradually a few and then more of the protestors began to file out of the western exit. It took ten minutes for all of them to leave before there was finally silence on the Temple Mount.

Walid turned and approached Esther and Uri. He bowed and said, "His Highness apologizes profusely for the attack today. He has already spoken to Prime Minister Abrams and has pledged his full support in bringing the attackers to justice. He will personally visit the family members of the fallen officer to express his condolences. This did not turn out the way any of us expected. When you return, we will ensure it won't happen again."

Uri's cell phone rang and he looked at the number.

"It's Akiva!" he said and touched the screen. "Are you okay?"

Solly's voice came on the line.

"Uri, it's Solly. We're at the Hadassah Medical Center. Akiva's wound has been sutured and dressed. After getting some fluids, he regained consciousness. He's going to be fine. He just won't be able to use his left arm for awhile."

Uri's face broke out in an enormous grin. "You tell him the Bulldog said that at least he still has use of his kosher hand!"

Two members of Esther's squad respectfully wrapped their fallen comrade in a black body bag. They zipped up the bag and slowly carried the body toward the exit. Walid led the remaining squad to the guardhouse nearby. The security agents and police officers entered the concrete building with guns drawn, but the room was empty except for hundreds of expelled bullet casings littering the floor. The attackers had slipped away with the rest of the mob.

PART 4

46

ISIS Headquarters, *al-Raqqah*, Syria

Sunset fell on the city of *al-Raqqah*, signaling the end of the daily fasting required during the month of *Ramadan* from dawn until sunset. While the Fox was a bloodthirsty and maniacal leader, he was also a highly intelligent man. He had invaded this peaceful city in January of 2014, executing the *Shia* Muslim residents and destroying their mosques. Then he turned his attention to eradicating the 10 percent of the people in the city who were Christians. ISIS ruthlessly beheaded many of them when they refused to convert to Islam and forced thousands more to flee the city of their ancestors in the shadow of smoldering churches. True to the Muslim warrior style, al-Bagahdi captured the beautiful Armenian Catholic Church of the Martyrs and converted it into his military headquarters.

Al-Raqqah then became the target of constant

retaliatory airstrikes from the Syrians, the Russian Federation, the U.S., France, Jordan, and other nations. However, al-Bagahdi had instructed his engineers to build a labyrinth of deep, sturdy bunkers underneath the church. The underground bunker system was so well constructed that it could easily withstand any bombing short of a nuclear explosion.

The underground system was quite comfortable and included cutting edge computer technology and massive servers connected through conduits to a central control center. Al-Bagahdi understood the value of social media, so he had also constructed a small filming studio outfitted with high definition cameras to house his own independent media company called *Al-Furqan*. Behind the scenes, however, this legitimate-looking media company surreptitiously posted hundreds of ISIS propaganda videos on dozens of global platforms. His trusted aide Ali el-Gamal, who had helped Dr. Saad in Jerusalem, was the well-heeled CEO of *Al-Furqan*. A stylish businessman who was also a cold-blooded killer, he had not hesitated to behead Christians in Libya. Per al-Bagahdi's orders, Ali's main role was to market ISIS and employ dozens of young geek-jihadists to troll social media sites, constantly looking for potential ISIS recruits.

While the Fox remained in his underground bunkers, inside the city of *Al-Raqqah* Muslims were busy observing the strict traditions of *Ramadan*. During this holy month of the Islamic faith, Muslims around the world were refraining from consuming food, liquids, smoking, and engaging in sexual relations during the daylight hours. Some particularly devout Muslims were also refraining from swallowing their own saliva, spitting out any moisture that formed in their mouths. Even in soaring temperatures, they wouldn't even swim during the day to avoid risking a drop of water entering their mouths.

Many restricted their movement to preserve their energy. Some slept for several hours during the day. But at sunset they celebrated with a feast each night that lasted into the early morning hours before dawn resumed again. As was the case throughout many Muslim countries during Ramadan, garbage pick-up would triple in *Al-Raqqah* throughout the month.

The Fox, however, did not allow his ISIS soldiers to rest during the day or to gorge on rich food after sunset. He believed that this was a time for prayer and enlightenment from Allah. Buried inside his television studio, he prepared to make another chilling ISIS recruitment video. The young cameraman named Ahmad gave Ali the thumbs-up signal, indicating he was ready to record. Ali stood beside the camera and began to count down in English, "Five, four, three, two ..." Then he pointed his finger at al-Bagahdi.

Ahmad panned the camera from the black ISIS flag to the right until al-Bagahdi came into focus. He was a man of average height dressed in the traditional black ISIS uniform and wore the ubiquitous black knit *tagiyah* on his head. His complexion was dark, matching his obsidian hair and thick eyebrows. He sported a full beard that hadn't been trimmed in years. By design his appearance both commanded respect from his soldiers and struck fear in the hearts of his enemies. Ahmad zoomed the camera out to reveal al-Bagahdi holding a fistful of hair belonging to a man kneeling at his right side. The captive's eyes were wild with fright. Duct tape covered his mouth, and his hands were bound behind him. He was dressed in Western clothes, including a disheveled coat and loose tie.

Al-Bagahdi held a long knife in his left hand. He stared into the camera and began to speak in Arabic as closed captions of his message in Russian, French, and English scrolled across the screen.

He began, "With praise to the most benevolent and merciful Allah, and with loyalty to his final Prophet Mohammed (Peace be Upon Him), I am the Caliph of Allah. He has called me to create his holy Caliphate on earth. He has called us in his holy *Qur'an* to bring death to the infidels."

He lifted the head of the prisoner higher until it was difficult for the man to breathe. "You recognize this man as the reporter James Anderson from the *New York Times*. He came to interview me, but I realized he was a spy. And now I will show you what we will do to all the infidels who oppose us!"

Without taking his eyes off the camera, the Fox suddenly moved his left hand across the neck of Anderson. Anderson closed his eyes in acceptance of what was next as the Fox tilted the man's head toward him and slowly drew the razor-sharp blade across Anderson's neck, severing his carotid artery. With his eyes still locked on the camera, the Fox twisted the spray of blood away from him as it pooled on the plastic sheets taped to the floor of the studio. After several seconds, the blood flow stopped and al-Bagahdi dropped the corpse.

A chilling smile separated the beard and moustache around his mouth. "This is the fate of every person who resists our Caliphate. We will destroy anyone—Jew, Christian, atheist, Hindu, Buddhist, Muslim—who resist our *jihad*."

The Fox pointed a bloodstained finger toward the camera lens. "Allah has told me that he will give a double reward for all the *Mujahideen* who sacrifice their lives killing the infidels during *Ramadan*. Your reward in paradise will be one hundred and forty-four voluptuous virgins instead of only the seventy-two promised in the *hadith*. So I call upon every true believer to strike down the infidel wherever you find him or her. Your reward will be great!"

The Fox wiped his knife on a nearby towel, inserted it back in its scabbard, and stared into the camera. "And now I have a message to those who call themselves Muslims but have perverted the pure faith of the Prophet. Unless you bow to me as the Caliph, we are also coming for you."

At Ali's direction, Ahmad panned the camera to a large image of the *Kaaba* in Mecca—considered the most holy site in Islam. The photograph clearly showed the cube-shaped building all Muslim men who are able must visit in their lifetime as part of their required pilgrimage or *Haj*. Al-Bagahdi looked in disgust at the image and said, "Allah gave the Prophet (Peace be Upon Him) warnings against any form of idolatry. Your black rock that you kiss in your *Kaaba* is the vilest form of idolatry. Your visits there are nothing but episodes of mass hysteria. We will destroy it, just like we destroyed the idols of the Christians. Muslims in the Saudi Kingdom—hear me now. You must join the Caliphate or die like the other infidels."

Then Ahmad zoomed in on a picture of the Temple Mount in Jerusalem featuring the Dome of the Rock. The Fox's dark eyes bored into the camera. "And to the Muslims around the world, and especially the Jordanians and Palestinians, I have a message for you. Your golden shrine to a slab of rock is nothing but a filthy idol as well. We are coming to destroy it and everyone who stands in our way. *Allah hu akbar*!"

The Fox continued to stare menacingly into the camera until Ali indicated to Ahmad to stop taping. When the recording ended, he stepped over the dead body at his feet, softened his fierce expression, and casually asked Ali, "How do you think I did?"

Ali slapped his leader on the back. "You are amazing, sir! We will prepare to post it on every video platform around the globe."

47

Temple Mount, Jerusalem

A week later Solly led a second wave of researchers onto the Temple Mount. Jordanian Ambassador Walid Obeidat had explicit instructions from the King Mashallah who was still stinging from the unfortunate earlier incident. Walid's small security detail had been replaced with two-dozen members of the Jordanian Special Operations Forces. These elite soldiers had received extensive training from U.S. Army Special Forces instructors in Fort Bragg, North Carolina.

True to his word, King Mashallah personally visited the family of the fallen Israeli officer. After entering their home, he had removed his shoes and sat *shiva* with them for six hours. Although he knew that it could not repay their loss, he had privately provided funds for the fallen hero's family to be comfortable for many years.

Esther also found herself commanding a much larger protective detail as a precautionary measure. In addition to twenty-four Israeli Police officers, she had been given a squad of sixty IDF commandos. Guarded by all these highly trained soldiers, the archeological team would enjoy a protective perimeter while they performed their tasks.

The unruly Palestinian gatekeepers of the *Waqf* had been dismissed from the public entrance near the Western Wall and replaced with Jordanian security agents. The large security force had also commandeered a Muslim-only entry point on the northern side of the Temple Mount and planned for the archeological team to enter that way instead. Unbeknownst to the Muslims, they would not be resuming control of this access point anytime soon.

An additional squad of Jordanian security forces was posted outside the *Al Aqsa* Mosque to ensure that the only activity happening there was prayer. To complete the security circle three IDF military helicopters flew a pattern that included the Temple Mount—nothing unusual for a city where active military exercises are common. The AH64 Apache attack helicopters remained in contact with all the forces on the Temple Mount. Everyone was confident that there wouldn't be another surprise attack.

Akiva was upright and feeling well enough after a week of rest to resume his activities. His left arm was in a sling, leaving him unable to perform physically demanding tasks. Since he was the brains behind the team, and Uri always provided the brawn anyway, Akiva received permission to enlist the help of one of his brightest forensic science Ph.D. students. Leah Dayan was in her early twenties, and the faculty at Hebrew University considered her a prodigy. Growing up on *Kibbutz Ein Gedi* in the Judean wilderness, Leah and her other *kibbutznik* friends spent their childhoods climbing the steep cliffs of the mountains. At almost six feet tall her frame was thin and rangy, but she was as sure-footed as the ibex that populated the rocky hills. She kept her long blonde hair tied up in a single ponytail that poked out from her favorite New York Yankees baseball cap. Her bright blue eyes were full of intelligence and humor.

Leah had trekked many times to the *Ein Gedi* spring that was less than a kilometer from her home and had spent seven years serving as a guide to lead Israeli schoolchildren to the famous spring. She thrilled them with stories of King David hiding in one of the many caves when King Saul was hunting him. Leah had personally climbed up and into all fifty-nine caves at Qumran where a shepherd boy had discovered portions of the Dead Sea scrolls. She was so nimble on the rocks that her childhood friends nicknamed her "Goatee." Leah could think of no better way to spend a day than out under the hot sun—especially being part of an important archeological project like this.

Akiva walked beside Uri and Leah who hoisted large backpacks containing a replacement for the Shaw portable drill that had been shot to pieces during the earlier attack. Several members of Esther's squad carried the other necessary equipment. The Hebrew University trio accompanied Solly, Ty, and Regan through the north gate following their armed guards. They went south onto the Temple Mount, passing two small Muslim monuments called the Dome of the Spirits and the Dome of the Tablets. After a three-minute walk they arrived back at the site just east of the Dome of the Rock where they had originally planned to drill. If they found extensive ancient traces of blood evidence in the soil here, it would support the popular belief that the Dome was built on top of the Temple location. If not, then many more possible locations would open up.

They removed the mangled remains of the portable drill and erected a new aluminum tripod in its place. Uri bent to pick up one of the stainless steel boring pipes and saw that the drill bit was still attached. He smiled and said, "It wasn't a total loss. All of the boring tubes are still intact. It's a good thing these were lying on the ground."

Akiva turned to Uri and said, "Remember, I'm just a spectator today. You and Leah will have to provide the muscle for the downward pressure on the drill."

Several of the IDF forces worked to set up a small tent as a makeshift lab with a metal folding table and various instruments to test the soil samples. The largest instrument was a battery-operated electron microscope powerful enough to examine individual specks of dirt for traces of blood.

Uri set up the drill and checked his work. He turned to Akiva and said, "I think I'll start the engine this time. I don't like what happened when *you* started it last time!"

Akiva grimaced in pain at the memory. He glanced around to ensure the security forces were in place and said in his crisp British accent, "Go for it, Bulldog."

Uri grabbed the starter handle and gave a mighty jerk. The engine coughed and sputtered before Uri gave it another pull and the little engine roared to life. He grabbed one of the butterfly handles on one side, and Leah grabbed the opposite handle. As they applied downward pressure, the diamond-encrusted bit dug into the mixture of dirt and rock. A fine dust cloud rising from the hole began to grow. Water from the pressurized tank fed into the tube to reduce the heat caused by friction from the drill bit.

After only about two minutes of drilling, the metal bore had sunk almost its entire length into the surface. Uri stopped the engine and disengaged the rotor from the bore. He raised the engine to the top of the tripod. Meanwhile, Leah quickly attached another hollow pipe to the lead bore and Uri attached it to the rotor underneath the engine. Each section of bore was numbered since every few feet of soil represented centuries of civilizations.

Akiva stood by, giving suggestions as they replaced each bore. Finally, they reached the desired depth. "Let's pull them up and see what we've got!" Akiva yelled above the sound of the engine. Uri flipped a switch to reverse the direction of the engine's rotation. The bores came out faster than they had gone in. Under the watchful eye of the security detail, they carried the samples to the lab tent and laid out twelve dirt-filled bores according to number.

48

The Temple Mount, Jerusalem

Solly watched with keen anticipation. "I guess you have some high-tech way of removing the soil samples and analyzing them?" he commented.

Akiva chuckled. "Well, yes and no. We actually have a very low-tech method to remove the soil from the bores." He simply inserted a wooden dowel into one end of the bore and pushed until a perfect cylinder of compacted soil came out the other end onto a metal tray.

"The water we use to cool the drill bit adds some viscosity to the dirt so it holds the shape," Akiva explained. "Then it's just like cutting slices of kosher salami and examining a few grains of each soil slice under the electron microscope. We also introduce a tiny amount of a chemical called Sodium 3-amino-phthalhydrazide.

"Luminol," Uri interjected. "When we introduce an oxidizing catalyst, it creates chemiluminescence."

"You lost me at Luminol," said Ty.

Uri grinned. "If there's blood in the soil, Luminol will make it glow like a swarm of lightning bugs."

Leah was adjusting the eyepiece on the microscope while Uri drew out a miniscule tube of Luminol and put a droplet onto a slide containing soil from the first bore, followed by a tiny drop of hydrogen peroxide. Leah clamped another glass slide on top and slid it underneath the microscope lens.

"Nope, nothing here," Leah said, adjusting the focus. "Let's test the other eleven bores."

After almost an hour of tedious testing, Leah looked up and wiped her tired eyes. "Based upon this forensic evidence, we can assert with almost complete certainty that there are only miniscule blood traces in this soil. If thousands of animals were sacrificed, it most definitely did not occur here."

Akiva's eyes lit up. "That's what I expected! We just scientifically proved that the Dome of the Rock is not built on the site of either of the Jewish Temples."

He turned to Solly and said, "Now that we know where the two Temples *were not* constructed, we must find the actual location. That, my friend, we'll leave up to you."

"Well I can assure you we aren't going to try to dig up the whole blasted Temple Mount," Solly said matter-of-factly. "We need to use another scientific method to determine a probable location. Then we'll dig in that position and see if we find what we're looking for there."

Solly cleared out a spot on the metal table under the makeshift tent, removed a cylindrical tube from his backpack and unscrewed the top. He took out a small map and spread it out on the table, using several of the empty bores to anchor the corners. The map was a diagram of the

Temple Mount showing the location of the Dome of the
Rock and the black *Al Aqsa* Mosque.

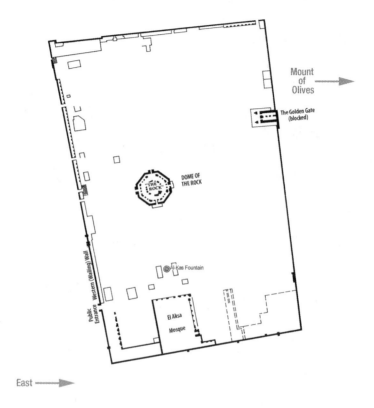

Solly leaned over and pointed to a gate drawn on the
right side of the diagram. "I've done some research over the
past week at Hebrew University and have determined that
this, my friends, holds the key to finding the right location
of the original two Temples."

He turned and pointed northeast from where they
had just drilled. "And there it is, right before our eyes—the

Eastern Gate, or Golden Gate as some call it!"

Regan and Ty stared in the direction of the gate, waiting for its significance to dawn on them. Leah, Akiva, and Uri were miles ahead of the Americans and began slowly nodding in agreement with Solly.

Solly continued, "To be fair, Jewish archaeologists are divided over whether what you see today is the exact original location of the Eastern Gate. There are no records of it ever being relocated. But no one disagrees that the Eastern Gate led straight into the Jewish Temple—as the bird flies, as you Americans say."

"Crow. It's as the crow flies," Regan said with a giggle.

Ty stared at the massive Eastern Gate's double arches. Solly grinned like a kid, pointing their attention back to the diagram. "If we believe some of the ancient writings, the Eastern Gate was built in a very precise location. Twice every year the beams from the rising sun would shine straight through the Eastern Gate into the Temple and illuminate the curtain concealing the Holy of Holies."

Akiva eyes lit up. "That's right! I remember! I've read the same claim. According to rabbinical literature, it would happen when the amount of daylight and darkness were equal. Those two days are, as I'm sure you already know, the vernal equinox in the spring and the autumnal equinox in the fall."

Solly crossed his arms and smiled. "You're correct. Now all of you look at our diagram and tell me what's wrong with this picture?" Solly waited patiently while they all studied it silently.

"Well," said Regan, "you need a straight line for a sunbeam to shine directly through the gate into the Temple, right?"

Solly nodded.

"And there's no way the sun could shine through the Eastern Gate and hit the Dome of the Rock. The angle doesn't work! It could only be done with smoke and mirrors..."

"Minus the smoke," Ty muttered.

"And they didn't use mirrors," Solly added.

"Why is the Eastern Gate sealed up with all those stones?" Ty inquired.

Solly explained that throughout history it had been opened and sealed multiple times. "The last time it was sealed was in 1541 by the Ottoman Sultan Suleiman," he noted.

Leah, an avid reader of history, added, "The reason they did that is because Muslims have been frightened of this gate for centuries. They know it's the gate through which the promised Messiah will enter Jerusalem. They sealed it up with heavy stones hoping to keep Him out! You've probably seen the cemetery just outside of the gate."

Ty and Regan nodded.

"That's not a Jewish cemetery. It's a Muslim cemetery. They buried their dead there on purpose because they think any Jewish Messiah worth His salt wouldn't dare desecrate Himself by walking over dead bodies."

Regan laughed. "You're kidding! When the Messiah comes..."

"Comes *back*, you mean," Solly interrupted.

"Right! When He comes back," Regan continued, "it

will take a lot more than gravestones to keep Him out!"

"Amen to that, Regan!" said Solly.

"We have two convincing proofs that the Jewish Temples could not have been built under the Dome of the Rock," Uri concluded.

Ty said, "So now what? Do we have to wait until the vernal or fall equinox to find the right spot where the sun shines through the Eastern Gate? That gate is all sealed up anyway, so isn't this all a moot point?"

"You're giving up too soon, Ty," Solly chided. "We have an even better plan, mate—and we don't have to wait for a certain date on a calendar. Tomorrow we're going to the Mount of Olives to meet a renowned astrophysicist named Dr. Malak Cantor. He has developed a fascinating method to simulate the exact location of the sunrise on the vernal and autumnal equinoxes."

Ty and Regan looked over at the Mount of Olives as Solly and the other team members started loading up all the equipment.

"Don't leave anything up here," Akiva cautioned. "We're being watched, and we wouldn't want to find some of our equipment sabotaged when we return."

Esther summoned her squad of policemen and IDF members to do a final sweep of their egress route. After hearing an "all clear" from the Apache helicopter pilots, she gave a thumbs-up to the Jordanian Special Forces members. Then she shouted to the team, "We're good to go. Civilians, stay within the protective corridor of the security detail. Let's move out!"

49

The Mount of Olives, East Jerusalem

The next morning Ty, Regan, and Solly arrived just after sunrise on the Mount of Olives with Esther leading a smaller security detail than the day before. Akiva, Leah, and Uri were not needed and remained at Hebrew University awaiting the results of the simulation Solly's guest would conduct.

Regan marveled at the amazing sight before her. It was a beautiful clear morning with the sun shining on the Old City of Jerusalem in a kaleidoscope of different colors and shapes. The Golden Dome of the Rock dominated the view. From this perspective directly across the Kidron Valley between the Old City and the Mount of Olives, it was easier to see that the Eastern Gate was nowhere near being in line with the Dome. To the naked eye it was clear that a shaft of sunlight shining through the gate would illuminate a point far north of the Dome of the Rock.

Regan turned her attention to the other sites she could see from one of the most unique vantage points in the world on the summit of the Mount of Olives. Solly followed Regan's gaze, eager to orient his guests to the historical feast before their eyes.

"See those golden onion domes jutting out below from the green vegetation? That's the Russian Orthodox Church of Mary Magdalene And that single grey dome marks the location of another church called *Dominus Flevet.*"

"What's that?" Ty asked.

"It's Latin for 'our Lord's tears' because it is built on the traditional spot where Jesus stopped on Palm Sunday during His triumphal entry to weep over the city of Jerusalem," explained Solly. He pointed out another large church on the bottom of the slope that marked the traditional spot of the Garden of Gethsemane where Jesus prayed the night before the crucifixion. But dominating the descending slope down the Mount of Olives were thousands of stark white boxes lined up like dominoes.

"Are those graves? Why are they here?" Regan asked.

"Those are actually bone boxes, Regan," Solly replied, seizing another teachable moment about Jewish customs. "Jewish burial customs go back thousands of years. When a Jewish person died, the body was placed in a cave or tomb and left there until all the flesh had decayed. Then the bones were collected, carefully separated at the joints, and placed in bone boxes called ossuaries. Orthodox Jews still follow that practice. The ossuaries are typically about two-and-a-half feet long in order to accommodate the femur, the longest bone in a human body." He pointed to his leg.

"And this," he continued, spreading his arms in front

of him toward the graveyard, "is a prime spot for religious Jews to await the coming of the Messiah. The prophet Ezekiel wrote that one day 'dry bones' would live again. These Jews took that promise literally. They wanted to be first in line when the Messiah sets foot on the Mount of Olives so He can bind their joints together and put flesh on them again."

Regan looked again at Jerusalem's skyline. "So much conflict for such a beautiful place," she said softly.

"People fight for what they love," Solly replied. "Jews, Muslims, and Christians all consider this their Holy City."

He looked beyond Regan to a green taxicab that had just pulled over to the curb. "I think that's Dr. Cantor there. Let me introduce you."

Solly led Ty and Regan to an elderly gentleman who unfolded his long frame from the taxi. Dressed as if he were going to undertake a long hike, he placed a white safari hat over his bald scalp and nodded toward them as his young assistant scurried out of the other side to remove several large suitcases from the trunk.

Dr. Cantor walked surprisingly quickly for an older man. He reached out a large hand, squeezing Solly's until Solly winced. "My old friend. I see you still have a sense of fashion about you!"

Dr. Cantor sported a full beard that was almost as long as Solly's.

Solly smiled. "As do you, my friend!" Both men grabbed the other's beard and pulled gently. "Malak, these are my two closest friends from America, Regan Hart and Ty Kensington."

Dr. Cantor greeted them as if they were long lost friends. "Any friend of Solly's ... has got to be a little crazy!" Everyone chuckled.

He turned to his assistant loaded down with the two heavy cases. "This young man is Gad Fielder. He's one of my students and he agreed to help us today." Gad nodded his greeting, sweat pouring off of his forehead.

"So I suppose Ziv Kessler briefed you on what we need?" Solly asked Dr. Cantor.

"Yes, and it's a fairly simple assignment. We're going to find the spot up here where the sun rises on the vernal and autumnal equinoxes."

Ty said, "That doesn't sound so simple to me, Dr. Cantor. How are you going to do it?"

"Gad, why don't you explain it to our American friends?" Dr. Cantor motioned toward his assistant.

Gad launched into his explanation. "Well, as I'm sure you know, the planet is constantly in motion. We're in orbit around the sun at a speed of about sixty-seven thousand miles per hour. In addition the earth is spinning so that every twenty-four hours we complete one rotation."

Gad took another breath. Listening intently, Ty and Regan both stood stock still, entertaining flashbacks of the Harry Caray lookalike, Dr. Chavitz, in their minds.

"So . . ." Gad continued without waiting for a response from his listeners, "we're spinning right now at about 1,040 miles per hour. But the earth is also tilting on its axis, which creates the four seasons. That's why the length of days and nights are different. In addition our solar system is rotating through our galaxy at about 800,000 miles per hour."

"I think I'm about to get motion sickness!" Ty muttered.

Gad stared at him as if he didn't get it. "Sorry to hear that. Anyway, there are two days each year when the length of daylight and darkness are equal – they are called the equinox. But we don't have to wait for those days on the calendar. We have computer programs that can tell us exactly where the sun rises at any spot on any given day anywhere in the world. Since we know the GPS coordinates of where the sun rises over the Mount of Olives on those two days, we can simulate the equinoxes right now."

Ty said hesitantly, "Okay, I think I get it. So where is that spot?"

Dr. Cantor pulled out a handheld GPS and read the small screen. "We're only about six hundred feet south of the right spot. Let's go for a little walk."

The group followed Dr. Cantor north up a busy street. After dodging tour buses, taxis, and aggressive street vendors with loops of olive wood cross necklaces and other souvenirs in both hands, they arrived at the location. They were standing in front of a Holy Land gift shop. Dr. Cantor entered the shop and spoke in Arabic to the owner. After a long and loud negotiation, they arrived at a price for the group to walk through the small shop to a back deck that offered a clear view of the entire Temple Mount.

Then Gad opened one of the suitcases that contained a powerful telescope, which he quickly mounted on a tripod. From the other suitcase he removed a small four-bladed drone with a tiny metal tube protruding at a right angle from the underbelly. The shop owner grew agitated until Dr. Cantor assured him that the drone was not a firearm.

"It's only a light, my friend," he explained in Arabic, pointing to the laser.

Gad attached a series of wires to a small laptop and punched in several coordinates. Dr. Cantor removed an electrical cord and asked the shop owner if he could rent a small amount of his electricity to charge the drone.

The shop owner protested loudly that his electric bill was already too expensive. After a few more minutes of haggling, a price was agreed upon. As he took the cord and turned his back to his guests in search of an outlet, the shop owner smiled at his fortune. He carefully inserted the plug.

Solly said, "Okay, you've got my curiosity now. What are you going to do?"

"According to the ancient writings," Dr. Cantor explained, "on the two days of the equinox the sun would rise from behind where we are standing here on the Mount of Olives. Seven minutes after sunrise, the angle of the sun would create a sunbeam shining straight through the Eastern Gate and illuminating the curtain inside the Temple for seven minutes. My theory is that Solomon's astronomers carefully designed the location and structure of the Eastern

Gate to capture this unique moment twice a year. I will program the drone to rise to simulate the speed of the rising sun and its laser will mark the exact spot of the sunbeam."

Solly said, "That's brilliant, no pun intended. But remember the entrance to the Eastern Gate is blocked with stones. How can we shine the laser so it hits the dirt on the Temple Mount in exactly the right spot?

Dr. Cantor smiled and smacked Solly on the shoulder. "That's beyond my pay grade, my friend. My job is to shoot the light to mark the spot. It's your job to dig me a hole!"

Solly winced as he thought about the militant response from the Palestinians if they made a hole in the Eastern Gate. Those men had nearly killed them for wanting to dig a tiny hole in the dirt!

But he shrugged his shoulders and asked, "So Dr. Cantor, how big a hole do you need?"

"That's the spirit," Dr. Cantor said as he turned to this assistant. "You're the math genius, Gad. Do the trig on your laptop."

Regan and Ty were glad to sit out on this conversation. It was definitely above their pay grades.

"Sure. No problem. I just need a few factors to determine how far the drone's laser will need to reach. The laser can easily hit the outside of the gate from here and calculate that distance. I just need to know how thick the gate is and the distance from the gate to our target inside the grounds of the Temple Mount."

Solly shook his head. "Sorry, mate. I don't have a clue."

He paused. "But I think I know someone who can give you that information."

He pulled out his phone and dialed David Shvaz at the Temple Institute, turning on the speaker. Solly relayed what they needed.

"Let me get Ariel on our call. He'll know." David pushed some icons on his phone's screen.

"Yes? What is it? I'm busy!" Dr. Chavitz shouted loudly.

Solly said cheerfully, "Hello there, Dr. Chavitz. It's Solomon Rubin here. We need some information about the Temple Mount that we think only you can give us."

"Go ahead." Dr. Chavitz enjoyed being the expert.

"First, we need to know the thickness of the Eastern Gate." He could hear Dr. Chavitz tapping keys on his computer.

"You understand that the gate is actually a chamber with a short hallway?" Dr. Chavitz asked. He went on to explain that the chamber's outer doors are double arches that face the Mt. of Olives. The chamber's inner doors open onto the Temple Mount. "Our scientists have used sonar and infrared from military helicopters to determine that the hallway inside the gate is not filled with solid rock as most people think," he said. "The chamber between the doors is actually empty, but it's deep. About twenty-five cubits."

Solly fought back a sigh. "I don't have my Bible handy, sir. Can you give that to me in meters?"

"Oh. Why didn't you say so?" Dr. Chavitz intoned. More tapping ensued, and he relayed the information to

Solly. "That's roughly thirty-one feet, Mr. Kensington, in case you were wondering."

Ty smirked.

"How about the thickness of the layer of stones sealing both sets of doors?" Solly asked. More tapping ensued.

"Let's see. It looks as if the outer gates are sealed to a thickness of about about twenty inches. The inner doors to the Temple Mount are about half that."

Dr. Cantor and Gad steadily plugged in the figures as Solly and Dr. Chavitz spoke.

"One last thing. Now we need the distance from the inner door of the Eastern Gate to the very spot inside the Temple where the curtain separated the Holy of Holies from the Most Holy Place," Solly said, nodding to Dr. Cantor.

"That will take me a few minutes. Hold on." They heard Dr. Chavitz drop the phone onto his desk with a loud thump, followed by furious tapping on the keyboard.

"Okay, I ran the numbers twice to make sure. The distance from the inner door of the Eastern Gate to the curtain is exactly 291.9 yards."

"Thank you, mate," Solly said. "That's all."

"Obviously you're calculating the exact angle of the equinox sunrise from the Mount of Olives into the Temple," Dr. Chavitz said. "Tell Dr. Cantor I said 'shalom.'"

"Right again," Solly said, winking at his friend. "Thanks for your help. We'll let you know what we find."

"I already know exactly what you're going to find," Dr. Chavitz said. And he hung up.

50

The Mount of Olives, East Jerusalem

"So, Gad, what size holes does Solly have to knock in those gates?" Dr. Cantor asked.

Gad looked down at his spreadsheet and said, "You need a circular hole in the outer gate with a diameter of six feet nine inches and a hole in the inner door with a diameter of four feet seven inches."

Ty started to ask why the holes were different sizes, but he didn't really want another lecture in trigonometry.

"Got it," Solly said. "But where exactly will I know to dig my hole? It's a rather large gate. And make it simple, please."

"We're going to use a combination of high-tech and low-tech methods to mark your spot," Dr. Cantor answered. He turned to Gad. "Is the drone charged yet?"

"It needs a couple more minutes," Gad said.

"Okay, while it finishes charging I'll explain the plan. First, take a look." Dr. Cantor motioned for Solly, Ty, and Regan to take a look through the telescope.

Each took turns staring at a magnified image of the

Eastern Gate. A detail of IDF soldiers had gathered in the
Muslim cemetery outside the Eastern Gate. Dr. Cantor
explained that they were guarding a small group from the
IDF Corp of Engineers. The engineers were maneuvering
a lightweight aluminum ladder against the exterior of the
Eastern Gate's double arches. In the early light of dawn
their presence would not be noticed.

Just then Gad brought out the small drone and the
control panel. "I'm all set, boss."

"I tried flying one of those little drones to take pictures
a few years ago and had a hard time controlling it," Ty
said. "How are you going to control the precise ascent to
simulate the sun rising?"

Gad answered, "Its flight path has been programmed
into the onboard computer. It will fly immediately to its
initial position of seven minutes after sunrise. Then it will
ascend slowly for the next seven minutes, compensating
for wind or temperature changes."

Dr. Cantor reached for his cell phone to contact the
lead engineer at the Gate. "We will launch the drone in one
minute. Quickly mark where the laser strikes the stones
sealing the gate. Are you ready? Good."

Gad pressed a single button and the blades started
humming like a hive of bees. He pressed another button
and the drone slowly rose in a straight ascent to a
predetermined altitude.

"The laser will emit in about ten seconds. Take a look,"
Dr. Cantor said, nodding toward the telescope.

Solly adjusted the focus on the telescope. There on the stones of the gate was an unmistakable bright blue dot. One of the engineers removed a large piece of chalk and marked its position. Over the next seven minutes the drone and the laser beam slowly rose incrementally. At each minute interval the engineer would mark another dot on the wall.

Gad, focusing on his laptop, finally said, "Time. Seven minutes elapsed." He turned off the laser. With a simple keystroke on his laptop the drone returned like a carrier pigeon to its roost. It flew to the back deck of the shop, landed, and powered down automatically.

"I want to see," said Regan. She looked through the telescope. The engineers had removed the ladder, and the IDF squad was now escorting them away from the gate. Their quick work had taken less than ten minutes to complete.

Ty took a turn at the telescope next. The vertical chalk line on the stone appeared to be about six feet long—the diameter of the hole they would need to dig.

When Solly took a final look he had a bad feeling in his gut. "*That* is a big hole," he said. Solly estimated that the marking on the gate was about ten feet above the uneven graveyard. Drilling a six-foot diameter hole up that high would be daunting.

"Right," agreed Dr. Cantor. "After you guys make your hole in the outer gate, then we'll shoot the laser again through it so the engineers can climb inside the chamber and chalk the smaller hole inside the inner gate."

Regan said, "Since we're digging from the outside, we'll technically be outside the Temple Mount area the whole time. So we shouldn't be under the scrutiny of the Muslims up there, right?"

"By the next morning everyone in East Jerusalem would see a gaping hole in their precious gate," he said, envisioning massive riots in the streets of East Jerusalem.

Regan piped in, "Not necessarily. From what I saw in the Temple Institute the Israeli engineers can replicate anything. Why couldn't they replicate a fiberglass cover with contours and colors to imitate these stones? They drill the hole, put the camouflaged cover on it, and then remove it when we need to shoot the laser?"

"You are a smart lady," Dr. Cantor replied. He motioned to Solly and Ty and said, "What are you doing hanging around with these two guys?" He then phoned the Israeli engineers and together they worked out an ingenious plan to make the hole nearly invisible. It was a plan so unusual and so crazy that it just might work.

51

Muslim Cemetery outside the Eastern Gate, Jerusalem

Ty remained a little skeptical into the next day as they walked along the wide paved walkway running parallel to the Eastern Wall of the Temple Mount. They wanted to inspect the engineers' work. Dr. Cantor, Gad, and the ever-present security detail under Esther's skillful hand joined them, carrying supplies and a ladder.

"Okay, so tell me again how you are going to get the fake cover to stay in the hole?" Ty asked. "Duct tape? That will fix anything, you know."

Gad said, "It can work. The engineers are constructing a metal circle on the inside of the hole, and magnets can be embedded in the inner rim of the fake cover. It will pop in and pop out like a cork."

As they approached the massive Eastern Gate, Solly could barely make out the vertical line of chalk left by the engineers about twelve feet above the ground. He paused and ran his hand down his beard, deep in thought. "I need ideas, guys. We can't just approach this wall with a wrecking ball. We need a more subtle approach."

Regan said, "The IDF Corps of Engineers are planning to drill the hole to our specifications, right?"

"Certainly," Solly agreed.

"I suppose they'll have to work after midnight and in total darkness. How long will it take them to drill?" Regan asked.

Dr. Cantor said, "They'll use water-cooled electric drills that don't make that much noise. Besides, medical helicopters fly through this valley much of the night on their way to the city hospital providing noise cover. The engineers could drill several large holes around the circumference of the circle. Then the middle could be punched out easily. I'd say allow a couple hours."

Solly looked at the ladder and asked, "Who wants to climb up and get the measurements for the cover?"

Gad pulled out his smart phone and snapped a couple of pictures. "No need. Our designers can use this picture of the vertical chalk line to calculate the right dimensions."

Ty asked, "So how long will that take?"

Gad said, "Oh, a few minutes. I just texted the pictures to our lab."

Regan smiled. "Problem solved."

Solly grimaced. Nothing was ever that simple.

***

After midnight Esther led a squad of sixty police officers as they strolled quietly through the Muslim cemetery, donning helmets equipped with night vision monocles and intercoms. Once they reached the Eastern Gate they set up a protective perimeter.

Within minutes a dozen IDF engineers loaded down with equipment joined them. Without speaking they quickly assembled the drills. Three engineers stepped into slingshot harnesses while three more fired metal anchors into the stonewall above the Eastern Gate. They looped ropes through belays attached to the anchors and the men began to rappel upward. The lead engineer removed a thick template from his backpack, unfolded it, and attached it to the stones with a strong adhesive to guide their drilling. They used trailing ropes to pull up the six-inch bore drills until they had them in hand.

The lead engineer whispered over his intercom mic, "Sergeant Major, we're ready to drill. Is everything clear?"

Esther checked in with her squad and whispered back, "All clear. Drill away."

Only a low rumble came from the sound-baffled gasoline generator, followed by three high-pitched whines as the drills started boring through the stones. Dirt and rubble flew in every direction, but the IDF engineers had wisely worn oxygen masks. The first drill made it through the wall in about ten minutes. Each engineer continued to drill around the perimeter non-stop for the next hour. They were vaguely aware of the sound of medical helicopters flying above delivering patients, hopefully masking the drills.

"There!" the chief engineer finally said. "We've drilled around the circle, leaving it intact at the bottom. If we cut through that, the rubble could fall in any direction – including on us."

Esther answered, "Roger that. What's your plan?"

The IDF engineer said, "There's nothing like good old fashioned manpower. When you cut a tree down and want it to fall a certain way, you have to force it in that direction. Our team is assembling a dozen long aluminum poles on the ground. I need some of your strongest men to stand below the gate with the poles pushing on the topside of the circle. We're going to finish drilling the bottom section. If all goes as planned, as your men push, the stones should cave into the empty chamber inside the gate."

Esther called the names of a dozen of her strongest officers and gave them instructions. Once the men holding the long poles were in place, the drilling continued at the bottom.

"Almost there! Now push!" the engineer said.

At first nothing happened, but then the huge circle of stone and rocks gradually began to tilt away from the squad. Once gravity took over, there was a huge crash as the remaining rocks and rubble fell inside the chamber. Dust came boiling out of the large round hole.

Within seconds the drilling crew fired up large sanding machines to even the edges of the hole. Then one of the men swung into the massive hole and used a powerful pneumatic hammer to attach a circular metal ring on the circumference of the hole. When he finished, two other engineers hoisted a lightweight fabricated circle rimmed with strong magnets. The camouflage of foam rock and stones was an identical match for the wall. They inserted it into the hole with a small click as the magnets seamlessly attached to the metal rim.

The only job left was to clean up. They removed the metal anchors and stowed all the equipment before everyone quietly vacated the area.

Esther glanced up at what had been a huge hole in the wall minutes before. She could barely tell where the hole was and thought proudly, *"That's Israeli engineering for you."*

52

Inside the Eastern Gate Chamber, Temple Mount, Jerusalem

The next night Esther led a smaller squad of security officers back through the Muslim cemetery along with a few engineers, Solly, and his friends. They all marveled at the realistic likeness of the fake cover in the outer gate. As Esther's men spread out, Solly, Regan, Ty and two engineers used a ladder to climb through the hole and into the chamber. Having been tightly sealed for centuries, the air inside was stale. Solly was secretly hoping to find something valuable hidden here – perhaps even the Ark of the Covenant! But he was disappointed to discover only dusty stones littering the interior. Whatever treasures had once been there had long since been removed.

Dr. Cantor and Gad were in position across the way on the Mount of Olives. At Solly's signal they planned to launch the drone and fire the laser through the hole in the outer door in order to trace another precise vertical line on the sealed inner door that led to the Temple Mount.

Dr. Cantor, who was on a cell phone with Solly,

announced the commencement of the laser. A sliver of blue light shot from the Mount of Olives once more across the Kidron Valley to the Eastern Gate. It passed through the large hole and appeared on the stones sealing the smaller inner door. There was no need for a ladder this time because the angle of the laser brought the level down to just five feet above the floor of the chamber. The lead engineer simply took out his chalk and noted the vertical line.

As he waited for seven minutes to pass, the engineer explained, "We're in luck. Since the laser beam is closer to the target on this inner door, this hole only needs to be four feet seven inches in diameter. And this sealed door is only half as thick as the outer one. This will be easy compared to last night's work."

Solly wanted to agree, but there was one big difference. "When this hole is drilled, we'll be looking right onto the Temple Mount. I don't need to remind anyone here that armed members of the Islamic *Waqf* could be waiting for us on the other side."

"It may be time to call in the help of our Jordanian Ambassador again," Regan suggested.

Solly was thinking fast. He turned to the lead engineer. "Can you just drill small holes through the rock around the circumference of the hole? That way the small drill holes could be seen from the other side, but we wouldn't breach their holy ground until I've briefed Prime Minister Abrams on our progress, and he can talk with Walid."

The engineer agreed and added, "It's going to get dusty in here. I suggest you guys head back out. We'll follow after we finish."

Solly, Ty, and Regan were glad to climb out of the musty chamber. Regan climbed down the ladder first, followed by Ty and Solly. Just as Solly reached the bottom rung of the ladder he heard Esther whisper urgently into her intercom, "Everybody down. Now!"

The security squad jumped for cover behind one of the dozens of Muslim tombstones. Solly, Ty, and Regan hit the dirt.

They heard several voices having a conversation in Arabic. In the darkness Esther could see a mob of eight young Muslim men walking toward them. They were smoking cigarettes and laughing. If they passed by without detecting their presence, it would be a miracle. She couldn't fire on unarmed Muslims. But their luck didn't hold. The group of men suddenly stopped and one of them pointed at the ladder leading up to the uncovered hole in the Eastern Gate. They decided to investigate.

Esther instructed her men over the intercom, "Move! Non-lethal methods only!"

The young Muslims screamed in terror as a squad of heavily armed policemen popped up from behind the tombstones and swarmed them. They physically detained all except one who took off running. Esther calmly loaded a rubber round into her pistol and shot him between the shoulder blades. He fell in a heap. A couple of policemen were there in a flash to detain him. The rubber bullet didn't penetrate his flesh, but it would leave a bruise.

Esther spoke in perfect Arabic, "You're under arrest for violating the city curfew. We'll take you in for questioning. Now place your hands behind your back." Her policemen applied plastic handcuffs to the wrists of the young men and led them away.

Solly said under his breath to Esther, "We've got to keep those boys quiet until we finish our work here. If word gets out to the Palestinians that we've breached the Eastern Gate, we will upset a hornet's nest of hurt."

Esther said, "I agree. The entire city is on curfew orders right now, so we can keep them under wraps for several weeks for the violation. Is that enough time?"

Solly said, "Let's hope and pray it is."

53

The Temple Mount, Jerusalem

The next morning Ambassador Walid Obeidat walked onto the Temple Mount like he owned the place. The Muslim *Waqf* offered him a wide berth, giving special consideration to the dozen or so Jordanian Special Forces soldiers surrounding him. Although the sun was broiling, Walid looked cool in his light colored Armani suit.

He led the team of soldiers over to the interior door of the Eastern Gate and examined it. Just as Prime Minister Abrams had described, he saw a circle of small, almost imperceptible holes drilled into the stones sealing the door.

Walid directed three of his soldiers to remove their packs and start using their battery-powered drills to finish opening the circle in the stones and mortar. The noise of three drills echoed across the area.

Four members of the *Waqf* came running over, their white robes billowing behind them. Their complaints toppled on top of one another in Arabic. "In the name of the most merciful Allah, you must stop this at once!" "You are desecrating this holy place. Are you looking for another fight?"

At Walid's command his soldiers leveled their AK-47s at the outraged men. When they finally stopped yelling, he explained in a calm voice, "I will remind you again that King Mashallah of Jordan holds supreme jurisdiction for this Temple Mount. You are only allowed here to pray by his merciful kindness. He has assured you that the Dome of the Rock and the mosque will not be touched or harmed in any way."

He pointed toward his men as they continued to drill. "This gate has been sealed for hundreds of years," he said. "His Highness is curious about what may be contained in the chamber. By right of treaty, he would own any treasures within. Go back to your praying, and don't bother me again."

The disgruntled Muslims reluctantly left, shaking their heads and calling Walid unpleasant names under their breath.

In a matter of minutes the soldiers had knocked out the opening. Walid peered eye-level into the chamber. Not wanting to spoil a perfectly good Armani suit, he pointed at one of the soldiers and instructed him to go inside and report what he saw.

The captain climbed into the chamber and switched on his flashlight. He waved it back and forth as he walked the length of the narrow hallway between the outer and inner doors of the Eastern Gate. After a few minutes he shimmied out of the hole.

"Sir, I didn't see anything of value in there," he reported. "Just a lot of old stones and dust. There is a large hole in the outer gate that seems to be sealed by some kind of artificial cover."

Walid nodded and thanked the captain. "Good work. I know about the other opening. We won't disturb it. Our job is finished. We may leave."

The captain asked, "Sir, do you want us to reseal this hole?"

Walid smiled and said, "No, that's too much work. Let's leave it open. That place probably needs a little ventilation."

As Walid passed the members of the *Waqf,* he gave them a stern warning. "Don't go anywhere near the gate. We have it under constant surveillance, and anyone who gets remotely near it will be shot immediately."

Walid left the Temple Mount via a private gate. His Mercedes was parked just outside with the engine running. He climbed into the back seat and took a moment to enjoy the chilly air conditioning. He pushed the speed dial number for the Israeli Prime Minister on his phone. Soon there was a familiar voice on the other end.

"Prime Minister, as you requested, the Eastern Gate is now open for your experimental business."

54

The Western Wall Plaza, Jerusalem

As soon as the sun sank over the western horizon, different teams started assembling at their designated locations. Ziv Kessler was directing tonight's operation.

Solly, Ty, and Regan were tasked with determining where the laser hit pay dirt on the Temple Mount. They teamed up with Akiva, Uri, and Leah to complete the forensic archaeology component.

Dr. Cantor and Gad were once more stationed up on the back deck of the gift shop on the Mount of Olives. They had their drone fully charged and ready. The gift shop owner had raised the rent each day, so he was happy for them to keep coming back. He even made sure his wife prepared hot tea and small lemon cookies for his guests this time.

The Jordanian Ambassador was absent, but he'd sent his Jordanian Special Forces soldiers to ensure there were no disruptions during this crucial final operation.

Esther commanded a team of sixty security personnel—a combination of Israeli Police and IDF soldiers. Overhead several Apache helicopters hovered near the area, giving the impression of another typical military exercise. When everyone was in place and briefed, Kessler radioed in and said, "It's go time!"

There was a flurry of footsteps as the Jordanian and Israeli troops ran onto the Temple Mount from the newly enlarged northern entrance. As expected, the place was basically deserted at this time of night. But it never hurt to be cautious.

Solly, Ty, and Regan walked straight to the Eastern Gate and looked through the hole that the Jordanians had cut the day before.

"I'll jump inside and help the engineers remove the camouflage cover to give the laser a straight shot," Ty offered. He climbed into the dark chamber and coughed as dust flew. Using his flashlight, he walked down the hallway to the other end and knocked two times on the cover. He heard one knock in return indicating two of the engineers were outside on ladders. Ty pushed hard on the cover to knock it off its magnetic rim and the engineers lowered it to the ground. Then Ty walked back through the hallway and crawled out to where Solly and Ty were waiting.

They walked due west from the gate until they came to an open area about two hundred feet north of the Dome of the Rock. There they met Akiva and his team who were preparing to set up their portable drill to begin sampling the soil.

Akiva said, "Wherever the laser hits the ground should

put us close to the actual location of the curtain separating the Holy of Holies from the Most Holy Place."

"This is so exciting," Regan said.

Solly pulled out his phone and punched in Dr. Cantor's number. "Malak, we're ready. Send the laser up."

"Launching the drone now," Dr. Cantor replied. "And remember to warn everyone to look at the ground and not up at the source of the laser."

In a couple of seconds a brilliant line of blue light shot through both openings of the Eastern Gate and onto the Temple Mount. The angle was lower than they had expected, so they had to move west until they reached the spot where the laser touched the ground.

Uri handed Solly two metal spikes and a mallet. He said, "We'll use these to mark the beginning and end of the line that the laser traces as it moves."

Solly drove one of the spikes through the broken pavement. They watched as the blue line continued to move westward as the drone slowly ascended, mimicking the rise of the sun. After seven minutes the laser dot disappeared. Solly drove in the second spike at that location.

"Wow! That is utterly amazing!" Regan shouted.

Everyone was smiling. Akiva, who had use of only one arm, instructed Leah to enter the data into his calculator. She announced the distance.

He said, "Leah, enter this as a home location on the GPS."

As she did so, she said, "This could be the most important GPS location on the planet, you know."

"According to the laser and our calculations," Uri said, "I'm standing close to where the Temple curtain hung outside the Holy of Holies."

Solly felt as giddy as a child. He looked due south and said, "Look around! We aren't anywhere near the Dome of the Rock. It's at least two hundred feet away!" He pointed to a random, thin column of rocks near Akiva that was about four feet high. "That column right behind you is what the Muslims call the Dome of the Tablets, named after the Ten Commandments that God gave to Moses."

Solly paused. "Wouldn't it be ironic if the Muslims inadvertently marked the very spot over the original location of the Ark of the Covenant containing the two tablets of the Ten Commandments?"

Ziv Kessler had joined the group by now. He had the Prime Minister on the phone.

"Yes, sir, we have confirmed by the laser test the precise location of what we believe would have been the curtain between the Holy of Holies and the Holy Place."

He paused and listened.

"Agreed. It is truly remarkable," Ziv said to the voice on the other line. "Yes, sir. I fully understand. We need additional scientific verification before we can present our findings to our friends and enemies. Akiva and his crew will begin sampling the soil as soon as I hang up."

55

The Temple Mount, Jerusalem

Now that they knew the location of the entrance to the Holy of Holies, it would be easy for Akiva's team to calculate the right distance to the bronze altar where they expected to find blood. The dimensions of the Temple were spelled out in the Bible. Akiva referenced a small notebook and said, "According to the Old Testament, the bronze altar was forty cubits from the entrance to the Most Holy Place. That's about sixty feet from the curtain to the altar. So let's walk directly toward the Eastern Gate for sixty feet, and we should be able to set up our drill over the location where thousands of animals were sacrificed on the altar."

There was little light on this deserted part of the Temple Mount, but there were plenty of flashlights as they walked about sixty feet to the spot where the altar should have stood.

"This is where we'll do our soil samples," Akiva announced. "With my bum arm it looks as if I'm going to be the observer again."

"That's okay, Boss," Uri said. "Leah and I know the drill."

"Nice pun," Leah said.

Uri pulled the starter cord and the little two-cycle engine roared to life. They got into a rhythm of drilling, adding bores, and drilling again until they had drilled through civilization after civilization until they had reached their target depth of twelve feet at the level of the Second Temple.

Akiva said, "Let's reverse the engine and get those bores into the lab."

Another tent had been set up farther north on the Temple Mount with a generator powering lights and the electron microscope. Uri and Leah gently carried the four soil bores into the tent and placed them on the table.

"Uri, let's start with the first one in," Akiva instructed. "If my calculations are correct, it should tell us something."

Uri took the wooden dowel and gently pushed out a cylinder of moist dirt. After Uri added the Luminol to the sample, she peered into the lens. She adjusted the focus and was silent for a long minute. Then she stepped back from microscope and looked at the anxious group.

"I've never seen anything like it," she said.

Uri bent over to look into the lens and sucked in a breath.

"Akiva, look at this!" he said.

Akiva stared into the lens and smiled. "That soil is lit up like a bunch of lightning bugs! There's not just a *trace* of blood in that dirt. It's *saturated*."

Regan, Solly, and Ty took turns examining the blood-soaked soil samples.

Over the next hour they examined dozens of soil samples to confirm their findings. All showed evidence of massive amounts of ancient blood that had soaked into the dirt.

Regan moved to the side of the tent to gather her thoughts. Instead of feeling happy that they had made the right discovery, she felt strangely frustrated. As she thought about the thousands of animals who died there, she thought how wasteful and useless these rituals were. They had done nothing to save people.

She suddenly felt a hand on her shoulder. "Regan, are you okay? What's wrong?" Regan turned to look into the concerned eyes of her new friend Leah and wiped her eyes. She was embarrassed to be so emotional.

"I just feel sick thinking about the slaughter of thousands of animals here. It was a broken religious system that was never able to forgive anyone's sins."

Leah raised her eyebrows in surprise and in solidarity with Regan. "I know what you mean," she said. Leah went on to explain that she was not a religious person, even though she grew up in a Jewish home where she learned the history of the sacrificial system. "To be honest, it always did seem a little strange to me," she confessed. "I'm not sure what the point was."

"I believe the point was symbolic," Regan said. "It's as if God used the sacrificial system and days like *Yom Kippur* to prepare the Jewish people for the coming of the true Lamb of God."

Leah looked a little skeptical. "Christians believe that Jesus was the Lamb of God, don't they? You are a Christian, right?"

"Yes."

"That takes a lot of faith. I've always been more of a scientist, and we always want proof."

Regan smiled. "That's okay, Leah. I never thought of faith having to be a blind leap. How well do you know the Messianic prophecies of the Old Testament?"

Leah frowned and confessed, "Well, I haven't actually read much of the Bible since my parents made me have a *bat mitzvah*."

The girls laughed.

"What if I could show you a list of predictions that the Old Testament prophets made about the Messiah, and then show you how Jesus of Nazareth fulfilled those prophecies?"

"Thank you, Regan. But I'm not really interested in exchanging my Jewish heritage for the Christian religion." Leah seemed suddenly uneasy.

"Hey, *religion* isn't for me either," Regan assured her. "To me, being a Christian is more like having a personal *relationship* with Jesus. He's a friend who is always with me."

Leah was getting more uncomfortable. "Well, we've still got work to do here, but maybe I'll look at your list sometime," she said.

"You're right. It's going to be a long night," Regan said. The girls walked back toward the tent in silence. Regan hoped she had not said too much and breathed a prayer for Leah.

Ziv Kessler had now joined them was talking to Akiva inside the tent. "Well, Dr. Hahn, tell me. Is this the spot of the First and Second Jewish Temples?"

Akiva sighed and said solemnly, "Mr. Kessler, I will stake my personal reputation and the reputation of the entire Forensic Science Department at Hebrew University on the irrefutable fact that we are standing above the ground where tens of thousands of animals were sacrificed over two-thousand years ago. Is that good enough for you?"

Kessler smiled. "It is, Dr. Hahn. And congratulations. You, Solly, and Dr. Cantor have proven what had only been a theory for years. Tonight we know without a doubt that the Dome of the Rock is *not* built on the site of the Jewish Temple. The ramifications of this discovery will be felt worldwide."

He then glanced at his Audemars Piguet wristwatch and saw that it was nearing 3:30 a.m. He lifted his communicator and radioed in, "All personnel, we are vacating the Temple Mount in ten minutes. Remove any traces of your presence here and exit through the north gate."

There was a flurry of activity as the crew disassembled the mobile lab, dismantled the portable drill, and packed up. Outside the Eastern Gate the faux stone cover was replaced. Solly, Ty, and Regan joined Esther's squad in egressing the Temple Mount. Regan was bone-tired and couldn't wait for a hot shower and a soft bed.

Kessler knew the Prime Minister would still be up. He punched his name on his speed dial list.

"Talk to me, Ziv," Abrams said.

"Sir, in my mind we are a 100 percent go for Jerusalem Protocol. It's just a matter now of the timetable."

"Meet me with our team in my office tomorrow at 0900 hours." Abrams paused. "And thanks, Ziv. This has been a masterpiece so far."

"But, sir, it can turn south at any minute."

"Don't I know it!" Abrams said as he hung up. He wondered for a moment if it was too early to call the Eastern Coast of the United States before deciding to give President Flowers a few more hours of sleep.

PART 5

56

Air Force One FL390 Over the North Atlantic

Air Force One, a specially equipped Boeing 747-200B, was cruising along smoothly over the icy North Atlantic. President Arthur Flowers was on an encrypted satellite Facetime call with Israeli Prime Minister Natan Abrams. CIA Director Tony Parker flanked him on his left, and Chief of Staff Frank Taylor sat nearby.

Two days earlier he had received an urgent but mysterious invitation from Abrams and Jordanian King Mashallah to join them at an emergency summit in Amman, Jordan. Flowers was still steaming from having to change his closely planned schedule to carve out two days for the trip to Jordan. He was giving Abrams an earful.

"Do you have any idea how many people and nations I have offended by cancelling my schedule to join you for this clandestine summit?" he barked.

"Mr. President, as you are aware, we have a copy of your personal schedule—just as you have one of mine," Abrams assured him. "I'm sure Prime Minister Mitchell of Granada will accept your apologies for rescheduling your meeting. And I don't suppose you have many strategic resources on the Island of Malta. Perhaps you're most upset about missing your weekly golf game at Camp David? If you wish, I can close down the Caesarea Golf Course so you and your friends can have the course all to yourselves."

Flowers turned from the video screen and yelled at Parker, "I thought my personal schedule was confidential!"

Parker shrugged his shoulders and said, "It is, sir. But as the Prime Minister indicated, they do know your schedule. And we know his."

Flowers returned to Abrams. "I suppose I can reschedule those events," he said with a small grin at the corner of his lips. "I didn't bring my clubs, but you'll owe me a round of golf next time you're in Washington."

He paused and grew serious. "But I need to know more about this summit in Amman before we land. If you don't give me some solid Intel on what's happening, I'll have my pilot turn this jet around and we'll be back at Andrews in a few hours. As soon as the Senate Foreign Affairs Committee learns I'm gone, they'll be all over this trip like ticks on a hound dog."

Abrams said, "Relax, Arthur. The press releases from our countries indicate that this is a last minute scheduled visit to strengthen ties between our nations in our united fight against ISIS. Nobody will argue with that. And it's part of the truth."

"*Part* of the truth?" Flowers snorted. "I need to know the whole truth about this meeting."

Abrams sighed. Although the President was already aware of the Jerusalem Protocol, he did not yet know about the recent findings regarding the location of the Jewish Temple. Still, he told Abrams, he did not think this new information was relevant since he too believed the Jews would be under too much international resistance from the Muslims if they tried rebuilding the Temple.

"King Mashallah has sworn me to secrecy about the rest of the details of this meeting, but I predict one thing. If you attend, it will be in the best interest of our three nations—and the leaders from other moderate Muslim nations who will be at the meeting."

"I figured you had an ace hidden up your sleeve. I've played poker with you enough to know that you never reveal your hand, Natan."

Abrams laughed. "But in my memory you're always the one who wins the biggest pot! I'll never be the poker player you are, Mr. President."

"Maybe not. But this time it looks like you're holding all the cards."

"It's going to be a good deal, trust me. And if there's ever been a time for our two countries to go 'all in,' it's now!"

"I'll have to trust you then, my friend. I'll see you in

Amman in a few hours."

Flowers punched "disconnect" on the video screen and called out, "Get me a turkey sandwich and a glass of milk in my stateroom. I need a few hours of sleep before I join the table for this high-stakes poker game!"

57

King Mashallah 1 Royal Airbase, outside Amman, Jordan

Air Force One landed a few minutes ahead of schedule. President Flowers walked down the airstairs to be greeted with a warm embrace from his old friend King Mashallah. There were no reporters or television cameras, just a huge support team of U.S. Secret Service Agents and Jordanian Special Forces agents keeping their eyes open for every possible threat of a sniper or ambush.

There were three Green VH-3D Sea King helicopters nearby, rotors spinning. They had been delivered twelve hours earlier aboard three massive C-5 Galaxy transports. The helicopter carrying POTUS would be designated as Marine One. The other two would be decoys. On cue various groups rushed into all three helicopters. From a distance it would have been difficult to see which helicopter POTUS and King Mashallah entered. The three giant helicopters rose and banked in three different directions.

As they climbed to a safe altitude, President Flowers

looked down to see the nose of the decoy Air Force
One 747 protruding from a large hanger. As with all
international trips, two identical 747s had made the trip.
The decoy had arrived eight hours earlier with a full crew.
Both were equipped with the same offensive and defensive
weaponry and were capable of mid-air refueling. He
glanced around the tarmac of the airport and saw several
other large private jets that he assumed were the heads of
state of additional Middle Eastern countries. As he sat
back in the soft leather, he thought, *"I wonder who'll be at the
table tonight? I'd better hold my cards close to my vest."*

Al-Maquar (Royal Headquarters) in Amman, Jordan

Marine One settled down softly on the back lawn
of the massive royal palace of King Mashallah. Security
details spread out in every direction to ensure the safety
of two of the world's most important leaders. It was only
a short walk through beautifully manicured gardens to a
huge patio with several tables loaded down with food and
drinks. Unobtrusive servants rushed about to refill drinks
and take empty plates from the men sitting at the tables. A
quartet of strings in the corner played soft classical music.
Arthur looked around and quietly marveled how much
it reminded him of a scene from a James Bond movie set.
He nodded a greeting to several heads of state who were

chatting and enjoying the light refreshments.

After about twenty minutes of making small talk, a servant approached. "Mr. President, His Highness King Mashallah requests your presence in the private conference room." The servant extended his hand to the left and said, "Please follow me this way."

POTUS, Director Parker, and Mr. Taylor proceeded across the expansive patio through the massive door. His secret service team was already in position. Ambassador Walid Obeidat sat next to King Mashallah. Once they were seated, King Mashallah began to introduce his other guests. Since everyone spoke English, it was the common language used in the meeting.

The King said in his cultured English accent, "Gentlemen, I welcome you to this historic meeting. Although everyone knows each other, allow me the honor to introduce each of you personally. We are pleased to have our friend, United States President Arthur Flowers. Next to him, we are honored to have the presence of His Highness King Nadeem from the Kingdom of Saudi Arabia."

Arthur raised one eyebrow and threw a look at Frank Taylor. Nadeem was the last guy he thought would come to a meeting where the Israeli Prime Minister was present. Now they had his attention.

King Mashallah moved to the next guest. "I believe you all know Egyptian President Adeem el-Boutros."

Arthur continued his private assessment of each

dignitary. He considered el-Boutros one tough cookie. He didn't tolerate jihadists or extremists. *"El-Boutros is just what Egypt needed to get them out of that mess,"* he thought. *"I'm glad he's here."*

Arthur nodded a greeting to el-Boutros as the King continued, "We are pleased that the Turkish President Necmettin Bilal Gulbaran could also join us. As we know, his nation has been a target for extremists more than others."

President Flowers beamed a genuine smile to the Turkish leader. Besides Israel, Turkey had become the United States' most valuable ally in the region.

The King continued, "Of course, we're pleased to have the honored Khalifa bin Shakir al-Din, President of the United Arab Emirates. And I'm sure you all know our friend, Emir Omar Nurullah, Monarch of Qatar. Thank you all for coming."

Mashallah paused and pointed to the end of the conference table. "Although I'm sure all of you know of him, you might not yet have had the privilege of meeting my friend and neighbor, Israeli Prime Minister Natan Abrams."

Abrams stood and said, "I am honored to be invited to join this historic meeting today. It is more imperative than ever that our nations learn to live together in peace."

King Mashallah introduced Ambassador Walid Obeidat last. "The purpose of this historic meeting is two-fold," the King continued. "I think it is important for the world to see nations of different cultures and religions forming a pact to fight against the scourge of radical Islam in general. We must join our nations to exterminate ISIS before they do any more harm to our region or around the world!"

This elicited heartfelt applause and nods around the table.

"Before this meeting is over, I'd like for the seven Middle Eastern nations to sign an agreement pledging our support in a joint effort against ISIS. I realize that the other Muslim nations, with the exception of Jordan, have never entered into any formal agreement with Israel before."

King Mashallah reminded those present of the details surrounding the peace treaty Jordan signed with Israel in 1994. "This agreement has been successfully honored by both nations," he explained. "It has been good for our economies, trade, and tourism. The outdated notion that Israel must never be recognized as a viable nation must be silenced for the good of us all. They are a strong nation and one that could be a great ally to each of us."

King Nadeem from Saudi Arabia raised his hand requesting permission to speak. "We still have the Palestinian issue. None of our nations wants them as refugees!" he said, earning hearty agreement around the table.

Prime Minister Abrams interjected, "We have repeatedly offered the Palestinians statehood and land, but they have always rejected our offers. The sticking point for them is that they want it *all*, and they want to kick Israel back into the Mediterranean Sea."

King Mashallah added, "With our signed treaty, we will be in a position to negotiate alongside Israel and the Palestinians. Perhaps we can help them see the advantage of accepting Israel's offer."

Egyptian President el-Boutros spoke up next. "Your Highness, I believe I know these men enough to predict that we will all sign the pact to unite against the scourge of ISIS. But you indicated that there was another issue to discuss. What is that?"

King Mashallah pointed to the Israeli Prime Minister. "Natan, why don't you tell them what else we want to do?"

Abrams stood up, buttoned his suit coat, and said firmly, "We believe the time has come for Israel to build a third Jewish Temple in Jerusalem."

There was stunned silence for a few seconds followed by a heated Arabic exchange that President Flowers was glad he couldn't translate.

58

King's Conference Room, The Royal Headquarters, Amman, Jordan

Several of the heads of state stood up so fast that they knocked over their chairs backwards. They all turned to leave the meeting, waving at their entourage to follow. But before they could reach the door, King Mashallah folded his hands on the table and said calmly, "I'm sure you are aware of the old Arabic proverb that says, 'The best answer will come from the person who is not angry.' Please, my friends, sit down and at least honor me by allowing me to explain."

Over the next hour King Mashallah and Prime Minister Abrams presented the recently proven scientific evidence that the construction of the Jewish Temple would interfere with neither the Dome of the Rock nor the *Al Aqsa Mosque*.

There was much initial grumbling and skepticism, but King Mashallah employed Ambassador Walid Obeidat's exceptional diplomatic skills to walk the leaders through the results of the experiments and scientific findings. President Flowers, having already been briefed by Abrams earlier, was on board with the plan from the beginning. The others were harder to convince.

King Nadeem remained silent during the debate. When there was a brief lull in the discussion, he raised his forefinger. Since Saudi Arabia was by far the richest and most powerful of the Arab nations, there was immediate silence. He looked around at every person at the table and said, "Let us not forget that the fool al-Bagahdi has threatened that ISIL will come and destroy the sacred *Kaaba* in Mecca because he considers it an idol. He has boasted that he will obliterate the Dome of the Rock in Jerusalem. All Muslim, Jewish, and Christian holy sites are at risk until every vestige of ISIL has been annihilated!"

President el-Boutros said, "You're correct, Your Excellency. But for decades Muslims have said that if Israel tries to build a temple, a million Muslim warriors will invade Jerusalem to defend the Holy Place to their last ounce of blood!"

King Nadeem nodded. "That has been our official position. It's been an effective deterrent. But that warning was based on the supposition that the Israelis would first have to destroy the Dome of the Rock to do so. We've heard today that this is not the case."

He paused.

"Besides, where are those million Muslim warriors coming from? Not from the *Shias* in Iran or the Asians in Malaysia! They would be coming from *our Sunni* countries! And if each of us agrees to this ambitious plan, we don't send our troops to attack Jerusalem. We simply keep our armies on alert and continue to fight as a united force against ISIL."

King Mashallah bowed toward the Saudi King. "You have spoken with the wisdom that comes with age, Your Excellency. But even if we all agree to the plan, the Palestinians will surely resist the Israelis. They will issue a call for our military to rally to their aid. We must agree that we will politely refuse or postpone our military support, citing our joint focus on defeating ISIS as our rationale."

The King looked at President Flowers. "In the Arab culture the response 'perhaps later' actually means 'no.'"

The men smiled a knowing smile. After much more verbal wrangling, it was clear that King Nadeem's initial approval of the plan had built the momentum needed to influence the other leaders to agree. It took supreme effort for Prime Minister Abrams to contain his surprised pleasure.

King Mashallah concluded, "Thank you for listening to reason, my friends. Now for the details of my proposal. I propose that we form a new political alliance of our seven Middle Eastern nations—united and devoted to defeating ISIS and bringing peace and stability to our region. I propose we call this alliance MEPA: the Middle Eastern Peace Alliance. This groundbreaking treaty will include the first multi-lateral alliance with Israel. Based upon our 1994 treaty with Israel, I can give you my personal guarantee that they will keep their part of the treaty. This coalition with Israel will make all of us stronger and ultimately safer."

The Turkish president spoke up. "I commend you for this plan, Your Highness. As ISIS has grown and spread, it has become apparent that desperate times call for radical alliances. Many of our citizens will not be happy with this alliance, but leaders often have to make the difficult choices."

President Flowers, who had remained quiet to this point, was prepared to speak. He briefly explained that because of America's ties with a variety of other nations around the world, including each one represented at the meeting, the United States could not be a part of the new alliance. However, he knew reiterating America's support for this historic treaty would go a long way. "I can assure you that my administration is in favor of this alliance," he said. "And we will continue to give favored nation status to all the countries that agree to be a part of MEPA. The United States pledges our full cooperation in defeating the scourge that is ISIS."

Because of the sensitive nature of what the Jews planned to do, he issued a warning to Abrams for the benefit of the other Muslim leaders. He continued, "I want to remind you all that we have been given every assurance from the Israeli government that the plans for a third Temple will not disrupt the Muslim worship on the Temple Mount. As an outside party, the U.S. will monitor this provision and ensure it is followed."

King Mashallah thanked President Flowers. Then he motioned to Walid who was now standing by the door. "Ambassador Obeidat has copies of an agreement that outlines the terms of our alliance. It basically states that our seven nations are sharing intelligence and military resources for the battle against ISIS. As with every organization, there must be a designated leader and a representative body. I am proposing that Ambassador Walid Obeidat be named the General Secretary of MEPA. Because of his longstanding relationship with Israel and with our nations, he is a logical choice. However, if any of you would like to propose another General Secretary, you are free to do so now."

No one spoke. The other leaders had been impressed with the ambassador's earlier display of impressive negotiating skills. King Mashallah continued, "Secretary Obeidat will receive funds from our seven countries on a per-capita ratio. He will enlist an administrative team comprised of members from all seven nations. Once this administrative team is formed, the Secretary will publically announce the launch of MEPA, and he will continue to coordinate our efforts."

Copies of the agreement were passed around the room and read carefully by each head of state. Their respective aides came alongside them to discuss points of the agreement with their leaders. After a few minutes King Mashallah asked, "Are there any questions?"

The president of the United Arab Emirates was a brilliant and astute businessman who had received an MBA from Harvard University. He was more westernized than any of the other leaders. He smiled and said, "Well, I guess I'll address the elephant in the room if nobody else will."

Some of the less modern leaders seemed confused. President Flowers even thought he caught one aide subtly glancing around as if to see if an elephant really were in the conference room!

King Mashallah smiled and said, "Go ahead, Mr. President."

President al-Din said, "We talked about it, but there's nothing in the written agreement about the rebuilding of the Jewish Temple. Why is that?"

Prime Minister Abrams spoke up. "Your Highness, if you don't mind I'll be glad to try to tame the elephant."

King Mashallah smiled and nodded his permission for Abrams to continue.

"President Flowers, King Mashallah, and I feel strongly that the building of the Temple is a separate concern and that it must be handled quietly in Jerusalem. It is such a controversial issue that we didn't want it to distract from the larger issue of the MEPA treaty to fight ISIS. All we ask is a gentleman's agreement that you will withhold your troops once the process of rebuilding begins. In this way your governments will be immune to the negative press that is bound to come from our effort. Therefore, we think it would be a mistake to make the Third Temple a part of this important treaty."

El-Boutros spoke up. "Sir, you are as wise as one of your famous ancestors who visited Egypt many centuries ago. Moses could have been one of our finest Pharaohs, but alas he chose to travel to your Promised Land. I believe we are all gentlemen here. I cannot speak for the others, but you have my word that we will give you room to rebuild your Temple."

In a moment of spontaneity Prime Minister Abrams walked over to el-Boutros who stood to his feet to receive him. Abrams took his hand firmly and said, "Thank you, Mr. President. I look forward to our alliance with you and these other nations."

Then Abrams approached each of the leaders of the other nations and shook their hands. He came at last to King Mashallah. And in the emotion of the moment, these two leaders embraced, symbolizing a new era of peace in their region.

Finally the meeting ended as all the leaders left with their entourages to board luxury business jets. On the way to the airport Abrams called Kessler. "You are a genius," Abrams told him. "It played out exactly as you promised it would. You knew that once a common enemy distracted our Arab neighbors, we could negotiate a treaty apart from the Palestinians—and you were right. The timing of this alliance is the perfect window of opportunity to build the Temple. Tell David Shvaz to activate the Jerusalem Protocol!"

Meanwhile President Flowers was aboard Marine One helicopter streaking back to the airbase where Air Force One was fueled and ready to go. He was still amazed by what he had just witnessed in the King's conference room. He turned to his chief of staff and said, "Frank, call the Secretary of Defense. Make sure all those Chinooks have arrived in Israel. They're going to need them after all."

59

Ramat David Israeli Air Force Base, Jezreel Valley, Israel

Over the past two weeks several squadrons of United States Air Force C-5 Galaxy transports had landed at the Ramat David Air Base located in the shadow of Megiddo, an ancient hill in northern Israel. Many biblical scholars thought of it as a fitting location for an Israeli air base since "Armageddon"—mentioned only once in the Bible—means "hill of Megiddo" and is the future staging point of the battle at the end of the world.

The massive four-engine transport plane was capable of carrying over eight hundred thousand pounds of cargo halfway around the globe at a speed of 570 miles per hour. The entire nose of the aircraft could hinge open, allowing large military vehicles and aircraft to be loaded into the mammoth cargo bay.

These C-5s had delivered a dozen Boeing CH-47 Chinook helicopters on loan to Israel from the United States Army. This twin-engine tandem rotor heavy-lift helicopter could easily carry a twenty-thousand-pound payload. With the addition of an upgraded laser landing system, the loadmaster could place the load on a location as small as a dinner plate.

Once the Chinooks had been offloaded and the rotors reattached, they were concealed in underground bunkers at Ramat. The U.S. Army air squad was under the command of Captain Jim Powell, a native of a small town in Texas. His liaison with the IDF was a Jewish officer, Colonel Isaac Silverman.

After introductions had been made, Colonel Silverman began his briefing. "You and your aircraft will be involved in one of the most important missions in the short history of our revived nation. We have been given the green light to proceed with building a Jewish Temple on the Temple Mount in Jerusalem." He paused for questions.

Captain Powell stood up. "Excuse me, sir. I don't know everything about Jerusalem, but isn't there a big golden domed building sittin' there where you want to build your Temple? Are you going to bomb it first? If you do, won't the whole Muslim world come down hard on us in a heartbeat?"

Colonel Silverman was confident in his reply. "That, sir, is a popular misconception. But our scientists have provided ironclad evidence that the location of the Jewish Temple was actually about two hundred feet north of the Dome of the Rock. As an extra precaution, your squad is tasked with dropping sections of a tall concrete wall to separate the northern and southern sections of the

Temple Mount. Muslims will continue to use the southern portion where the Dome of the Rock and *Al Aqsa* Mosque are located. Israel is staking claim to the northern part of Temple Mount for our purposes. The Jordanians exercise control over the whole Temple Mount, and they have approved this plan."

Captain Powell was not satisfied. "If we fly in broad daylight with concrete wall sections, won't we be shot out of the sky by all those radical Muslims with RPGs? My understanding from the briefing my men received is that the Muslims will defend their holy site to the death." The other U.S. airmen nodded.

"That's a valid question," Colonel Silverman responded. "There may be some fierce opposition, but we have several factors in our favor. First, we're going to drop in the wall sections at 0200 in the morning when most of the Palestinians are asleep. Second, there aren't that many armed Muslims in the Old City. We have inside intelligence about the cell groups within the Old City and we have raided and arrested all the radicals we know. Most of the bad guys are in the West Bank and the Gaza Strip, and those borders are going to be locked shut. Third, you're going to have a convoy of Israeli Apache attack helicopters escorting you for cover."

Captain Powell grinned. "I'm liking the sound of that. Sir, brief us on the mission details."

Colonel Silverman displayed a map on a digital screen. He pointed to a spot and explained, "We're here at the airbase which is to the north of part of the West Bank." He pointed to another spot and said, "And here's Jerusalem about ninety miles southeast of our position. We'll take off and fly west toward the Mediterranean Sea to get separation from the West Bank. The first leg will not have a load, so you can make good time. Once we get our feet wet over the Sea, we'll head south. When we get to Tel Aviv, we'll turn east toward Jerusalem. Five miles from the Old City is an old concrete plant where the wall sections have been constructed and are being kept undercover. This is our staging area for loading."

He zoomed in on the Temple Mount. "Upon arrival at the staging area, our men on the ground will connect your hoisting cables to embedded titanium hooks in the top of each wall section. Once the sections are secured, it will be a short flight of only five minutes to the Temple Mount. Your GPS track will take you around the Temple Mount toward the Mount of Olives. Then you'll circle back and descend inside the north end of the Temple Mount and release your load. You'll be in radio contact with our engineers on the ground. They have the GPS coordinates for the exact location of each section of wall, and they will connect all the adjoining sections. The wall will run at an angle from just south of the Eastern Gate, beside the Dome of the Rock, to the upper location of the Western Wall."

Captain Powell was doing the math in his head. "So what is the total length of the wall? How many trips will it take to complete the task?"

"The total length of the wall will be a little less nine hundred feet. The base is six feet thick, tapering to a thinner width at the top. Think of them as giant highway dividers. Each section will be thirty-two feet long and forty feet high. We've calculated the weight to ensure that it fits within the lifting profile of the Chinooks. If everything goes as planned, it will involve thirty round trips. We are also going to space out the arrival time of each Chinook by fifteen minutes. There won't be more than one Chinook over the Temple Mount at any given time. With the regularity of medical helicopters flying over this area, not to mention frequent Israeli military air patrols, it won't seem as if the apocalypse is happening!"

The Colonel paused. "Are there any questions?"

One U.S. airman raised his hand. "Sir, when do we get this party started?"

Colonel Silverman looked at this watch. "It's 1900 hours now. We'll be wheels up at 0100, so get some grub and some rest because it's going to be a long night."

The Army aviators jumped to their feet, high-fived each other and yelled, "Hoo rah!"

60

0200 hours over Jerusalem

For the few people awake at this hour, the first sensation they detected was a slight pressure change in their ears. It seemed as if a large fan were sucking the air out of the room. A moment later they heard the distinctive *whump whump whump* of helicopter blades as the huge tandem rotors of the first Chinook sliced through the nighttime sky.

Some in the Old City could not sleep through the eerie invasion of noise. Others got out of bed and went outside to try to identify the sound, but they were disappointed. All they could see were a few dim lights and the sound of a single large helicopter moving across Jerusalem from west to east. The residents went back to bed, assuming this was just another military exercise of a vigilant IDF.

0200 hours Temple Mount, Jerusalem

Solly, Ty, and Regan had been up all night on the Temple Mount waiting for the arrival of the helicopters.

Dr. Akiva, Uri, and Leah joined them, also filled with anxiety as well, despite the large contingent of armed policemen and IDF soldiers providing tight security.

They passed around cups of hot coffee from a thermos as they checked the sky for any sign of activity. Uri stomped his feet, not because it was cold but because of nerves.

Earlier in the day, the IDF Corps of Engineers had laid out the drop zone for the wall using a laser geodolite to shoot a line from the Western Wall to a predetermined point just south of the Eastern Gate.

They soon saw a massive Chinook with a huge section of wall suspended underneath it slowly moving toward them. Intervals between each Chinook were timed so that there would be no lingering over the Temple Mount.

The Chinooks had a cutting edge offloading system that took the guesswork out of delivering the payload. On the bottom of each section of wall a small but powerful sensor had been attached. As the loadmaster in the Chinook lowered the payload, the engineer on the ground simply had to "paint" the landing spot with a laser marker. The system locked into the winch controls as the pilot gently descended and automatically adjusted the load until it reached the precise target. It worked perfectly. After a pair of engineers unhooked the cables, they gave a thumbs-up. The powerful Chinook minus its load silently disappeared into the night sky to return to the staging area to get next load.

Solly yelled, "That's one down and twenty-nine to go!"

The next Chinook arrived a few minutes later. The ends of each wall section had a tongue-and-groove joint. As the next Chinook lowered the wall section, it slid into a perfect fit with the first section. Engineers on the ground inserted huge bolts through pre-drilled holes to make it even more secure.

The team got into a rhythm of watching the next Chinook line up and lower another wall section. They were a little more than half-finished when Regan thought, *"This is easier than I thought it would be."*

"Yep, this is the easy part," Solly said.

Regan would never understand how Solly seemed to be tuned in to everyone's thoughts!

"But in the morning this wall will be the lead news story on every major network in the world," he added.

Ty shook his head. "How are we going to deal with that? I don't know about you, but the thought of the entire Muslim world aiming their missiles at us is not a pleasant one."

Solly responded, "The leaders who get the big shekels will be the ones answering the tough questions! We're just going to do whatever we're told."

61

Northern Half of the Temple Mount, Jerusalem

After three hours of constant airlifts, the wall was finally completed just as the faintest glow of the approaching sunrise painted the sky. As the engineers bolted the last section of the wall in place, the Chinooks winged their way west toward the Mediterranean Sea to return to the Israeli airbase.

For the first time in history a massive wall towering forty feet high now separated the north and south areas of the Temple Mount. It was no ordinary concrete structure. The wall featured electrified elements embedded in protruding metal rebar. Motion sensors built into the base of the southern side of the wall facing the Muslim section were so sensitive that an approaching cat would set off an alarm! Video cameras encased in protective steel cages dotted the top of the wall. As a final precaution, the southern face of the wall was coated with a chemical that made it impossible to write or paint graffiti on it.

As the first Muslim men appeared on the Temple Mount for morning prayers in the *Al Aqsa* Mosque, they screamed in horror. They pulled out their cell phones, started taking pictures of the wall. They screamed into their phones in graphic Arabic reporting the ugly desecration of their Holy Place.

Within minutes a huge mob of protestors had gathered, chanting, "Death to Israel! Death to the Jews!" Some approached the wall and threw rocks toward it. As soon as they drew near, a column of IDF soldiers and Israeli Police appeared on the scene with guns leveled at the crowd. It was obvious that they would not tolerate any attempts to approach or damage the wall.

The word of the new wall spread like wildfire over social media and the Internet. Al-Jazeera was the first international news organization to arrive on site to report on the construction of what they called "a breach of international law." Soon the other news reporting sources picked up the story, and it became breaking news on every international news outlet.

The BBC and all of the American broadcast networks soon got their hands on an aerial view of the wall. The response from the Palestinians was predictably insolent. However, to the surprise of the news networks, the majority of other Muslim nations in the region had no comment. Only Iran was forthright to condemn the wall as illegal, but even they practiced bewildering restraint. They had no love for the Palestinians, but they appeared to be caught off guard by the lack of response from their fellow Muslim nations.

In preparation for this anticipated backlash, Israel had set up roadblocks to prevent any Palestinians from entering Israel from Gaza or the West Bank. Palestinian President Fatallah Ayman appeared on camera vehemently condemning the action of the Israelis. He issued an urgent call to all Muslim brothers to join their *jihad* to remove the wall and to remove the Jews from the Palestinian homeland. His urgent phone calls to the leaders of several nations asking for military aid were shuttled off to lesser politicians who complained that their forces were stretched too thin dealing with ISIS. When he heard "perhaps later" for the third time, Ayman began to suspect that King Mashallah of Jordan was behind this.

Across the world Muslim communities launched protests against what they saw as Jewish intervention on the Temple Mount. They demanded military action against Israel, but military leaders remained mute—quietly monitoring the protests in their countries to ensure they didn't become violent.

After twenty-four hours of talking heads giving their opinions, King Mashallah of Jordan issued a brief press release that shocked the world:

> "In 1994 Israel and Jordan signed a treaty concerning the control of the Temple Mount. Israel has maintained military oversight, while Jordan has maintained religious oversight. It has recently come to our attention that it is possible to

build a third Jewish Temple without disturbing the holy sites of the Dome of the Rock or the *Al Aqsa* Mosque in any way. The construction of a Wall of Peace was the only way this could happen. I have given my blessings and authorization for the nation of Israel to practice their religious sovereignty on the northern portion of the Temple Mount. I give my assurances to Muslims around the world that we will defend the preservation of the Dome of the Rock and the *Al Aqsa* Mosque. In the near future several Middle Eastern nations will be announcing a new coalition to unite in our fight against ISIS."

The next day the IDF Corps of Engineers began the process of constructing the new Temple.

62

The Jewish section of the Temple Mount, Jerusalem

While the global controversy over the divided Temple Mount continued unabated, Israeli engineers opened a large entrance in the northern wall for heavy equipment to enter the construction site. The first order of business was to remove several small Muslim relics and domes that were on the northern half of the Temple Mount. They carefully removed the Dome of the Tablets and loaded it on the back of a transport truck. They also removed a smaller relic, the Dome of the Spirits, which they loaded beside the Dome of the Tablets. The remaining two relics, the Dome of Solomon and the Dome of Suleiman Pasha, were then dismantled and loaded on a separate truck. These relics would be carefully preserved and returned to the Jordanians who would eventually reconstruct them on the Muslim section of the Temple Mount.

When the northern section was clear of any Muslim artifacts, the chief architect for the project, Dr. Ariel Chavitz, walked onto the site with eight of his Temple Institute technicians. They were loaded down with equipment for a portable construction office to oversee the work.

As Dr. Chavitz approached the place where the Holy of Holies would be built, tears filled his eyes. He reverently knelt down and kissed the ground, his white hair grazing the chalky pavement. He whispered in private prayer, *"Thank You, Oh gracious Maker, for allowing Your servant to be in this holy place. Empower us to build a place where Your Holy Name can once again be revered in the world."*

After a few minutes he rose and walked back to the location near the Eastern Gate where his technicians were already setting up the construction tent. He noticed that Solly, Ty, and Regan had joined them.

Solly removed his hat and said, "Dr. Chavitz, this has to be a dream come true for you. I really do feel as if I'm standing on holy ground."

Dr. Chavitz tried hard not to weep as he spoke. "This… has been the dream … and prayer of millions of Jews since 70 CE." Then he pointed to the ground and said, "We aren't quite standing on holy ground yet. Wait until we remove twelve feet of soil to get to the exact level of the Second Temple!"

The soil would be removed by heavy equipment, but it would then be delivered to the Israeli Archaeological Institute. Experts would carefully sift through the layers of soil for important archaeological evidence from the last two thousand years.

IDF engineers were busy crisscrossing the Temple Mount using several laser Geodolites to mark the corners of the actual building. They drove down high-tech stakes in a number of locations outlining the main areas of the

Temple complex: the court of the priests, the Most Holy
Place, and the Holy of Holies. Each marker fed data back
to Dr. Chavitz' laptop computer in the construction tent.

Dr. Chavitz showed Solly, Ty, and Regan what they had
outlined thus far. "Here, you can see from these blinking
icons where they are staking out the Temple's footprint."

Ty was fascinated. "I'm surprised," he said. "I thought the
Temple was going to be much larger. The pictures we've seen of
Herod's remodeled Second Temple show a massive building."

"As I've told you, Herod tried to build that Temple to
match the size of his ego," retorted Dr. Chavitz.

He punched a couple of keys and the screen brought
up a Bible passage from Exodus 26 written both in Hebrew
and English. As he scrolled down the screen, he said, "The
dimensions for the first Holy Tabernacle are still listed here
in the Bible. From the beginning the Temple Institute has
followed the precise instructions that the Maker gave to Moses
regarding the much smaller dimensions of the Tabernacle."

He then explained how Solomon's Temple and the
Second Temple included expanded areas that were never
part of the Maker's original plan. Instead of gold and silver,
Moses had to avail himself of the materials he had on hand
in the wilderness. The walls were woven yarn, and the roof
was made of finely twisted goat hair.

He continued, "In that tradition we will be using the
materials we have at hand, but we will follow the original
dimensions of the Maker's instructions to Moses."

Solly said, "What size are we talking about, mate?"

Dr. Chavitz did the mental calculations quickly. "The outer courtyard for the Priests will be about one hundred and fifty feet by seventy-five feet."

"So that's like what…a basketball court?" Regan asked Ty.

"Good guess, Regan!" Ty said. "A college basketball court is ninety-four feet by fifty feet, so we're talking about the courtyard being just a little larger than that."

Dr. Chavitz seemed slightly annoyed with Ty's basketball illustration, but he continued his explanation.

"There was only one entrance to the courtyard from the east." He pointed to the Eastern Gate. "That's why Solomon built this beautiful gate you see. The Maker instructed His people to enter from the east with their backs to the rising sun. This was in direct rebellion to pagan religions that worshipped the sun.

"The Third Temple's courtyard will be open to the sky, but the actual building will only contain the Holy of Holies and the Most Holy Place, separated by a thick curtain. As the Maker instructed Moses, this two-roomed building will be forty feet long and only fifteen feet wide."

Ty turned to Regan and interjected, "In the Marines they ran out of space in the barracks, so several of us lived in a single-wide mobile home that was about that size, so maybe that helps…"

Dr. Chavitz interrupted Ty, clearly irritated now. "Why this mobile home nonsense?" He ran a fat hand over his forehead. "The size of the Temple has nothing to do with the greatness and majesty of our Maker!"

Ty and Regan looked down apologetically.

"As I've told you, the only people who entered these rooms were specially assigned priests. There was no need to accommodate a congregation as in a synagogue or church. Temple sacrifice was the work of the priests only. The people brought the sacrifices to the court of the priests, and then the priests offered them to the Maker."

Dr. Chavitz glanced at the computer screen and said, "Oh, good. All the electronic stakes have been placed."

"How long will it take to complete the construction?" Regan asked, already envisioning spending the next few months in the King David hotel spa.

"Starting tonight and using advanced construction techniques, the Temple can be rebuilt in seventy-two hours."

There was stunned silence for a few moments. Solly finally spoke up and said, "Well, that's a grand sight better than the time it took Solomon and Herod!

"How is that even possible with city permissions and code inspections? It would take months, even years in America!" Ty said.

"We already have our building permit, the Bible," Dr. Chavitz said nonchalantly. "As you know, the materials have all been manufactured and are stored underground only minutes away. Our team of engineers will be working around the clock." He paused and stared at the barren site, although in his mind he could already envision God's Temple back in its proper location. "Besides, *Yom Kippur* is less than a week away … the perfect time to rededicate the Temple."

63

ISIS Headquarters, Al-Raqqah, Syria

The Fox watched Al Jazeera's live feed of the Temple Mount on one of the multiple large flat screen televisions in his bunker. The camera showed an aerial view of the activity on the Northern Temple Mount. He could see eight heavy frontloading earthmovers scooping up huge portions of soil and carefully dumping them into massive dump trucks.

The Al Jazeera reporter said in Arabic, "It looks as if the Israelis are going to proceed with the construction of a Jewish Temple just north of what the Jordanians are calling the Peace Wall. We are baffled by the lack of resistance being given by the major Islamic nations to this intrusion. But we have also been informed that a new alliance has been formed and will be announced soon. We have not learned anything further about the identity of the members or the nature of the alliance."

The longer he watched, the angrier al-Bagahdi became. Ali, quietly reading a magazine, was the only other person in the bunker with him. Suddenly al-Bagahdi jumped up and unstrapped his Kalashnikov rifle. He aimed it at the televisions, screamed, and started firing. The televisions exploded in a spray of glass and metal. His rage-gauge was in the red. Ali quickly took cover to avoid being injured by flying debris or ricocheting bullets.

When the magazine was empty, the firing stopped, but al-Bagahdi continued screaming. He threw the weapon at the nearest demolished television, turned to Ali and yelled, "Get to your feet!" Ali stood up and carefully brushed the dust from his expensive slacks.

The Fox's eyes glowed with cold fury. "We were on our way to set up the Holy Caliphate, but now the Jewish pigs have changed our timetable. I was saving Jerusalem for later, but now I must change my plan. It will be our next target."

Ali knew that al-Bagahdi would never endure anyone questioning his strategy. He had seen other ISIS officers shot on the spot for disagreeing with the leader over something trivial. "Of course, sir. How can I help you with the attack? I know Jerusalem well."

Al-Bagahdi motioned for Ali to follow him out of the main room of the bunker to a locked iron gate down the hall. He punched a seven-digit code, swung the door open, and switched on an overhead light that illuminated a set of stairs. Ali followed the Fox down the steep steps into a deeper bunker that Ali had not even known existed. At the bottom of the stairs he arrived at a huge walk-in vault with two separate tumblers. Positioning his body to obscure the combination, the Fox entered the right combination of numbers on both dials. He swung a huge steel bar up to the right and pushed opened the door on silent hinges. Ali noticed that the lights in the safe came on automatically and that the air was climate-controlled. He expected to find money, drugs, or gold stores, but instead there was a single storage box about the size of a large trunk with handles on the sides. He waited for the Fox to speak.

Al-Bagahdi unlocked the thick clasps on the side of the box and lifted the lid on its hinges. Inside the box Ali saw a green cylinder less than four feet in length. The circumference was larger on one end than the other. The larger end gave the appearance of an oddly shaped mushroom head. Ali noticed two round holes in the bottom of the smaller end of the cylinder.

Al-Bagahdi smiled as he turned to Ali and asked, "Do you have any idea what this is?"

Ali shook his head, afraid to give the wrong answer.

"This, my friend, is a nuclear bomb."

"I've never seen a bomb that small. Where did you get it?"

"It was made in the good ol' U.S.A. before it was stolen from the U.S. years ago by Soviet agents. I was able to buy it from my explosives expert in Chechnya. He is the man who taught the heroic martyr how to make the bombs used in Boston."

He pointed to the device with the same pride of a horse breeder pointing to his prime thoroughbred. This is an American-made Mk-54 SADM, which stands for Small Atomic Demolition Munition. It was manufactured in the early 1960s, but my expert assures me that it is still lethal. The explosion is equivalent to sixty tons of TNT, but the most devastating effect is the nuclear radiation."

"You mean a dirty bomb?" Ali asked.

"That's exactly what I mean. I had been planning on detonating this on American soil, but now the Jews have forced our hand."

64

THREE DAYS LATER
Northern Half of the Temple Mount, Jerusalem

Three days later David Shvaz led Solly, Ty, and Regan onto the Temple Mount through the renovated northern entrance. They were stunned by what they saw. The Third Jewish Temple gleamed in the bright sunlight. The wall surrounding the Holy of Holies and Most Holy Place was about seven feet tall and was made of the off-white Jerusalem limestone that was prevalent throughout the city. The Eastern Gate was open, leading straight into an area designated as the court of the priests. But what drew their gaze the most was the splendor of the Temple that rose from within the small wall. Its brilliant white marble featured a row of thin translucent alabaster lining the top of the building. Although the footprint of the Temple was rather small, its soaring sixty-foot scale made it appear as a miniature skyscraper.

Regan was the first to speak. "It's beautiful!" she blurted out. "I never imagined that it would be so white."

"Not many people know this," David said, "but starting

in 1967 the building code for all new construction in Jerusalem required the use of off-white Jerusalem limestone. Of course, this was in anticipation of the day the Temple would be rebuilt—the only building in Jerusalem of pure white marble."

"And I thought that the Jerusalem limestone you see everywhere *was* white!" exclaimed Ty. "But compared to the Temple, it's like looking at a white horse after a snowfall. You realize that the horse wasn't that white!"

"This is brilliant, just brilliant!" Solly said in his melodious Australian tongue. "And I'm not just talking about the luster on the Temple. It is simply brilliant how your people designed and built this in only three days."

David shrugged and said, "Dr. Chavitz deserves the credit. He had every step of the construction pre-planned." He explained that workmen had been training for months on the construction process, laboring around the clock to shorten each task to the closest minute and even the nearest second. While one team was performing a job, the next two teams figured out a way to overlap their work so there was no lost time.

Regan was dumbfounded. She felt she might be standing inside a historic moment on the cover of *Time Magazine*. She told Solly that she was picturing Jesus standing nearby two thousand years ago saying, "Destroy this Temple, and I will build it back in three days."

"People thought He was speaking literally when He was predicting His resurrection," she said. "But the Jews have now literally fulfilled His statement."

Solly shook his head in amazement. "Regan, you're right. I never thought of that until now."

Ty wanted to shift the subject away from Jesus. He turned to David and asked, "What's going on north of the Temple?"

David replied, "That's where the contractors are working on the Hall of Hewn Stones. It is a wing of the Temple that will be the future meeting place of the reconvened Jewish Sanhedrin. As you can see, its exterior is also Jerusalem limestone. The interior will provide comfortable working accommodations for the rabbis and their assistants, as well as use the latest technology including high-speed Internet ports and video-conferencing capability. Because of the extensive wiring, it will take a few more days to complete."

Solly asked, "So what's left to do?"

"The Sanhedrin elected the new High Priest yesterday, Chief Rabbi Yitzak Rabin. You remember him," David replied.

Solly remembered being rebuffed by Rabbi Rabin on more than one occasion. "Yes, I remember him. It sounds like it's all coming together. But I never got to ask a question that's been bugging me since my first meeting about the Jerusalem Protocol."

"What's that?" David asked.

"Why now? I know you've had these plans to rebuild the Temple for years, but I'm curious about the timing."

"The short answer is ISIS," David replied. "The longer answer is that our government was waiting for a time when our neighboring countries would be so distracted by another common enemy that they would be reluctant to divert resources to oppose our efforts. You've heard the old proverb, 'The enemy of my enemy is my friend.' What we did not anticipate is that not only would we have a new Temple but also a new alliance with countries who were formerly our enemies."

Solly silently mused how David seemed to know more about the cryptic alliance King Mashallah referred to in his press release. If David was part of the inner circle of MEPA, what else must he know? Solly wasn't entirely convinced he would ever find out.

"No wonder it's so quiet here," Ty said. "There are Muslim protests going on all around the world but hardly a peep from them here, aside from the initial violence. I guess going nose-to-nose with the armed IDF shut that down. But what happened to all the news helicopters flying around the city a few days ago?"

"We've closed the border between Israel and the West Bank," David replied. "Three rings of defensive IDF forces now surround the Old City. The Palestinians are still waiting for military help from their friends before they attack. They may be waiting a long time. Also, our government made the entire city a no-fly zone. Now only designated military and medical aircraft have clearance over Jerusalem. The news networks are still here, as you can tell by all the satellite trucks parked around the city. But the Temple Mount itself is off limits to the press."

David continued, "Strangely, the most recent and most vocal resistance we've encountered are the protests led by PETA, Greenpeace, and ASPCA."

"You're kidding," Regan said.

"Oh, no," David replied. "They are violently opposed to the idea of sacrificing animals for worship. We have assured them that the sacrificial animals will be handled with respect and that the meat will be cooked and distributed to the priests and the needy citizens of Jerusalem. Still, that rationale doesn't appease them."

Satisfied with David's answers, Solly asked one more question. "So when will the priests begin their work?"

"High Priest Rabin is scheduled tomorrow to perform the purification process using the ashes of the red heifer. The first scheduled sacrifice is for *Yom Kippur*, the Day of Atonement, which is less than a week away. That's also the day that Walid Obeidat, now the General Secretary of MEPA, will formally announce the new alliance mentioned in the King's press release."

Solly tempered the euphoria over what was happening on the Temple Mount with a nagging suspicion. There was some remaining detail teasing his mind that something about this entire picture wasn't completely kosher.

65

ISIS Headquarters, Al-Raqqah, Syria

Al-Bagahdi began to lay out his dirty bomb strategy with Ali and another trusted ISIS warrior named Fatih Nagi. Fatih, whose name means "conqueror," had volunteered months earlier to be a suicide bomber. Since then he had lived in luxury and been treated like a celebrity by other members of ISIS.

"We will load the device under the cargo area of an *Al-Furqan* satellite television truck," the Fox explained. "Fatih, you will be the driver. Ali, you will go with him. We have obtained fake Jordanian passports and press credentials for both of you. You will drive into Jordan at night through a checkpoint where we have already bribed the crossing guard to let you through. Then the next morning you will cross into Israel by way of the King Hussein Bridge. Do not attempt to bribe the Israelis. Just use your credentials to get you through. And pray that they won't dismantle the entire truck upon inspection! When you arrive in Jericho, we have friends there who will allow you to hide the vehicle under a covered garage."

Al-Bagahdi looked at Ali and said, "You are too valuable to me as CEO of *Al-Furqan* to risk losing you. In Jericho your only responsibility will be to arm the device by inserting two blasting rods into the slots in the bottom of the bomb. Then you'll be provided a ride back through Jordan to return to our base here. Fatih will join with another warrior named Jalal Zaman in Jericho, and together they will make the twenty-minute drive up to Jerusalem. They must time their arrival so that the bomb detonates at noon."

Ali nodded his head and noticed he was sweating through his tailored shirt. He was relieved because he was no longer certain he was willing to die for this man as the leader of the Caliphate. As he removed his silk handkerchief to wipe his brow, the thought even occurred to him that he would be a much better leader of the Caliphate. Where he once thought Al-Bagahdi was crazy like a fox, Ali feared he was really losing it now.

Fatih had expected to strap an explosive belt around his body to attack his target. But once he learned of the scope of his new assignment, he beamed with pride thinking about the greater reward he would receive in Paradise. His name would be honored throughout the Muslim world, and his family would be revered for their sacrifice.

"Fatih, don't worry about the bomb accidentally detonating before you reach Jerusalem," the Fox said. "It is safe until the two blasting rods are inserted. There are also two separate plunger triggers that must be pressed simultaneously."

Fatih nodded that he understood.

"You'll have one plunger and Jalal will have the other," he explained. "The GPS will take you to a road in Jerusalem that runs just east of the Temple Mount. The waypoint for you to detonate has been pre-programmed. Stop immediately when the GPS indicates that you have reached your destination, and arm the bomb. The blast will destroy everything on the Temple Mount, including the hated Western Wall. Also the churches of the infidels on the Mount of Olives will be obliterated. The radiation fallout will kill thousands, and Jerusalem will soon be a nuclear wasteland. It will be uninhabitable for years. This, my friend, will be the greatest act of *jihad* in history! Allah be with you!"

"*Allah hu akbar!*" said Fatih.

"*Allah hu akbar!*" al-Bagahdi and Ali shouted in return.

"Before you depart I want you to record a video message from me claiming responsibility for this act," the Fox said to Ali. "Then I want you to load it on all of our social and media platforms so that it will be released five minutes after the blast. That way the world will know without a doubt that Abu Bakr al-Bagahdi planned and carried out this glorious act of *jihad* for Allah."

Ali pulled out his cell phone and punched in the speed dial for his videographer. "Ahmad, prepare the television studio immediately." Although it pained him to feign respect for a man he now considered insane, Ali knew his life was at risk until the Fox was out of the picture. He added, "Our great leader is coming to tape an important announcement."

Ahmad Karim had worked as the chief videographer for Ali and *Al-Furqan* for the past eighteen months. Filming recruitment videos was his only responsibility for ISIS. He stayed on call and lived in a small apartment attached to the modern television studio. With computerized controls, it was a one-man operation. He controlled the lighting and sound and did all the editing for the ISIS propaganda videos. Born in Nazareth, he was an Israeli citizen. He grew up planning to become a Muslim cleric. However, as a teenager he demonstrated an amazing aptitude as a computer programmer and hacker. Once he entered the shadowy underworld of cyberspace, he lost all interest in being a cleric.

When he was eighteen years old, he grew bored of hacking into corporate computer systems. One night he tried to hack into something more challenging—the *Mossad* computer system. He was good, but not good enough. After he penetrated several levels of their firewalls, he lost track of time trying to get through the next layer of security. Before he realized it morning had come. That's when he heard pounding on his family's front door.

When his father opened the door, Israeli policemen immediately arrested Ahmad. He was convicted of computer crimes and spent three years in an Israeli prison. *Mossad* had secretly recruited him in prison to work for them. They recognized his exceptional computer skills and trained him to join ISIS as a mole.

His senior *Mossad* handler was Solly. Ahmad used the double-encrypted Confide app to communicate with *Mossad.* Solly had warned Ahmad to only use it if he had valuable Intel.

To create his cover Ahmad had received credentials and a birth certificate indicating he was an Iraqi citizen. He had memorized all of the carefully crafted details of how he grew up and when he attended school in Baghdad. Solly and other *Mossad* officers briefed him numerous times about his backstory until he could recite the slightest nuance when questioned. Under *Mossad's* direction Ahmad moved to Baghdad and started following ISIS social media sites. He was soon communicating with Ali, who proposed that his technical skills could help ISIS. After six months of contact, all the while spouting the poisoned ISIS rhetoric, he had been hired. Since that time Ahmad had carefully protected his true identity, waiting for a breakthrough of important intelligence. This seemed to be his opportunity.

66

The King David Hotel, Jerusalem

Regan had invited Leah Dayan to her hotel suite to finish their earlier conversation about faith. Solly and Ty joined them in the sitting area where they were enjoying soft drinks and snacks.

Leah looked around the room. "Wow," she commented. "This is a nice suite in the nicest hotel in Jerusalem. I like your style."

Ty snickered and said, "Don't let her fool you, Leah. She makes a lot of money without doing a lot of work."

Regan cut her eyes at Ty and retorted, "He doesn't know what he's talking about, as usual. Actually, Solly's employer has graciously provided our lodging."

Leah asked, "Who's your employer, Solly?"

Solly smiled and stroked his beard. "I could tell you, but then I'd have to kill you."

"It's one of those 'need-to-know' kind of things. He enjoys being a man of mystery." Regan paused and took a sip of her soft drink. "Leah, I enjoyed talking about religion with you the other day. Tell me some more about growing up Jewish."

"As I mentioned, growing up at the *Ein Gedi* kibbutz, we weren't a religious family. At my *bat mitzvah* I read some of the Torah. But that was just a rite of passage for the young people at the kibbutz. I haven't read much of the Scriptures since then."

Regan nodded and smiled, encouraging her to go on.

Leah drew a breath. "I like my job, but I don't know. Something seems to be missing. I can't quite put my finger on it. I'm sure you've felt like that before."

"There's a longing in that girl that all the scientific knowledge in the world just can't fill," Regan thought.

"I know the feeling exactly, Leah," Solly offered. "When I first came to Israel as a young man, I was basically an agnostic. But a professor of Hebrew archeology mentored me and got me interested in the Scriptures. He was the most brilliant man I've ever known. He wouldn't label himself a Christian, but he believed that Jesus of Nazareth was the Jewish Messiah. As I was learning Hebrew, he would have me read an Old Testament prophecy about the Messiah, and then he would read the fulfillment of that prophecy from the New Testament. It took many months, but he convinced me to put my faith in Jesus as the Messiah and as my Savior. I shared some of these prophecies with Ty last year, but he's still a skeptic."

Ty rolled his eyes dramatically and Leah giggled.

"That's because Ty is just hard-headed," added Regan. "He likes coming across as the bad boy, but I know that he's a softy at heart. Besides, I'm convinced he will believe sometime."

For once Ty chose not to draw his verbal sword and parry with Regan. He just sat back and stayed quiet.

"You have me curious at this point," Leah said to Regan's surprise. "What prophecies are you talking about?"

Solly pulled out his phone and called up his Bible app. He said, "Regan, you have the list of Messianic prophecies I sent you. Why don't I read the Old Testament prediction, and then you read the New Testament fulfillment?"

Regan removed her phone from her purse and activated her Bible app. "Sounds good. Let's do it."

Solly read, "*Therefore the Lord himself will give you a sign: The virgin will conceive and give birth to a son, and will call him Immanuel.* That's from Isaiah 7:14. As you know, Emmanuel means, 'God with us.'"

Regan touched her screen to scroll down to Luke 1. She began to read about how God sent the angel Gabriel to tell a virgin named Mary that she would give birth to a son.

She continued, "*How will this be,*" Mary asked the angel, "*since I am a virgin?*"

The angel answered, "*The Holy Spirit will come on you, and the power of the Most High will overshadow you. So the holy one to be born will be called the Son of God.*"

Leah raised her eyebrows. "So I suppose a virgin having a baby would be a pretty unique sign. Do you really believe the whole virgin birth claim?"

Solly and Regan answered together, "I do."

They laughed.

"This *isn't* a marriage ceremony, by the way," Regan said.

"Here's another one," said Solly. He scrolled down his phone to find Micah 5:2. He read, *"But you, Bethlehem Ephrathah, though you are small among the clans of Judah, out of you will come for me one who will be ruler over Israel, whose origins are from of old, from ancient times."*

As Regan scrolled down her phone, Leah said, "No need to read that one. Even I know that Jesus was born in Bethlehem. I know the whole Christmas story. That's two. What's next?"

Over the next hour Solly and Regan read thirty-three more predictions that Jesus fulfilled precisely. Leah listened intently.

"So you're really not making this up? That's really in the Bible?" she asked incredulously. "Couldn't Jesus have just read those predictions and set out to fulfill them?"

Solly said, "Sure. But we also read about how He would be betrayed by a friend for thirty pieces of silver. How could He control that? We read that His executioners would gamble for His clothing when He was stretched out with His hands and feet pierced. How could He have predetermined that?"

"But throughout history there have been dozens of men who claimed they were the Messiah," Leah objected.

"That's true, but only Jesus fulfilled every Old Testament prophecy," said Regan.

"Think about this. Nobody ever produced His corpse after He was crucified," Solly added. "And hundreds of eyewitnesses went to their tortured deaths insisting they had seen the risen Christ. People don't die for a lie."

Leah's face darkened. "Now, that's where you're wrong, Solly. Muslim suicide bombers are dying for a lie every day at an alarming rate."

"I stand corrected. Those terrorists are dying on behalf of an entire false system that teaches hatred and violence against infidels. Compare that to the message of love that Jesus proclaimed."

Leah seemed confused. "I guess you're right. I don't know much about what Jesus taught. But you sure have me thinking."

Solly loved a teachable moment and appreciated Leah's interest in the subject. He suggested they take another approach. "Let's imagine that you were climbing in those caves near *Ein Gedi* and found an undiscovered clay jar containing a papyrus scroll. And when you read it, you found that it was carbon dated to 1,300 CE, seven hundred years ago. Upon further research you learn that some Jewish mystic who lived alone in the desert had penned it. It contained a prediction that in 1950 a boy would be born in Singapore to Jewish parents. His parents would name him Solomon. As a boy he would move to Sydney, and as a teenager he would excel in debating. He would also come to doubt the whole Holocaust story until he met some Holocaust survivors. Then he would move to Israel where he would become an archeological tour guide and have a long white beard and wear a Stetson cowboy hat."

Leah laughed. "That's you, Solly!"

Solly joined in with a chuckle. "Exactly. There are almost seven billion people on this planet, but I'm the *only* one who could fulfill those twelve detailed predictions. And that's just a dozen details. There are at least sixty detailed predictions about the Messiah that Jesus fulfilled. To me, that is convincing proof."

Leah was silent as she pondered these ideas. "The scientist in me wants to pull out my calculator and figure up the random odds of that happening by chance."

"You don't have to do that because it's already been done," Solly said. He explained that Dr. Peter Stoner was a scientist and mathematician at a secular college in California. He computed the odds of one person fulfilling just eight predictions. He estimated that eighty-eight billion people have lived on earth since these prophecies were written.

"The odds of one person randomly fulfilling just eight predictions is 1 in 100 quadrillion," Solly explained. "That's a 1 followed by 17 zeroes! And the odds increase exponentially as you increase the number of prophecies."

"Those are numbers I can't comprehend," Leah said. "It sounds like astronomical odds of it happening randomly."

Solly smiled. "As a scientist, I'm sure you've heard of Occam's Razor."

"I was just thinking about that actually," Leah said.

"Well then you know Occam's Razor was proposed by a Franciscan Friar named William of Ockham," Solly added for Ty and Regan's benefit. "It's often used by scientists to develop the most likely theoretical models. As a scientist, how would you apply Occam's Razor to what we have been talking about?"

Leah was quiet for a moment and thought through her answer. "Well, to paraphrase Occam's razor, *'The simplest explanation is usually the correct one.'* In this case the simplest explanation of these overwhelming odds is that Jesus did fulfill many Old Testament prophecies."

Regan wanted to add a personal note to the argument. "Logic is nice," she began, "but the bottom line is this. I don't believe in Jesus because of the prophecies being fulfilled. Those only increase my confidence in my faith. I believe because I learned that God loves me. Then I learned that my personal sin separated me from enjoying the benefits of God's love. Jesus said, 'God so loved the world that he gave his one and only Son, and that whoever believes in him would never perish but have eternal life.' I learned that the consequences of my sin would earn me eternal separation from God, but God offered me the free gift of eternal life. When I was a teenager, I put my trust in Jesus and I've been following him ever since then. My life isn't perfect, but I have a perfect peace knowing that God has forgiven me and gives me strength and purpose to live every day."

Leah was quiet. She quickly wiped away a tear that was slowly falling down her cheek. "I'm sorry. I don't know why I'm crying. But what you just described is what I think I've been looking for. How can I have what you have?"

Solly took Leah's hand and said softly, "Faith to believe

is a gift that God gives us. The Bible says, 'For as many as received Jesus, to them he gives the power to become a child of God.'"

Leah said, "That's what I want. How can I do that?"

"Why don't you just talk to God and tell Him what you want in your own words?" Regan suggested. "It helps if you will pray the words aloud."

Leah was silent for a long time. Finally she closed her eyes, bowed her head, and said, "God, I don't know how to say this, but I believe in you. And I believe in Jesus. I want my life to be different. I need your strength. Help me, God. Please, help me."

Regan slipped over and put her arm around Leah. "That was a beautiful prayer. God heard every word. You may not see fireworks or have chills up your spine, but this is the first step of a new direction for your life. And we'll be here to help you. The main thing that identifies followers of Jesus is that we really love each other."

Solly's cell phone rang just then and he excused himself to take the call outside. Regan and Leah spent a few more minutes talking about what Leah could do to grow in her faith. Soon everyone called it a night. After Leah left, Solly and Regan broke into huge smiles. "Great job, Solly. You really know your Bible prophecy! I think she just took her first step of faith!" Regan said.

In the excitement neither of them noticed Ty was still seated in his chair with his head bowed. When Regan glanced at him she assumed that he had fallen asleep.

PART 6

67

**Al-Furqan Television Studio,
ISIS Headquarters, *al-Raqqah*, Syria**

Ahmad rushed around to set up the studio for the
arrival of Ali and al-Bagahdi. He didn't have to wait
long. The Fox came storming through the door with Ali
following. He walked over to the familiar spot with an "X"
taped on the floor and said impatiently, "Ali, let's get this
done quickly! You and Fatih must leave tonight."

Ali turned to Ahmad. "Is everything ready to roll?"

Ahmad gave him a thumbs-up sign. Ali started the
countdown and pointed to al-Bagahdi. He looked sinister
in his black military outfit and his checkered *keffiyeh*. He
had wrapped it around his head, obscuring the bottom part
of his face.

The Fox began to speak slowly, "With all praise to the
most benevolent and merciful Allah, and with loyalty to

His final Prophet, Mohammed (Peace be Upon Him), I am the Caliph of Allah. I have been called to establish the global Islamic State. Allah has called me to bring a swift death to the infidels. This includes all Christians, Jews, Buddhists, Hindus, and even false Muslims who have forsaken the pathway of Allah revealed in the *Qur'an*. Allah has appointed me to destroy all the temples, shrines, and idols that infidels worship."

He stared into the camera a few seconds before speaking again. His voice grew in volume and intensity. "By the time you view this video, the whole world will already know of our unlimited power to strike wherever we wish. At noon today the Islamic State detonated an American-made nuclear bomb in Jerusalem. I'm recording this beforehand so that there will be no question that the Islamic State is claiming responsibility for this act of glorious *jihad*! *Allah hu akbar*!"

He paused again, and Ali directed Ahmad to zoom in on the face of al-Bagahdi. As the lens trained even closer on the Fox, he made a surprising move. He removed the *keffiyeh* from the bottom of his face, revealing his full beard and a wicked smile. He pointed toward the camera and said, "And America, you are next. We are coming for you. There is nowhere you can hide from our *jihad*. Convert to Islam, or die!" He continued to stare menacingly at the camera until Ali signaled Ahmad to fade to black and end the recording.

The Fox stormed out of the studio in a flash and said over his shoulder, "Ali, instruct your man on exactly when to launch that video. The timing must be perfect. No mistakes!"

Ahmad waited a few seconds to make sure they were alone. "Is he really going to do this?" he asked his boss.

Ali grimaced. "He is. And I'm going to be riding in the *Al-Furqan* satellite television truck where the device is hidden."

Ahmad was astonished. "Ali, where did the Fox get an American-made nuclear device? I never pictured you as a suicide bomber. I thought you were too valuable to the Fox and ISIS to die."

Ali let out a nervous laugh, "Yeah, and I'm glad the Fox agrees with you. I'm just riding as far as Jericho. That's where I'll arm the device, and Fatih and another fighter will drive it to Jerusalem to detonate it. By then I'm going to be as far away from that area as possible! From what the Fox told me, years ago the Russians stole the bomb from the U.S., and the Chechens in Eastern Europe stole it from the Russians. The initial explosion will be small, destroying everything within five kilometers, but the radiation will be the real killer. The Fox has chosen to create the explosion at exactly noon tomorrow on *Yom Kippur*, the Jewish holy day."

Ahmad was working hard to memorize all of these details to relay to Solly later.

"We're leaving *al-Raqqah* immediately," Ali continued. "It's critical that you launch the video at precisely five minutes after noon tomorrow. I predict that it will become the most famous video footage of history. Your work will be more exalted than the videos of our brothers flying jets into the World Trade Towers."

Ahmad tried to hide his nerves and keep Ali talking. "But aren't you afraid that the bomb might accidentally explode before you get to Jericho?"

"Yes, I'm afraid! But our explosives expert has told us that the American-made dirty bomb is harmless until the two blasting rods are inserted. Plus, there must be two simultaneous detonations of the rods for the bomb to explode."

Ali turned to leave. "You have your instructions. Follow them exactly. After this we must relocate or dig some deeper bunkers for all of us. The payback from Israel and the U.S. is going to be devastating."

Ali left the studio. Ahmad realized that getting in touch with Solly about this information would likely lead to his discovery and possible death. However, when he was certain he was alone, he retrieved a throwaway cell phone that he had been hiding for months.

He entered Solly's Confide address and quickly punched in the most important text message he would ever send. As he typed, a plan began formulating in his mind to escape tonight after loading the video to automatically play thirty minutes before noon tomorrow. If the Israelis failed to stop the truck, at least they would have a few minutes' warning. He kept a dirt bike hidden in one of the storerooms for this very moment when he might need to escape. *"By the time the video plays,"* he thought, *"I should be hidden in the Mossad safe house in Baghdad if I can make it in time."*

68

King David Hotel, Jerusalem

As the sun set that afternoon, *Yom Kippur* officially began. With the establishment of the Third Temple, word had spread throughout Jerusalem that this would be the most important Day of Atonement in two thousand years. Not long after sunset Solly's cell phone chimed. He had a Confide message from a number that he immediately recognized. Knowing that the text message would disappear as soon as he read it, he opened his voice memo app and recorded the message as he read it aloud. The Confide message read:

```
ISIS will explode a small dirty nuclear
device at noon tomorrow near Temple
Mount. Device hidden in Al-Furqan TV
truck arriving at Jericho in morning. Ali
will arm it there and evacuate back to
al-Raqqah base. The Fox recorded video
claiming responsibility with instructions
to post after explosion. Instead I will
post video at 1130. Cover soon blown.
Leaving for Baghdad tonight.
```

Solly's mind reeled as he considered the impact of Ahmad's information. He played back the voice memo to make sure he had the details memorized. His first call was on an encrypted line to his boss, Asher.

"Boss, our deep cover in ISIS just reported al-Bagahdi has a nuclear device that he is planning on detonating at noon tomorrow on *Yom Kippur* near the Temple Mount. It's hidden in an *Al-Furqan* television truck that is arriving in Jericho tomorrow morning."

There was silence for a few seconds until Asher said, "I would say you are kidding, but I know you would never kid about something like that. We have time to stop it. If it were just explosives, we could find the truck and bomb it to hell before it gets close to Israel. But nuclear—that's another matter."

"Right," agreed Solly. "We don't have clearance for our jets to fly in Syria or Jordan. And we don't want to wait until it's in Israel to risk detonation. Just when we have the trust of some our Muslim neighbors, we can't be responsible for the first atomic bomb exploding in the Middle East. We've got to handle this carefully. We must stop the attack, but you don't use a hammer to crack a fragile egg."

Asher paused. "Solly, you're the senior agent on the ground. What do you have in mind?"

"I don't have it all figured out yet, but, with your approval, by morning my friends and I will work out a plan to take out the truck and its occupants without blowing up half of this region."

"This decision is above my pay grade. I'll have to talk to Prime Minister Abrams. But we can't let this circle get too large because we suspect ISIS may have a mole or two in our government."

Solly, "I agree. If ISIS gets a whiff that we are on to their plan, they will certainly change it. Talk to Abrams and see what he says."

Thirty minutes later Solly's phone rang. "What did Abrams say?"

"He was mad, as anticipated. He wanted to find the truck and bomb it to shreds. But Ziv was with him, and they finally agreed to give you until the morning to come up with a Plan B. If we don't like your plan, we're using the hammer." The line went dead. Solly opened the Confide app and texted Ty:

```
Grab Regan and meet me in my room ASAP.
```

Five minutes later they joined him, and he gave them an update. "We've got to come up with a plan to stop them," he said, "without detonating the bomb ourselves and without the suicide bombers detonating it early at the slightest suspicion that they are discovered. I can't discuss why, but this cannot be a military operation. It's up to us."

Over the next three hours the trio floated dozens of ideas. Most of them were eliminated after they were discussed in depth. It was long after midnight when Ty and Regan returned to their rooms. They would be able to grab only a few hours of sleep before they presented their plan to the Prime Minister.

69

Jericho, West Bank, Israel

Ali and Fatih had taken turns driving through the night. Each had grabbed short snatches of sleep when they weren't driving. It had taken them over eight hours to drive from *al-Raqqah* to Jordan. They had stopped only to refuel with gasoline and coffee. They didn't have any trouble crossing the border into Jordan because of the guard who had pocketed a generous bribe from ISIS. There were more questions at the border between Jordan and Israel after they crossed the King Hussein Bridge. Their Jordanian credentials were impeccable. After an agonizing thirty-minute wait they were finally cleared to enter Israel. The crossing guards had briefly examined the television equipment in the back of the truck, but everything was legitimate. Ali was glad there were no Geiger counters or bomb sniffing dogs at the border.

After entering Israel it was only a short forty-five-minute drive to Jericho. They arrived just as the sun was rising above the ancient hills of Moab on the eastern shore of the Dead Sea. Their pre-programmed GPS took them toward the oldest section of Jericho to a large automotive repair shop with a massive garage. As soon as they drove in the garage, the overhead door lowered behind them.

Four men dressed in the traditional ISIS uniform of black combat fatigues greeted Ali and Fatih. They all had their AK-47s drawn and were ready for any threat. When the truck stopped, they raised their guns over their heads and greeted them with a hearty, "*Allah hu akbar!*"

Ali climbed out of the passenger seat and noticed the four guards were barely eighteen years of age, if that. He said wearily, "All of you, just settle down and shut up! We need a few hours' sleep and a hot meal, so save the victory shouts for later."

The four young jihadists were disappointed. They lowered their weapons and sheepishly pointed their important guests to sleeping quarters behind the garage.

Three hours later Ali and Fatih were digging into plates full of hummus, roasted pita bread, falafel filled with scrambled eggs, and roasted lamb while downing cups of strong, sweet Arabic coffee. Ali wondered if Fatih was thinking about this being his last meal.

Ali was postponing arming the bomb as long as he could. He was fearful that he would do something wrong and be vaporized on the spot. The thought turned his stomach sour. It was only a twenty-minute drive up to Jerusalem, but he wanted to arm the bomb and evacuate as early as possible.

At 900 hours he turned to Fatih and said, "Let's do this."

When they entered the garage, there was only one man there. He was dressed in Western clothes to fit his role as a television technician. He held out his hand to Ali and said, "My name is Jalal Zaman. I am honored to carry out this glorious *jihad* against the infidels. Al-Bagahdi has cleared me to join Fatih."

Ali took his hand and said, "Congratulations, Jalal. You and Fatih will be honored as the greatest martyrs in all of Islam." But he was really thinking, *"Better you than me."*

Fatih raised the back door of the truck. He and Jalal climbed in and moved aside some of the television equipment. Fatih used a cordless drill to remove the nuts securing the door to a hidden compartment. Once the cover was removed, they carefully raised the storage box containing the Mk-54 SADM dirty bomb. They unlocked the clasps and opened the lid.

Ali used the drill to remove the back of what appeared to be a video-editing console. He carefully removed a thin metal case from inside the console and gently opened it to reveal two long blasting rods designed to fit into the slots in the bottom section of the bomb. He realized he was sweating again and his hands were shaking.

Ali carefully removed one of the rods. It was made of dark metal, about two-feet long and thicker than his thumb. It had a silver tip that would be inserted first. It was also surprisingly heavy. He took the rod and gently inserted it into one of the holes according to the arrows painted on the rods. Then he repeated the process with the other rod. He was so scared by this point that he felt nauseated, expecting to be engulfed in a blinding flash at any second.

But when he finished inserting both rods, he was still there. He carefully closed the case. Fatih and Jalal closed the cover and lowered the bomb back into the hidden compartment. Jalal used the drill to replace the bolts for the cover. Then they moved heavy cases of video equipment to cover the hidden payload.

Ali removed another small case from the inside of the video-editing console. He opened it and removed two detonators that had been disguised to appear as felt tip markers. He handed them to Fatih and Jalal.

"Now listen carefully," he told them. "These are small transmitters, each tuned to the frequency of one of the blasting rods. To detonate the bomb you must twist the cap of a marker clockwise one full turn until it stops. Then you just push down on the cap of the marker at the same moment."

He produced two real markers for them to use for practice. He handed one to each of them. "Don't worry. These aren't detonators. Pull off the cap and you'll see."

Both men were sweating profusely through their clothing, their pungent body odor filling Ali's nostrils. The young men removed the caps to confirm the felt tip of the black markers.

"Both of you twist the cap one full turn."

They followed his instructions.

"Now I'm going to count it down. Three, two, one, push!"

Fatih and Jalal successfully pressed on the tops of the pens at the same time.

Ai said, "That's good."

Fatih smiled as he thought about the glory and fame that would be his when they really detonated the bomb in just a little while.

Ali looked at his watch and said, "I'm leaving. Stay here until 1130 hours, and then drive slowly up to Jerusalem. It's important to time the explosion at exactly noon. You can't take any cell phones that might be traced. Once you start your trip, don't carry any identifying papers. You will be out of contact with any of our leadership. You must complete your mission at Jerusalem, or die in your effort. If you are prevented from reaching the Temple Mount, detonate the bomb wherever you are. You cannot be captured."

70

The Third Jewish Temple, Jerusalem

On the morning of *Yom Kippur* the Jewish nation fulfilled a two-thousand-year-old dream. They had a Temple again. Today would be the first day of ritual sacrifice since the Romans destroyed the Temple in 70 CE.

High Priest Rabin was not an emotional man, but he couldn't hold back the tears as his fellow trained *Cohen*— special priests—dressed him in the High Priest's clothing. The Temple Institute craftsmen had carefully recreated the unique garment according to the description provided in Exodus 28.

Over a white robe the High Priest wore a garment called an ephod. It was made of fine linen with gold, blue, purple, and scarlet and was worn on both the front and back of the body like a breastplate made in two parts. These parts were clasped together over the shoulder by two onyx stones set in gold. Each of these onyx stones was engraved with the names of the twelve tribes of Israel—six on one side and six on the other. Every time the High Priest entered the Holy Place, he symbolically bore the names of all the Israelites before the Lord.

The Hall of Hewn Stones had been completed as a wing adjoining the Temple. The members of the Jewish Sanhedrin were seated and already in session. Invited guests packed the courtyard around the new Temple. With its small footprint there was only room for around three hundred Jewish men in this area called the court of the Israelites, as described in the Old Testament. A short fence protecting a narrow area had been designated as the court of the women. There was not yet an area designated for the court of the Gentiles.

The invitees included a Who's Who of prominent Jews from around the world. Many wealthy Jews in the U.S. had contributed large sums of money to the Temple Institute, and they were in attendance. Israeli leaders from the government, education, science, and the arts had also been invited. Some of the American Jews had joked that a ticket to the day's event was harder to obtain than a skybox at a Super Bowl.

Forty *Cohen* followed a carefully choreographed ceremony for *Yom Kippur* following the precise directions from Scripture. They led two identical male lambs toward the brazen altar. One ram would be sacrificed, while the other would be allowed to live. This was called the "scapegoat." The High Priest would place his hands on the head of the scapegoat, symbolically transferring the sins of Israel onto the animal. A priest would then transport the ram far into the wilderness outside of Jerusalem to symbolically "carry away" Israel's sins.

While High Priest Rabin lifted his hands and offered a prayer in Hebrew, another priest gently cut a small incision in the neck of one of the rams. Another priest stood by with a silver bowl to catch the blood. When it was full, the remaining blood drained into the bare soil.

As he continued to pray in Hebrew, High Priest Rabin was given the branch of a hyssop tree. He dipped the branch into the bowl of blood and started slowly walking into the Most Holy Place. The priest holding the bowl of blood walked beside him, careful to catch any drops of blood that dripped from the branch. As he solemnly approached the curtain separating the Holy of Holies, a choir of priests began to sing several of the Psalms in beautiful Hebrew harmony. The air was electric as people realized they were witnessing the restoration of a tradition that was the central part of Jewish life thousands of years ago. This moment in history bore the weight of justifying the struggle of the Jews for millennia.

High Priest Rabin approached the curtain leading into the Holy of Holies. He was conscious of all the stories of High Priests who had died in the presence of the *Shekinah* glory. *"I wonder if I will be considered worthy?"* he thought. *"Will the Shekinah glory even be in there? There's only one way to find out."*

Two priests lifted the corner of the curtain, making sure not to look inside. Rabin nodded. One of the priests then tied a long silk rope to Rabin's ankle. Rabin silently prayed that they wouldn't have to pull his corpse from the Holy of Holies.

With a deep breath he entered the Holy of Holies while reciting aloud another prayer in Hebrew. The room was empty. He paused and used all his senses to detect anything different about this space. He didn't sense any Divine Presence. He didn't have any feelings of awe or wonder. Terror seized him suddenly, and he wondered if he was the right man to do this job.

He noticed a dim light filtered down from the thin alabaster windows at the top of the room. Rabin shook the hyssop branch in the place where the Ark of the Covenant would have been placed. The Talmud required that he remain in the Holy of Holies praying for three hours. There was no place to sit down, so he tried to be comfortable standing and then kneeling.

"I'm part of the most momentous event to take place in Jewish history in thousands of years," he kept telling himself. He and the hundreds of people gathered for this momentous *Yom Kippur* had no inkling that a madman in Syria had a plan in place to make this the worst day of their lives.

71

Jericho to Jerusalem Highway

Fatih had never made the trip from Jericho to Jerusalem, but Jalal had driven it many times. Jericho is located near the Dead Sea, the lowest point on earth, almost fourteen hundred feet below sea level. Jerusalem, less than twenty miles to the west, sits on several mountains at an elevation of two thousand five hundred feet above sea level. In the space of a few miles, drivers on the highway from Jericho to Jerusalem must climb almost four thousand feet in elevation.

Thankfully, the Israelis built a modern four-lane highway that twists its way through the Judean hills as it makes its way up to the Old City. Jalal was glad they did not have to drive along the old Jericho road that had been used since the time of the Romans. Parts of the old road that the modern highway replaced could still be seen at times snaking in and out of the hills and gullies.

They decided that Jalal would drive. At 1120 hours they backed the bomb-laden truck out of the garage and drove it carefully through the deserted streets of Jericho. Within five minutes they had reached the turn to the

highway to Jerusalem. This was their last chance to abort
the plan. They turned right and started uphill toward their
final destination.

After driving for only ten minutes they were more than
halfway to the city. Traffic was very light on *Yom Kippur*
because most of the Israelis were on holiday enjoying time
with their families.

Up ahead Jalal saw that the traffic was slowing down
to a crawl. "What is this?" he yelled. He pounded the dash
with his fist. "We can't be late! There is no room for error."

Fatih opened the passenger door and stood on the step
to see what was causing the delay. He saw that the highway
ahead was undergoing some construction. The pavement
was torn up and there was a big sign in Hebrew, Arabic,
and English that said, "ROAD WORK. DETOUR."

The other sign had an arrow pointing to the right. Fatih
could see the cars and buses taking the detour and re-
entering the highway about half-a-mile ahead. He climbed
back into the cab of the truck.

"It's okay. It's just a short delay. We have to drive around
this road construction." He looked at his watch. "We
should still make it on time."

Jalal turned the truck to the right at the detour sign
and bounced over the poorly paved temporary road that
was part of the old Jericho highway. Around the next bend
Jalal could see the line of traffic passed through a Bedouin
encampment scattered in the hills between Jericho and
Jerusalem. Jalal hated these nomads descended from Arab

and Syrian wanderers. "'Desert dwellers,' they call them," Jalal thought. "More like sewer rats."

For centuries the Bedouin had moved from place to place living in tents and herding goats and camels. Modern Bedouin in Israel no longer relocated. Instead of tents, they lived in more permanent shanties, although the occasional satellite dish was attached to some of their dwellings!

Several Bedouin men were approaching the slow-moving vehicles, holding up their jewelry and scarves and trying to make a quick sale. Some of the cars had stopped to shop and do business through the open windows. Most were ignoring the Bedouins. A tired camel stood nearby looking irritated at all the commotion. The Bedouin loved charging unwitting tourists to have their picture made while sitting on the smelly beast.

Jalal eased forward slowly.

Fatih yelled, "Let's go! Is there any way to drive around these cars?"

"No! This is a narrow one-lane road. The Bedouin have their tables set up too close to the edge. Just hang on. We'll be back on the main highway in a few minutes, and we can still make it in time."

Two stooped Bedouin men approached the television truck holding up fists full of jewelry. They donned worn out robes, and their filthy feet were contained in dirt-encrusted sandals that had seen better days. Faded *keffiyehs* covered their heads and faces so that only their eyes were visible. The older of the two approached the driver's side and yelled through the closed window in Arabic, "Please, you must buy my jewelry. My family is starving. I sell to you for good price! Please!"

Jalal ignored him. The man started tapping insistently on the glass.

Jalal shook his head and continued to ease the truck forward. The other Bedouin walked along the passenger side. He didn't speak, but he was holding up jewelry showing it to Fatih. Fatih was waving him away when he noticed something strange. He could only see the eyes of the Bedouin, but they were an icy blue.

"What's going on?" he wondered.

At that moment an old Bedouin woman covered from head to toe in the traditional black robe and head covering limped in the front of the truck and stopped. She held up a handful of beads while she pounded her other hand on the hood.

Jalal stomped on the brakes, slammed the truck in park, and was going to blow his horn at the haggard woman. But before his hand reached the horn, the woman dropped to the ground in front of the truck. At the same moment the two Bedouin men whipped out Uzi machine pistols from their robes and shot through the truck windows, shattering the glass and instantly killing the two bombers. The shooters had both fired from behind the side windows, avoiding any crossfire. Jalal slumped forward, his body causing the horn to emit a continuous blare. Fatih slid sideways, his body covered with broken glass.

The older Bedouin ripped off his *keffiyeh,* revealing a full white beard.

"Solly! Are you okay?" Regan yelled, climbing to her feet from in front of the truck.

Solly shouted into a shoulder-harnessed intercom clipped under his robe, "Clear! Clear! Clear! Bomber one is down!" On the other side of the truck Ty ripped off his head cover and said, "Confirm! Clear! Bomber number two is down! I repeat. The threats have been neutralized."

Regan quickly ripped off her black head covering, releasing a cascade of blonde hair. She moved out of the path of the still idling truck and began removing pieces of broken glass from her robe and dusting herself off.

Solly jerked the driver's door open and shoved Jalal's body to the side silencing the annoying blare from the horn. He turned off the ignition and pulled up the emergency brake handle.

The other dozen Bedouin men threw off their robes that had concealed their IDF Special Forces uniforms. They rushed to the back of the truck with guns raised and quickly raised the door to ensure that there were no other terrorists. The leader of the squad said, "All clear! Truck is clear!"

At *Mossad* headquarters in Jerusalem Asher Hazzan had been anxiously tracking the action from the live video feed of three surveillance drones. Asher barked, "Roger that. The drones have been watching the truck since it left the garage in Jericho. We aren't picking up any traffic. We did send in an armed Predator drone to follow one of the principals who left Jericho for Jordan around 0900."

"That would be Ali el-Gamal," Solly replied. According to our ISIS mole, he is the one who armed the nuclear device. He's also the bad guy who helped Dr. Saad kidnap Regan. He was going to deliver her to be a personal prize for al-Bagahdi. Take him out if you can."

Asher said, "He passed into Jordan a couple of hours ago, and he's heading north. We can't engage him in Jordan without permission. I'll call the Prime Minister."

At sunrise that morning Solly had told Asher the plan that he, Ty, and Regan had hammered out the night before. They needed some kind of diversion to force the bombers to stop the truck long enough to allow Solly and Ty to approach without alerting them. Regan volunteered to be the one to stop the truck.

After approving the plan Asher dispatched heavy earthmoving equipment before dawn to dig up a section of what until early that morning had been a perfectly good highway. Detour signs had been erected, and the Bedouin who lived in that area had been reluctantly rounded up and driven to another location amid much loud complaining. The surveillance drones flew low enough in front of the television truck to relay video I.D. of the two occupants. Facial software even identified Jalal as someone on the terrorist watch list.

Solly wondered about the fate of Ahmad and hoped he had made it safely to Baghdad. So far the plan had worked like clockwork, but no one was in the clear just yet with the Fox still on the loose.

72

ISIS Headquarters, Al-Raqqah, Syria

Al-Bagahdi had been kneeling on his prayer rug for the past thirty minutes. He rose, strapped his AK-47 over his shoulder, and entered his bunker office at a quarter before noon to prepare to watch the breaking news on a newly installed set of flat screen televisions that replaced the ones he'd destroyed. He glanced at the various network feeds and was surprised to see his face posted on every channel.

He checked his watch again. "What's going on?" he screamed at the small gathering of ISIS soldiers in the room.

The Al-Jazeera reporter was saying, "This video was posted by ISIS at 1130 Israel time. In it Abu Bakr al-Bagahdi makes a mysterious claim asserting that ISIS has already set off a bomb in Jerusalem. Authorities in Jerusalem have been put on emergency alert. But so far there has been no report of any explosion. We'll be back with updates as they occur."

The Fox turned his gun on the new televisions, blasting every one of them. "Why didn't you tell me about this?" he demanded.

The soldiers cringed in fear. "We didn't want to disturb you from your prayers, sir. And we thought this was perhaps some brilliant strategy of yours," one of them said.

Al-Bagahdi's faced clouded with dark anger. "That dirty dog Ali and his wonder boy were instructed to launch the video *after* the attack! Now they have ruined the plan and made me look like a fool!"

He slammed another clip in his weapon and ran to the television studio looking for Ahmad. He kicked the door open and yelled, "Come out of there, you traitorous pig!" He looked around, but the studio was deserted. He saw lights blinking in the uplink equipment. That became his next target.

When he finally expended all his energy, he looked at his watch. It was 1155 in Israel. A wicked smile creased his face and he took a calming breath. *"They can't out-fox the Fox,"* he told himself, remembering he'd instructed his explosives expert to set a hidden internal timer inside the blasting rods to automatically detonate at noon. *"I suspected I couldn't trust those fools,"* he thought. *"Even if the Israelis stopped them, the bomb will still detonate at noon."*

The Fox would make Ali pay dearly for his bumbling attempt that sabotaged the timing of his attack. He pulled out his satellite phone and dialed Ali's number. It went straight to his voicemail—marking the first time that Ali had not taken his call.

73

The Old Jericho Highway, outside Jerusalem

Solly turned to the soldiers, some of whom were also members of the Bomb Disposal Unit, and said, "Let's get this bomb defused. The bombers may be dead, but the bomb is still live. It could be detonated by an explosion or by another remote device we don't know about."

They went to work. There was no need to wear protective suits because they wouldn't be of any use against a nuclear blast. Captain Abraham Kahn had the critical task of disarming the dangerous device. IDF soldiers quickly removed all the video equipment, taking care to check for hidden compartments. Meanwhile, Captain Kahn opened the doors to the cab of the truck and began looking for anything that might be a detonator. He didn't see anything obvious, so he ordered the men to remove the two bullet-ridden bodies and place them on the ground face up.

He slipped his hands into a pair of surgical gloves and began to search the driver's body for a cell phone. There was none. He felt a small cylinder in the driver's jacket pocket. He carefully removed it and saw an instrument designed to look like a felt tip marker. But it was too heavy to be a marker. He carefully handed it to one of his team members and told him to hold it gently in the center without touching the top. He found a similar device in the pocket of the passenger. After removing it carefully, he handed it to another IDF soldier. He knew that these were electronic transmitters because there were no wires connecting them to the bomb. He also knew that their range couldn't be very far since they could only be powered by small lithium batteries.

In his years of dealing with bombs he had learned an important maxim based on Occam's Razor: *"Always try the simplest solution first."*

He turned to both soldiers holding the devices. "We need to get these devices as far away from each other and out of range of the bomb as quickly as possible." He pointed toward the main highway and said to one of the men, "You start walking away in that direction, and don't stop until you reach the main highway. One of our highway repair trucks will drive you north for two miles. Stop there."

Captain Kahn turned to the man holding the other device. "You start walking down the old highway. The range between the detonators is likely only a few yards, but go south as far as you can just to be on the safe side. When you are both about a half-kilometer away from the bomb, the detonators will be out of range of the bomb. Hold them carefully, however, and don't touch the tips. I'll send someone to retrieve you when I've finished my work here."

The two soldiers anxiously started walking in opposite directions, holding the detonators in front of them as if they were going to explode. Captain Kahn went to the back of the television truck and looked inside. He immediately saw the cover to the hidden compartment.

"Take that cover off and let's see what's in there." He glanced at his watch and saw that it was 1150. The intelligence they had received said the bomb would explode at noon. *"I wonder if this thing is just on a simple timer?"* he asked himself. *"We'll find out in the next few minutes."*

As Solly watched Captain Kahn, his com beeped. "Go ahead."

It was Asher. "We've gotten clearance from the Jordanian Kingdom to take out Ali."

Solly winked at Ty and said, "Another one bites the dust."

74

20,000 feet above Safawi, Jordan

The American-made Predator Drone was the most lethal Unmanned Aerial Vehicle in the skies. Israel had purchased a dozen of the UAVs from the United States. This particular drone had the capability to fly without fueling for sixteen hours and was equipped with two deadly Hellfire air-to-surface missiles.

It communicated via satellite uplink with the Ground Control Station at Ramat David Air Force Base. The Israeli flight control officer monitoring the target received a call from his commanding officer.

"Yes sir. Right away, sir."

Over the com link he said to the twenty-year-old Israeli drone pilot, "You have clearance to engage the target. I repeat. You have clearance to engage."

"Painting target now with laser. Firing in three, two, one. Missile away! Time to impact thirty seconds."

On the ground speeding along in the backseat of a Mercedes C class sedan, Ali had been sleeping for much of the trip back to Syria. He was mentally and physically exhausted. He glanced at his watch for the hundredth time. The bomb should be detonating in just a few minutes. He closed his eyes to savor the global impact this would have on his recruiting more young fighters for ISIS. He smiled as he thought about how he could become the Caliph once the Fox was out of the way. This one act in Jerusalem that he helped bring to fruition would turn the tide and win the global war for the Caliphate.

Ali never heard the Hellfire missile that slammed into the roof of the car. He was dead before he could even hear the explosion.

75

The Old Jericho Highway, outside Jerusalem

Time was running dangerously short. Captain Kahn instructed a couple of soldiers to lift the crate out of its hiding place and carefully slide it to the doorway of the truck to receive more light. He glanced at his watch again. 1155. He carefully examined the outside of the crate for trip wires to trigger a detonation. Finding none, he opened the two clasps and removed the cover. Sweat was dripping down into his eyes.

What he saw brought a tiny smile to his lips. He immediately recognized it as the Mk-54 SADM. This was a simple device that every Bomb Disposal Unit trained on in their first year. Once the blasting rods were removed, the bomb could not be exploded. The only residual danger might be a leak from the radioactive core. Captain Kahn deliberately removed each blasting rod. He handed one to Ty and one to Solly. Remembering his simplicity mantra, he said, "To be safe, throw those bars as far away as you can. Do it right now!"

Solly and Ty quickly turned and hurled the bars in

different directions into the Judean desert. They landed with a thud in the sand. Captain Kahn ran a Geiger counter over the nose of the bomb and announced, "We're safe."

"These are normal readings," he continued. "Without the blasting rods this is just a lead-lined case of Uranium 235. We'll place the device in a lead container and let the Americans add it to their other stockpile of nuclear waste."

Solly glanced at his watch. "Way to go, team! We've done a good day's work, and it's not even noon yet."

Everyone jumped at the sound of two small explosive blasts that sounded like shotguns. The noise came from the vicinity of where the two blasting rods had just landed in the desert. They could see small clouds of sand rising from the source of the blasts.

Captain Kahn's face turned pale.

Solly said, "Does that mean what I think it means?"

The Captain nodded. "I suspected it. Every good bomb maker always builds in a redundancy. If we hadn't removed those rods when we did, this could have been a very bad day for us all."

With a shaky voice Solly pressed his com link and reported to Asher. "Sir, we're all good here. The bomb has been defused. We are giving the all clear."

Asher had been watching the whole scene on the video feed from the hovering drones. "Thanks. Solly, I assume you don't want to tell me about those two small explosions in the dirt, right?"

Solly replied coolly, "No sir. It was nothing."

Nobody spoke for a few seconds, realizing just how close everyone had come to certain death. Ty tried lifting the mood. "Hey," he said, "maybe the blasting rods just detonated on their own when they hit the dirt."

Regan, still staring out into the desert, said, "You were always a terrible liar."

76

The Hall of Hewn Stones, Temple Mount, Jerusalem

It was after sunset. *Yom Kippur* had ended without incident in Jerusalem. Dignitaries filled the beautiful Hall of Hewn Stones on the wing of the Temple that night—the same people who had earlier witnessed the first Temple sacrifice. This evening event was a press conference to announce the formulation of the MEPA treaty between seven nations.

General Secretary Obeidat looked as assured as always as he stood to begin the conference. Almost overnight he had gone from an obscure Ambassador to a trendsetting global leader.

"I have a short statement to make tonight. I won't be taking any questions," he began. He looked down at his prepared notes and continued, "I'm here tonight to announce a world changing treaty. This is an alliance between seven nations, some of whom were enemies only a few years ago. The seven-nation alliance is comprised of Jordan, Israel, Egypt, Turkey, The Saudi Kingdom, The

United Arab Emirates, and Qatar. I have been named as the General Secretary of what is now called the Middle Eastern Peace Alliance. We have also formed a MEPA council comprised of high-ranking officials from each of the nations."

Walid paused to take a sip of water.

"These seven powerful governments have all signed a peace agreement for the duration of the next seven years. They are united in their fight to destroy and eradicate the scourge of ISIS. We are committed to share resources and intelligence to make the Middle East a safer region for every country and every religion. Thank you."

The Hall filled with thunderous applause. Walid raised his hands in victory as he smiled for the dozens of photographers and cameramen present.

77

The King David Hotel, Jerusalem

Solly, Ty, and Regan had ordered room service while they waited for the broadcast announcing the launch of MEPA. Solly had his phone to his ear. "Yes sir. You're welcome. I completely understand." Regan and Ty made small talk while Solly finished his call.

"That was the Prime Minister," he told them. "He asked me to convey his deepest gratitude to you. This incident is being buried, and the official spin is that al-Bagahdi's video was just the benign raving of a madman intended to spread fear. He also informed me that there would be no medals or public recognition for you. Sorry."

Ty said, "That sounds familiar."

"You don't want to be famous, Ty. You'd lose the ability to have dinner without being hounded by reporters," Solly chided.

He turned toward the large television and said, "It's time for Walid to speak." He pointed the remote at the screen and turned up the volume.

***

Thirty minutes later they had finished their meal. After they placed their used dishes in the hall for the hotel staff to retrieve, they sat down to debrief the day.

Regan asked Solly, "So what do you think about MEPA?"

"I really have mixed emotions."

"What do you mean?"

"As an Israeli, I'm relieved that we now have some powerful allies who have been our enemies for as long as I can remember. But there was something about Walid's announcement that made me feel uncomfortable. It came to me as he was posing for pictures after his announcement."

Ty said, "What is it?"

Solly pulled out his phone and opened the Bible app. "Of course, the Jewish people have desired and prayed for another Temple for many centuries," he said. "But rebuilding the Temple in Jerusalem is also a missing part in a prophetic jigsaw puzzle that leads to the return of the Messiah."

He scrolled down to find a particular scripture on his phone. "Listen to this. In Matthew 24 Jesus' disciples asked Him for some hints or signs that would predict His return."

He scrolled some more. "Here it is." He read it aloud:

Jesus said, "So when you see standing in the holy place 'the abomination that causes desolation,' spoken of through the prophet Daniel—let the reader understand— then let those who are in Judea flee to the mountains."

Regan and Ty seemed confused, so Solly paused and continued. "I read that for years and missed something important. Jesus talked about letting the *reader* understand. He usually talked to his audience about having ears to *hear* since the common people did not know how to read. When Jesus spoke these words, they hadn't been written down in the Bible yet. However, He knew that it would be written and read at some point in the future."

Regan said, "As in, today? I've also always been confused about that abomination thing."

"Sure," Solly said. "Daniel wrote about it in chapter 9. Many scholars believe he is making a prediction about the Antichrist. Let me read it:

He will make a firm covenant with many for one week (that means a week of years, or seven years), but in the middle of the week he will put a stop to sacrifice and offering. And the abomination of desolation will be on a wing of the temple until the decreed destruction is poured out on the desolator.

"I didn't miss the fact that Hall of Hewn Stones is a wing of the new Temple, did you?" Solly asked.

"I still don't understand what you're trying to say," Ty said.

Solly returned his phone to his pocket. "Many scholars believe that some charismatic global leader will appear on the world scene around the time when the Messiah will return. He will give every appearance of being a man of peace. He will broker a historic seven-year treaty, but in the middle of that period his true evil nature will come out and he will want to be worshipped. That's an abomination to any Jew. They would move out of the Temple in an instant if that happened."

"So this brand new Temple would be left desolate by that act abomination?" Ty asked. "I get it. But are you really saying Walid is this Antichrist character? I kind of liked the guy myself. And you have to admit he was so helpful to us."

Solly held up his palms and said, "Whoa, mate. I'm not saying anything for certain. Let's just keep our eyes on what happens over the next few months."

Solly patted his thighs and jumped to his feet. "Enough gloom-and-doom and Bible prophecy for one night. It's been great to be with you guys again. I'm going to miss you when you head back to the States. Are you up for one more adventure before you leave?"

Ty and Regan said together, "Sure!"

78

Sunrise, Masada, Israel

Solly called Ty's room first and then Regan's room and awakened them at 0400. He was far too cheerful so early in the morning. "Put on your hiking clothes and meet me downstairs."

When they made their way downstairs into the lobby, Solly was waiting for them out front behind the wheel of a black Range Rover. They jumped in, and Solly drove through the deserted streets of Jerusalem then out toward Jericho. They were quiet on the drive, lost in their personal thoughts. Past Jericho they turned right and drove along the shore of the Dead Sea for almost an hour. When they arrived at Masada National Park, it was closed and the gate to the entrance to the parking area was locked. Solly produced a key and opened the gate for their private visit.

As the eastern sky started to glow with orange tints, the three of them climbed up the snake trail that crossed back and forth up the side of the flat-topped mountain that was Masada. Ty and Solly had run this same trail many times together in the past. Solly had timed their arrival to reach the top of Masada just as the sun started rising over the mountains of Jordan and the Dead Sea.

This was Regan's first visit here. She spun around slowly to take in the panoramic 360-degree view. "Wow! This is one of the most beautiful spots I've ever seen, Solly." She hugged him spontaneously. They were all silent for a few minutes, comfortable with the silence that good friends can enjoy.

Then Ty said, "Solly, would you excuse us? I'd like to show Regan the Northern Hanging Palace that Herod the Great built."

Solly grinned and said, "Sure, mate. You kids run along. I'll be here when you get back."

Ty explained to Regan all about the excavations of the massive food storehouses and the ornate Roman baths King Herod had built on Masada, his private palatial retreat. They finally reached the northern cliff of Masada. They walked down a series of wooden steps to reach the remains of Herod's magnificent "hanging palace." It was given this name because it seemed to be precariously dangling off the side of the mountain. They gazed at the beautiful mosaic that could still be seen on the floor, although two thousand years had passed since the time it was installed.

Ty broke the silence.

"Regan, I've been meaning to tell you something. The other night in the hotel room...when Leah was praying her prayer...something happened. I felt a huge weight on my chest, and I had to fight to hold back tears. I realized then that I also wanted what it is that I've seen in you. So that night I finally placed my faith in Jesus. I was praying when Leah left the room. Ever since that night I've been thinking about my life from a different perspective."

Regan reached out and embraced Ty. "Ty, I'm so happy for you! You have no idea how long I've been praying that you'd come to this point!"

Ty held her at arm's length, and Regan noticed moisture in the corners of his deep blue eyes. When he regained his composure he said, "Well, there's something else I want to tell you."

Regan smiled. "Yes, Ty?"

He stumbled over his words like a shy schoolboy. "Regan, I have also known for a long time that I love you. But lately..." he paused.

Regan searched his eyes trying to figure out where Ty was going with this.

"Lately, I've come to realize that I can't live without you. So . . . will you marry me?"

Regan hesitated.

"I will," she said coyly, "but on one condition."

"Name it."

"You drive us to our honeymoon instead of flying!"

As a beautiful pink sun rose over the Dead Sea, Ty and Regan embraced and sealed the deal with a kiss. It was the first of many to follow.

AUTHOR'S COMMENTS

The Jerusalem Protocol is a sequel to my earlier novel, *The Cloud Strike Prophecy*. If you haven't read *The Cloud Strike Prophecy*, you will enjoy that story now that you know the characters from *The Jerusalem Protocol*. Both books are available in print and as e-books from Amazon or other online bookstores.

As many of my friends know, the character of Solomon "Solly" Rubin is loosely based on my good friend and Israeli tour guide, Reuven Solomon. I have taken liberties with his character, but he will always be a hero to me. I appreciate his willingness to lend his appearance and wisdom to create Solly. If you have the distinct privilege of meeting Reuven, know that he never worked for *Mossad*. So he claims!

Although this is pure fiction, there is a widespread belief that the Dome of the Rock is not built on the site of the Jewish Temple. In 1983 Dr. Asher Kaufman, a Professor at Hebrew University in Jerusalem, proposed the theory that the Jewish Temple was actually built to the north of the Dome of the Rock. Other Jewish scholars have proposed similar theories. You'll see my modified version of Dr.

Kaufman's full diagram in the back of this book.

The Temple Institute in Jerusalem has been in existence since 1987. They are located in the Jewish Quarter of Jerusalem's Old City. The Temple Institute is dedicated to every aspect of the biblical commandment to build the Holy Temple of God on Mount Moriah in Jerusalem. If you visit Jerusalem, I encourage you to visit The Temple Institute. They have manufactured all the implements and instruments to resume sacrificial worship. You can access YouTube to see the 3-D plans for the proposed future construction of the Hall of Stones and the Temple itself.

The most factual part of this novel is the reality of dozens of Old Testament prophecies that were fulfilled in Jesus of Nazareth. I have also attached a list of Messianic Prophecies with the New Testament fulfillment. To anyone who has an open mind this should provide convincing proof that is difficult to ignore.

As always I'm thankful to the Green Acres family who provide me with the time and support to travel, train, and write.

Special thanks to Fluency, Inc., for their excellent work in publishing both my non-fiction works and my novels. I'd also like to thank Bill and Sharon McKenzie for allowing me the use of their family's lake cabin to have uninterrupted time to write.

David Orlo Dykes
Tyler, Texas

Solomon's Temple: Holy of Holies over Dome of Tablets
(Based on Asher S. Kaufman's view, 1983 AD)

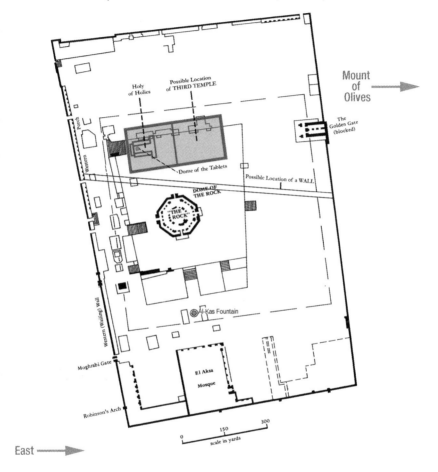

CONVINCING PROOF

The Jesus Prophecies
David O. Dykes

There are dozens of prophecies about the Jewish Messiah, and only one individual has ever lived who has fulfilled all of them – Jesus of Nazareth. The following is a list of Old Testament predictions about the Messiah and how Jesus fulfilled each one in the New Testament. This is convincing proof.

(Old Testament / New Testament Fulfillment)

His Identity

1. Offspring Of A Woman
    Gen. 3:15 / Matt. 1:18-20, Gal. 4:4

2. Gained Victory Over Satan
    Gen. 3:15 / Heb. 2:14, Rom. 16:20

His Lineage

3. Line Of Abraham
    Gen. 12:3 / Matt 1:1, Rom. 9:1-5

4. Descendant Of Isaac
    Gen. 17:19 / Luke 3:34

5. Descendant Of Jacob
    Num. 24:17 / Matt. 1:2

6. From The Tribe Of Judah
    Gen. 49:10 / Luke 3:33, Heb. 7:14

7. Heir To David's Throne
    2 Sam. 7:12-13, Is. 9:7 / Rom. 1:2-4

His Birth

8. Born Of A Virgin
    Is. 7:14 / Luke 1:26-31

9. Born In Bethlehem
    Mic. 5:2 / Luke 2:4-6

10. Timing Of His Birth
    Dan. 9:24, Neh. 2:1-10 / Matt. 2:1

11. He Is Called Emmanuel
    Is. 7:14 / Matt. 1:23, Col 2:9

12. Kings Bring Him Gifts
    Ps. 72:10-11 / Matt. 2:1-11

13. Slaughter Of Innocents
    Jer. 31:15 / Matt. 2:16-18

14. Called Out Of Egypt
    Hos. 11:1 / Matt. 2:14-15

His Ministry

15. Called A Nazarene
    Is. 53:2-3 / Matt. 2:21-23

16. Announced By A Forerunner
    Is. 40:3 / Matt. 11:7-14

17. Ministry In Galilee
    Is. 9:1-2 / Matt. 4:12-17

18. Anointed By God
    Is. 42:7, 61:1-2 / Luke 4:18-21

19. Zeal For God's House
    Ps. 69:9 / John 2:14-17

20. As Prophet
    Deut. 18:15 / John 5:46, Acts 3:22-26

21. As Miracle Worker
    Is. 35:5-8 / John 20:30

22. As Spirit-Filled Preacher
    Is. 42:1 / Matt. 12:18

23. Teaches In Parables
    Ps. 78:1-3, Is. 6:9-10 / Matt. 13:10-17

24. Lifted Up Like Moses' Serpent
    Num. 21:7-10 / John 3:14-18

25. A Kinsman Redeemer
    Ruth 4:4-9 / Mark 10:45, Eph. 1:3-7

26. Cornerstone Rejected By Builders/Stumbling Stone
    Ps. 118:22, Is. 8:14, 28:16 / Luke 20:17-18, Acts 4:11

27. Brings Glory To The 2nd Temple
    Hag. 2:6-9 / Luke 2:27-32

28. A Light To The Gentiles
    Is. 9:2, 42:6, 49:6 / Matt. 4:16, John 8:12

29. A Priest Like Melchizedek
    Gen. 14:18-20, Ps. 110:1-4 / Heb. 5:5-6

30. Rejected By The Jews
    Ps. 56:1-6, 69:7-8; Is. 29:13, 53:1-3 / John 1:10-11,
    Mark 3:20-22, Matt. 15:1-9

His Suffering And Death

31. Entry Into Jerusalem
    Zech. 9:9, Ps. 118:25-26 / Mark 11:1-11

32. Betrayed By A Friend
    Ps. 41:7-9, 55:12-14 / John 12:4-7

33. A Reward For Betrayal
    Zech. 11:12-13 / Matt. 26:14-16

34. Blood Money Returned/Thrown In The House Of God
    Zech. 11:13 / Matt. 27:1-5

35. Money Used To Buy Potter's Field
    Zech. 11:13 / Matt. 27:6-10

36. Deserted By The Disciples
    Zech. 13:7 / Mark 14:27; 14:43-51

37. Accused By False Witnesses
    Ps. 35:11, 15-17 / Matt. 26:59-67

38. Spit Upon And Struck
    Is. 50:6 / Matt. 26:59-67

39. Silent Before His Accusers
    Is. 53:7 / Matt. 27:12-14, Luke 23:7-12

40. Wounded And Bruised
    Is. 53:5 / Matt. 27:27-31

Prophecies From The 22nd Psalm

41. Forsaken By God
    Ps. 22:1 / Matt. 27:46

42. Ridiculed On Cross
    Ps. 22:7-8 / Matt. 27:39-44

43. God's Beloved From The Womb
    Ps. 22:9 / Luke 2:6-7

44. Surrounded By Vicious Men
    Ps. 22:12-13 / John 19:1

45. Body Stretched On Cross
    Ps. 22:14 / John 19:16-18

46. Heart Melted
    Ps. 22:14 / John 19:31-34

47. Thirsts
    Ps. 22:15 / John 19:28

48. Hands And Feet Pierced
    Ps. 22:16 / John 20:25

49. No Bones Broken
    Ps. 22:17, Ex. 12:46, Num. 9:11-12 / John 19:32

50. Men Gambled For Clothing
    Ps. 22:18 / John 19:23-24

51. Lives To Sing Praises
    Ps. 22:22 / Heb. 2:11-12

52. Crucified With Thieves
    Is. 53:12 / Luke 23:32-33, 39-43

53. Prayed For His Persecutors
    Is. 53:12 / Luke 23:34

54. Offered Vinegar To Drink
    Ps. 69:21 / John 19:28-29

55. People Shook Their Heads In Shame
    Ps. 109:25 / Matt. 27:39

56. Friends Watched From A Distance
    Ps. 38:11 / Luke 23:49

57. Darkness Over The Land
    Amos 8:9 / Matt. 27:45

58. Committed Himself To God
    Ps. 31:5 / Luke 23:46

59. Died For Others
    Is. 53:4-16, Dan. 9:26 / 1 Pe. 2:24, 3:18

60. Buried In A Rich Man's Tomb
    Is. 53:9 / Matt. 27:57-60

61. Ascend To Right Hand Of God
    Ps. 68:18, 110:1 / Acts 1:3-9, Eph. 4:7-10, Heb. 12:2

62. Return In Glory
    Zech. 14:4-8 / Acts 1:11; 3:17-21

63. Have Eternal Dominion
    1 Chron. 17:11-14, Is. 9:6-7, Dan. 7:13-14 /
    1 Corin. 15:24-25

DAVID ORLO